Crossing the
Lion

Crossing the Lion

A *Reigning Cats & Dogs* Mystery

Cynthia Baxter

BANTAM BOOKS
NEW YORK

A Bantam Books Mass Market Original

Copyright © 2010 by Cynthia Baxter

Published in the United States by Bantam Books, an imprint of The Random House Publishing Group, a division of Random House, Inc., New York.

BANTAM BOOKS and the rooster colophon are registered trademarks of Random House, Inc.

ISBN 978-1-61664-751-3

Cover design: Marietta Anastassatos
Cover illustration: Bob Guisti

Printed in the United States of America

To Carol, Anna, and Ba

Crossing the
Lion

Chapter 1

"It is better to be a lion for a day
than a sheep all your life."

—Elizabeth Kenny

How on earth did I get myself into this situation? I thought miserably, zipping my jacket up to my chin and wondering why I'd ever put so much faith in Polarfleece.

On a dreary November evening like this one, I usually preferred snuggling up in front of a fireplace with my brand-new husband, Nick, and sipping hot chocolate, mulled cider, or some other beverage that was really good at adding warmth to the human body. It wouldn't have hurt to have my pets around me, as well, since my two dogs and two cats happen to be pretty good at that aforementioned snuggling.

Instead, I found myself in the middle of Peconic

Bay, huddling inside the cold, damp cabin of a boat that, at the moment, was being thrown around as if the turbulent waters were gearing up for a replay of *The Perfect Storm*.

Even though I didn't remember having had a problem with seasickness before, the churning in my stomach told me that could be about to change.

Icy rain pelted the windowpanes, through which I could see that darkness had settled around the dense gray fog surrounding the vessel. I was beginning to understand why all those sailors on the HMS *Bounty* had decided to mutiny. Right now, nothing sounded better than dry land.

At least my traveling companions didn't come close to the Captain Bligh category. In fact, for what it was worth, they looked almost as miserable as I felt.

Beside me, Betty Vandervoort Farnsworth sat hunched over, with her arms folded and her legs crossed. The oversize parka that nearly devoured her slender frame was the same shade as overripe limes, as if it had been designed to scare away bears. Even less fashionable was the multicolored wool cap she'd yanked so far down that it nearly concealed her sapphire-blue eyes. Her hat also covered most of her hair, although a few strands of her usually neat white pageboy stuck out at wild angles.

Her husband, Winston, looked as if he was on his way to a Halloween party dressed as the Gloucester fisherman. He wore a bright yellow slicker topped by one of those hats that looks as if it's really good at redirecting rain toward the guy behind whoever's wearing it. Being British, he was doing a much better job of keeping a stiff upper lip. The only thing that gave him away was the slightly green tinge of his skin.

Frederick looked a little green, too, although it was harder to tell, since he was covered with tan fur. It was also impossible to discern whether the wirehaired dachshund tucked beneath Winston's coat was trembling because of seasickness or because he was simply terrified by the storm.

I might have been amused by the way Betty and Winston looked, if I wasn't wrestling with a slew of conflicting emotions. After all, they were the ones who'd gotten me involved in this in the first place.

It had all started a few hours earlier as I lay on the bed in Betty's guest room, working my way through a stack of veterinary journals. I'd lived in the former gardener's cottage on her estate for years, but recent events had rendered it uninhabitable. Since June, Nick and I had been staying in Betty and Winston's residence, a luxurious nineteenth-century mansion I'd nicknamed the Big House.

While Nick and I had every intention of looking for our own place, neither of us ever seemed to find the time. After spending a few years as a private investigator, Nick had decided to change careers. He was plowing through his second year of law school, which meant he spent every waking hour studying. There's a saying about law school: The first year, they scare you; the second year, they work you; the third year, they bore you. And year two was turning out to be as demanding as it was reputed to be. As for me, I run my own veterinary practice out of a twenty-six-foot clinic-on-wheels. That means I routinely put in ten- to twelve-hour days driving all over Long Island, making house calls.

Besides, people who've been married for only five months can find much better ways to spend their free time than searching for apartments on Craigslist.

Just like hunting down real estate, keeping up with my reading was one of those to-do items that was hard to squeeze in. So I was taking advantage of a few free hours on a gray rainy Thursday afternoon, exactly one week before Thanksgiving, to curl up on our comfy canopy bed with the *American Journal of Veterinary Research*.

The fact that my dogs and cats had snuggled up with me made the atmosphere even cozier. Max, my adorable Westie, was pressed against one leg, his furry white head resting on my thigh. Every few minutes he let out a sigh, although I couldn't tell if he was expressing joy or was simply annoyed over having his reverie interrupted by the sound of pages turning. Still, every time I reached over distractedly to fondle his ears, he fixed his big brown eyes on me and appreciatively thumped his stub of a tail—a sad reminder of his previous owners.

Catherine the Great, better known as Cat, was curled up against my other leg. My dignified gray pussycat suffers from arthritis, and I hoped she found the heat from my body soothing. The other feline love of my life, Tinkerbell, was lying on my chest. She'd first gotten into the habit of acting like a lobster bib back when Nick brought her home after finding her abandoned in a cardboard box, and she'd immediately taken over as top dog—er, cat. But now she was fully grown, big enough that I had to hold my journal high in the air to keep her orange fur from blocking the pages.

Lou, my Dalmatian, was stretched out at the end of the bed. He happened to be doing a terrific job of keeping my feet warm. Like Max, he bears a sad souvenir of his earlier life: He has only one eye. At the moment, he was dozing, making cute snorting noises that led me to suspect he was dreaming about chasing tennis balls.

The other two animals that were part of my family were downstairs in the kitchen. I could hear Prometheus, my blue-and-gold macaw, screeching, probably trying to bully Betty into bringing him an afternoon snack of an apple or some other treat. At least Leilani was quiet. Then again, most Jackson's chameleons aren't very noisy, even when someone takes them out of their tank. Usually they just stare, lazily blinking the eyes on the sides of their heads.

I couldn't have been more content—or more relaxed. It helped that I was dressed in sweatpants and a white T-shirt with a picture of a Dalmatian and the words *Got spots?* My straight dark-blond hair, which usually hangs around my shoulders, was pulled back into a low ponytail.

As I perused an article about the relationship between canine hip dysplasia and body weight, I couldn't resist glancing up every once in a while to admire not only my menagerie but also the room that Nick and I were sharing. The large bedroom looked like the finished product from one of those home-design shows on TV. The walls were painted a serene shade of powder blue. In addition to the fairy-tale bed, the room was outfitted with lustrous wooden antiques, a beautifully crafted marble fireplace, and two huge windows that overlooked the back of the estate.

In fact, I was gazing out those very windows from bed, wondering if venturing out into the gray drizzle with Max and Lou would be exhilarating or simply uncomfortable, when I heard a soft knock. Glancing up, I saw Betty and Winston standing in the doorway.

Ordinarily, I would have assumed they'd stopped by to invite me for a cup of tea or a game of backgammon. But the distressed expressions on their faces told me this was no social call.

"What's wrong?" I asked. I picked up Tinkerbell and, cradling her in one arm, began to extract myself from Max, Cat, and Lou.

From the serious look Betty shot Winston, I knew my first impression was correct: It was bad news that had brought them to my room.

"Jessica, Winston and I wondered if you could possibly help us with something," Betty said.

"Of course," I assured her. "Just name it."

She cast her husband another wary look before saying, "I think I'd better sit down."

An alarm sounded inside my head. I pulled myself over to the edge of the bed, stroking the velvety fur on Tink's head. Betty plunked down on the opposite side, wedging herself between Max and Lou, while Winston lowered his lanky frame into a cream-colored upholstered chair that was as elegant as it was comfortable. Cat was only too happy to stretch out smack in the middle of the mattress.

"Jessica, Winston and I received some terrible news a little while ago," Betty said, her tone earnest. "The wife of one of Winston's friends called to tell us the poor man died last night."

"That's terrible!" I exclaimed. "I'm so sorry. Is it someone you were close to?"

"Linus and I had been friends for years," Winston said somberly. As always, he spoke with an English accent that reminded me of the classic television series *Upstairs Downstairs*—with him being decidedly upstairs. "He and I belonged to the same club in New York City for... goodness, it must have been several decades."

Smiling sadly, he added, "I met Linus Merrywood for the very first time during a rather heated discussion of whether Ronald Reagan or Jimmy Carter was likely to win the upcoming presidential election."

"Linus Merrywood," I repeated, running my hand along Tinkerbell's back. Even though I couldn't place him, I had the nagging feeling there was something familiar about the name.

"The man was quite a mover and shaker in the business world," Winston went on. "He was the president and CEO of Merrywood Industries, which for the past few years has been named as one of the Fortune 500. It was a family business, which his great-grandfather founded in the late 1800s. He started in steel—making parts used in building railroads, I believe. But over the years the company expanded into all kinds of metals, opening factories all over the world that manufactured everything from aluminum cans to hubcaps.

"Linus was the most successful businessman in his family's history, which is how he came to earn his nickname: Linus the Lion. I've heard that he tripled his net worth over the course of his lifetime." Thoughtfully, he added, "I've also heard that that's a modest estimate."

"Wow," I said simply. I wondered if maybe I should start using Nick's subscription to *The Wall Street Journal* for more than just lining the bottom of Prometheus's birdcage.

"But even though he was phenomenally successful, he never lost his humanity," Betty interjected. "Linus was almost as well known for his philanthropy as he was for his skill in business. He supported so many good causes. Education, primarily. Especially literacy. And not only with his checkbook but also with his time."

"He sounds like a wonderful man," I commented. "How did he die?"

"I'm afraid I don't know the details yet," Winston replied. "Charlotte was too upset to say very much."

"This is all very sad," I said, "but what does any of it have to do with me?"

Betty frowned. "Just a few days ago, Winston got an extremely troubling phone call from Linus."

Winston took a deep breath before adding, "He said he thought someone was plotting to kill him."

"What?" I cried, causing both Max and Lou to raise their heads. "But—but—did he say who? Or why?"

"All he would say," Winston answered in a strained voice, "was that it was somebody close to him."

"And do you have any reason to believe him?" I asked.

Winston shrugged helplessly. "To be perfectly honest, Jessica, at this point I don't know what to think. Which is why Betty and I hoped you might be willing to help us."

"How could I possibly be of help?" But even as I asked the question, I had a feeling I knew what the answer was going to be.

I had a history of solving mysteries—or, as some people saw it, butting my nose in where it didn't belong. It turned out I had kind of a knack for it, too.

Then again, not everyone was happy with this tendency of mine. That included Norfolk County's chief of homicide, a rather unsavory individual named Anthony Falcone. For some crazy reason, he believed that the police were the only ones who should be investigating murders.

That thought led to my next question.

"What do the police think happened?" I asked.

"At this point," Winston said, "everyone seems to be assuming that Linus's death was from natural causes. We haven't told them about Linus's unsettling phone call." He frowned. "At least not yet. We didn't want to upset his wife, Charlotte—and we certainly don't want to see the family dragged into the headlines if it turns out there's no reason for it. We're still hoping that Linus was simply dramatizing some family squabble."

"But Winston and I agree it's something we have to pursue," Betty added, "especially since the police might not even suspect foul play."

"How old was Linus?" I asked.

"He was in his mid-seventies," Winston replied.

"But still going strong," Betty pointed out. "Linus was the picture of health, as far as anyone knew. Didn't he once mention that his father and his grandfather both lived well into their nineties?" she asked Winston. Turning back to me, she added, "While Winston knew Linus for decades, I got to know Linus and Charlotte only over the past year. The four of us got together shortly after Winston and I became an item, then continued to meet for brunch or dinner whenever we could find the time. It was always a pleasure, since they were both such lovely people."

Wanting to focus on what I was hearing, I plunked Tink down on the bed, next to Cat. The two felines eyed each other warily, then curled up a good four or five feet apart.

"What about the last time you saw him?" I asked. "Did he mention that anything out of the ordinary was going on?"

"Not that I recall," Winston replied thoughtfully.

"We haven't seen much of Linus since spring. Wasn't that the last time we all had dinner in Manhattan?"

Betty nodded. "You're right, we haven't seen the Merrywoods in a while. But I do remember him and Charlotte talking about the fact that they'd begun spending less time at their apartment in the city and more and more time at the estate they'd always thought of as their country house. It's on an island they own in Peconic Bay."

I gasped. "Not Solitude Island!"

Winston raised his eyebrows. "Yes, as a matter of fact."

All of a sudden I knew why the name Linus Merrywood had sounded familiar. Solitude Island was a valuable piece of real estate that amazingly had been owned by the same family for hundreds of years. It was located between the two forks of Long Island— or, in more graphic terms, between the two tailfins of an island that to most people looks like a fish. Solitude Island's original owner, back in the 1600s, was Epinetus Merrywood, one of the first colonists who came over to Long Island from England. Not only had he prospered wildly in the New World; for four centuries, his descendants had expanded the family fortune even further, maintaining their position as one of the wealthiest families on Long Island.

And from what I recalled, the Merrywoods were as well known for their obsession with privacy as they were for their affluence.

"But how could I even get close enough to the

Merrywoods to find out what really happened to Linus?" I asked.

"Charlotte asked us to come to the house for a few days to help her get through this difficult time," Betty said. "We thought you might be willing to join us."

"It makes sense for you two to go, since Winston was friends with Linus and Charlotte for such a long time," I mused. "But why would the Merrywoods—especially his widow—want a stranger like me around at a time like this?"

"Because I told her that you're like a daughter to us," Winston said matter-of-factly. "She said you'd be more than welcome to come along."

Betty added, "Which means the only questions that remain to be answered are whether you're willing to help—and whether you'll be able to take off a few days from work so you can come with us to Solitude Island."

My mind raced. The last thing I'd been expecting was a request to drop everything and accompany Betty and Winston to an isolated private island to poke around a possible murder. Still, I'd already told the two of them that I'd help however I could. And I had to admit that the idea of getting a peek at the Merrywoods' estate was pretty enticing.

Besides, the week before Thanksgiving was always pretty quiet, work-wise. Most people were too busy with turkeys to make other appointments. As for the few routine checkups I already had scheduled over the next couple of days, I could easily ask my assistant, Sunny, to rearrange them. I was even free from my weekly television spot on local cable television, which usually aired live on Friday mornings. In order to give everyone a little breather right before the holiday weekend, the producer had decided to repeat one of my earlier shows.

Before I knew it, I heard myself saying, "Of course I'll go to Solitude Island with you. I'll do whatever I can to help."

"Good," Betty said with a nod. For the first time since she'd stepped into the room, I noticed just a hint of a twinkle in her blue eyes. "Especially since I already told Charlotte to expect you."

For the next three hours, I felt as if I was running on fast-forward, as I threw clothes into a suitcase, called Sunny to go over the necessary schedule changes, and sent Nick what was possibly the longest text message in history. I explained that Betty and Winston's friend Linus Merrywood had died and that they'd asked me to accompany them on a condolence call at his weekend retreat. I didn't see any reason to burden Nick with the truth about my real mission, so I left out the part about investigating the poor man's murder.

I also asked Nick to take on the jobs of house sitter for Betty and Winston's place and caretaker for my pets, now his step-pets. As much as I would miss my animals, I wasn't sure how welcome they'd be at the Merrywoods' estate—especially my two dogs, who sometimes struck me as the canine version of Beavis and Butt-Head.

As for Frederick, Winston had decided his spunky

dachshund was small enough and well behaved enough to come along with us. After we packed him into the car with our suitcases, we raced along Long Island's North Fork in Winston's cream-colored Rolls-Royce to the Merrywoods' private dock where we drove onto a ferry-size boat the family also owned.

Even though going to Solitude Island had sounded like a good idea at first, I wasn't as convinced now that I was sitting on a roller coaster of a boat, shivering amid the fog, rain, cold, and sadistic waves. But I forgot all about my yearnings for both the creature comforts and the creatures themselves the moment the cotton-candy-like fog thinned just enough to give me my first glimpse of the island and the enormous mansion in the middle of it.

As I pressed my face against the window, the first thing that struck me was that the Merrywood estate looked anything but, well, merry.

Looming a few hundred yards in front of me was a sprawling building centered on the island. Thanks to the lightning that periodically lit up the sky, I could see it was made of rough gray stone, its shape reminiscent of a medieval castle. A dozen irregular towers and turrets spiked into the air, their tops disappearing into the dense fog. While a few small windows dotted the seemingly impenetrable façade, I could see no signs of life inside the house, from this distance, at least.

As for the land surrounding the mansion, it looked equally uninviting. It was smothered in a dense blanket of tall trees that looked as if they'd been free to thrive on their own for decades or even centuries, their branches reaching out greedily to consume as much space as they desired. Because it was late November, the trees had already lost their leaves, exposing a chaotic tangle of bare, gnarled branches.

Most of the island appeared to be ringed by a white-sand beach, which was all that separated dry land from the deep, dark waters the storm had converted into such a formidable foe. The ragged white peaks of the waves kept lunging toward the island. It was almost as if they were seeking out some poor unsuspecting beachcomber they could drag into their midst.

Yet even though my new home away from home looked like a set from *The Munsters,* I had to admit that the scale of the place was pretty impressive. And it wasn't only because the Merrywoods' house was big enough to be converted into a couple dozen condos—or that it was surrounded by at least a hundred acres of gardens and grounds. What was truly mind-boggling was the fact that a single family could own a private island so close to New York City and leave it completely undeveloped, except for their not-so-humble abode.

Betty must have read my mind—as she so often does—since she chose that moment to comment, "It doesn't exactly scream 'welcome,' does it?"

"It's certainly big," I replied diplomatically. "Have you ever been here before?"

Betty shook her head. "No. Neither has Winston, since he mainly saw Linus at the club. And whenever we got together with Linus and Charlotte, it was either at their apartment on Park Avenue or at a restaurant in Manhattan."

"It's hard to believe all this belongs to just one family," I observed.

"And I don't think the children come out here much anymore," Winston said, patting Frederick soothingly. The more the boat slowed down, the more excited the dachshund became, as if he knew he'd soon be back on dry land and could hardly wait. "The whole family spent lots of time out here when they were growing up, especially on weekends and vacations. But they're all adults now and they've got their own lives. They probably find it easier to see their parents in the city. I seem to recall that all but one of Charlotte and Linus's children live in New York."

"How many children do they have?" I asked.

"Three," Betty replied. "Two sons and a daughter. They're all in their thirties. Linus had just turned seventy-five, but Charlotte is about fifteen years younger. I believe she was right out of college when they got married."

"How about Linus and Charlotte's children?" I asked. "Are any of them married?" Now that I fell into the lawfully wedded category myself, I'd developed a new interest in other people's marital status.

"Only one," Betty said. "Their daughter, Melissa— Missy. Winston, you went to her wedding a few years ago, didn't you?"

"That was certainly a memorable event," he agreed. "Quite extravagant, even by our club members' standards. Well over five hundred guests attended. Linus wanted to hold the reception at the club, but it just wasn't big enough. Instead, it took place in a tremendous ballroom in one of New York's finest hotels. The event had everything from bagpipers leading the guests from the church on Park Avenue to the hotel to a five-course dinner complete with lobster and pastries flown in from Paris."

Whoa! I thought. As someone who had recently planned a wedding of her own—with a great deal of help from her mother-in-law, I should add—it was hard not to compare. And even Winston's brief overview of the event went a long way in helping me understand the extent of the Merrywoods' wealth.

"What about their two sons?" I asked.

"I seem to remember Linus mentioning something about his oldest boy having been divorced once or twice," Winston replied after a bit of thought. "I also recall that Taggart's inability to settle into family life was something Linus was quite upset about. As for the youngest of the Merrywoods' three children, Brockton, I don't believe he's ever been married."

He sighed, then added, "Linus was desperately hoping for grandchildren who could one day take his place presiding over the business. Sadly, he died before he had a chance to see that dream come true."

"What about those three children of his?" I asked, surprised. "Why couldn't one of them take over?"

"Linus felt that none of them lived up to their potential," Winston explained. "His contention that not one of them ever accomplished what he'd hoped for was a constant source of unhappiness in his life."

"Maybe he had unreasonably high expectations," I suggested.

Winston cast me a wary glance. "You can make up your own mind once you get to know them. Loving your children is one thing. Passing on the responsibility of running a Fortune 500 company is something else entirely.

"In fact," he continued, "that's one of the reasons Linus brought someone else into the organization as his number two man. Harrison Foss—Harry. Linus expected that one day he'd take over the reins."

By that point, the ferry was pulling up to a dock. Given the size of the mansion, I was surprised that the dock was little more than a stretch of uneven, rough-hewn boards. Jutting up at the far end was a small, dilapidated boathouse.

But as I stepped off the boat, I wasn't thinking about architecture. I'd had enough of the deep blue sea—and worrying that I was going to end up crammed in Davy Jones's locker like a sweaty gym suit—but I braced myself for what lay ahead.

Now that I was close to the house that up until this point had merely loomed in the distance, I wasn't exactly looking forward to entering. As far as I was concerned, the place looked downright scary.

I only hoped the family inside wouldn't turn out to be just as frightening.

Chapter 2

"I never thought much of the courage of a lion tamer. Inside the cage he is at least safe from people."

—George Bernard Shaw

Even though I hadn't spotted any signs of life from the boat, I'd assumed that was simply because we were so far away from the mansion looming upward in the center of Solitude Island.

But as we stood on the front doorstep, huddled together in the pouring rain, the place looked just as desolate.

"Do you think anyone's home?" I asked Winston, my voice unusually thin. I peered through one of the two narrow stained-glass windows that framed the front door, trying to see inside without success.

I was hoping his answer would be no—and that he'd suggest we turn around and go back home.

Instead, he boomed, "Of course they're home! They're expecting us!"

With that, he reached for the tarnished brass knocker shaped like a lion's head. I squinted at the animal's narrowed eyes and sculpted snout, noticing that its features made it look an awful lot like a man's face—a man who had dead eyes and was in serious need of a haircut. In fact, it reminded me of the knocker on Ebenezer Scrooge's front door in Charles Dickens's *A Christmas Carol,* which eerily transformed into the face of Scrooge's dead business partner, Marley, right before the bad-tempered old miser was visited by three ghosts.

There's no such thing as ghosts, I reminded myself as Winston rapped the brass handle against the door. The jarring noise prompted the poor wet dachshund tucked under his free arm to let out a startled yelp.

I felt like yelping myself. But I remained quiet enough to hear the loud metallic knocking echo through the cavernous rooms I was picturing inside the house.

I was about to voice my own feelings about the wisdom of hightailing it out of there when the heavy wooden door opened slowly, creaking as if its hinges hadn't moved since 1928. We found ourselves standing opposite a man who had to be the Merrywoods' butler.

The tall, emaciated gentleman, probably in his early forties, was dressed in a black tuxedo, complete with tails. With it he wore a blindingly white shirt, a dark bow tie, and immaculate white gloves.

Yet while his formal attire reminded me of someone on his way to a prom, he didn't look like someone who was ready to party. His demeanor was pretty grim, but I had to attribute at least some of that to his unusually gaunt face and his unattractively pasty skin.

I was considering suggesting that he spend a few hours in the sun when he drawled, "Ye-e-e-s?" while looking us up and down as if we were beggars.

"Good evening," Winston greeted him heartily, despite the fact that we were all up to our ankles in puddles and icy rivulets were running down the backs of our necks. "Is Charlotte in? She's expecting us."

"Ah. You must be the Farnsworths," the butler said in an English accent that was even thicker than Winston's. He made no move to let us in.

Jeepers, I thought miserably. Not only was he expecting us, but you'd think he would have noticed that we were getting soaked, standing in the pouring rain.

"May we come in?" Betty finally piped up, sounding uncharacteristically impatient.

"Ye-e-e-s." Reluctantly, the butler stepped aside.

The three of us moved considerably faster. In fact, we burst through the door, leaving our suitcases outside and practically tripping over them in our effort to get someplace warm and dry.

Winston immediately set Frederick down. That made four of us dripping rainwater all over the highly polished marble floor.

"Mind giving us a hand with our luggage, old sport?" Winston asked as he peeled off his dripping-wet slicker. For some reason he'd resorted to expressions commonly associated with his homeland, at least back in the days when he still lived in Jolly Olde England.

"Sorry." The butler gave a helpless shrug. "Bad back."

What exactly are *this guy's buttling skills?* I wondered crossly as I dragged my suitcase across the threshold. At this rate, it wouldn't be long before I too would start complaining about a bad back.

Yet I forgot all about how hard it is to find good help these days as soon as I got my bearings. I was too busy looking around as I shrugged off my wet Polarfleece, wondering if the Merrywoods' butler was able to handle coat hangers.

Not surprisingly, the interior of the Merrywoods' mansion was totally consistent with the exterior— meaning big, dark, forbidding, and downright dismal. The front hallway stretched toward the back of the house, which, from where we were standing, appeared to be very far away. Its walls were covered in dark-wood paneling that greedily sucked up all the light.

The only illumination came from an elaborate chandelier over our heads, which looked as if it weighed a couple of tons. It was comprised of dozens of tarnished brass curlicues intertwined like a bunch of those nasty carnivorous vines that are frequently featured on the Discovery Channel. Yet despite its monstrous size, it gave out hardly any light. That was probably because the dozen or so lightbulbs hidden among all that blackened brass appeared to be about ten watts each.

Even in the dim light, I could see that the hallway served the role of a museum. It was lined with various items that were meant to be looked at, rather than touched or used. On the walls hung big, dark oil paintings of octogenarians wearing black garments that had been out of style for at least a century. In most of them, the only accessory was a sour expression. I was sure I was simply imagining that the piercing eyes of the people in the portraits were focused directly on us.

Positioned on either side of the hallway were two suits of armor that looked as if they hadn't been polished since King Arthur's posse wore them. Dusted, either. Given the Merrywoods' wealth, I wondered why they hadn't found themselves a good cleaning service. Or maybe dusting was part of the butler's duties, and his bad back and determination to keep those gloves nice and white kept him from doing a very effective job.

A few other large, decrepit-looking items took up space in the hall: an ornate Chinese chest of carved wood, painted in bright red; a nearly life-size snarling tiger made of marble; and a giant ceramic urn. I didn't even *want* to know what that thing contained. Right above the urn was a sword with a jewel-studded handle, hanging by a tarnished silver chain. Centered above it was a dagger. The smaller weapon was substantially shinier, but it still looked old enough to be a collector's item.

As I surveyed the place that I'd be calling home for the next few days, *The Rocky Horror Picture Show*'s theme song began playing in my head: *Let's—do—the—time—warp—again!*

I reminded myself that I wasn't an extra in a cult movie. This was real.

I focused on the butler once again, since he appeared to be the only living thing around. More or less. I wondered if I dared comment on his outfit, since it looked as if it had been designed by the costume department. Before I could decide, Winston did it for me.

"My goodness," he said with his lyrical, upper-crust British accent. "Are white gloves still worn in this day and age?"

"Skin condition, m'lord," the butler replied, polite but aloof.

The better to keep from leaving behind fingerprints, I thought cynically, suddenly remembering why I was here in the first place.

In fact, I was wondering if that overused phrase *the butler did it* might turn out to be true this time. It wouldn't have surprised me if this guy's name even turned out to be Jeeves.

I was about to ask, when Betty turned to him and said, "I'm Betty Vandervoort Farnsworth." She extended her hand, then abruptly withdrew it—probably because of the glove business. "And you are...?"

"Jives," the butler replied. "Mortimer Jives, actually, but Jives will do. I'll have Gwennie bring your bags up to your quarters."

"Thank goodness," Betty said, in a voice so soft only I could hear her. "Somewhere around here there's a big hulking he-man who's willing to lift something heavier than a tea cozy."

Before I had a chance to reply, Jives added, "I believe she's almost finished getting the rooms ready."

Betty and I exchanged an amused glance.

"If you want something done," I whispered, "give the job to a woman."

Her nod told me she'd been thinking the exact same thing.

"In the meantime," Jives continued, "Mrs. Merrywood has requested that you join her for refreshments. Won't you step into the conservatory?"

"The *conservatory*?" I whispered to Betty with amusement. "That's a word I haven't heard anyone utter since the last time I played Clue."

Betty covered her mouth to control her laughter. "Why not meet in the billiards room," she whispered back, "or the lounge?"

But Betty, Winston, and I dutifully left our suitcases and followed Jives to the end of the hall. Frederick trotted alongside us, his toenails clicking against the marble.

After passing through a pair of double doors, we found ourselves in a large room with ornate antique furniture, a faded dark-red Oriental rug, and a stone fireplace with a huge fire crackling inside. An elaborately embroidered screen that looked Chinese and was probably made of silk stood in one corner of the room. It must have been gorgeous once. Now, however, the colors were badly faded in spots, making it look splotchy.

One wall was made up entirely of windows— which, I realized, was what made it a conservatory. I remembered seeing a segment on the Home and Garden Channel about conservatories, which are basically greenhouses that have been added onto a house. They became popular in England in the 1800s, not only for growing rare plants but also as the setting for tea parties.

But there were no plants in this conservatory. In fact, the floor-to-ceiling windows were framed by heavy dark-blue velvet drapes that looked as if they had been designed to block out the sun, not let it in. At the moment they were partially closed, making the room feel claustrophobic.

Then I noticed another ominous touch: A beady-eyed raven was perched on a four-foot column, glowering at all of us. I couldn't tell if he had once been alive or if he was simply a replica. Either way, he looked as if any minute now he was going to utter that single famous word: *Nevermore.*

But not all the animals in the room were inanimate. Two dogs lay on the hearth, basking in the warmth of the fire. A somewhat overweight basset hound, mostly black and brown, glanced over curiously, then pulled himself up on his short legs and lumbered toward me. Like most members of his breed, he had a mournful look in his big brown eyes. But while his body moved as if in slow motion, his long tail wagged enthusiastically, letting me know that, appearances aside, he was happy to make my acquaintance.

His buddy was considerably more sprightly. The fluffy white dog jumped up from the hearth, his long, curled tail whipping around energetically. I noticed that while his tail was white on top, the underside was brown, the same shade as his ears and head. But he had touches of gray on his remarkably sweet face. I wasn't positive, but I thought I saw both shih tzu and Lhasa apso in him. He charged over, as excited as if we were long-lost friends.

"Hey, pal!" I greeted the smaller dog, crouching down to give his neck a good scratching.

The basset reached me a few seconds later. I gave him just as warm a welcome.

Finally! I thought with relief. *Somebody I can relate to.*

Unfortunately, I wasn't going to be able to limit my interactions to those with four feet while I was a guest here at the Merrywood estate.

"Come sit with me, Jessica," Betty said. As she patted the couch cushion beside her, a cloud of dust rose up from the dark-red velvet upholstery. She cast me a startled look, then calmly said, "I can't wait for you to meet Charlotte. You're going to love her."

"I'm looking forward to getting to know her," I said sincerely.

I sank onto the couch next to Betty as gently as I could. I was afraid that if I let any more dust loose in that room, we all might have to resort to wearing hazmat suits.

I was pleased that the Merrywoods' two dogs lowered themselves onto the floor next to me. Not wanting to be forgotten, Frederick jumped up and put his two front paws on my knee, asking if he could sit in my lap. One thing about dogs: They can always be counted on to figure out who's the best ear-scratcher in the room.

"Quite a house, isn't it?" Winston remarked. He was standing next to the fireplace, pretending to admire a pair of tarnished silver candlesticks on the mantel but probably trying to get his body temperature back up into the normal range.

"Amazing," I said noncommitally. The little white dog was trembling with excitement, and I worked on his ears with one hand, hoping to calm him down. I scratched the basset's ears with the other, grateful that I was fairly ambidextrous when it came to keeping canines happy. Frederick, meanwhile, curled up contentedly in my lap. Sometimes I wonder if that dog is part cat.

We sat in silence until Betty, ever the polite houseguest, finally commented, "This is such a lovely room." Glancing around, she added, "Charlotte clearly has a real passion for old things."

She'd gotten that right. The room was such an anachronism, in fact, that I half-expected someone to come along and offer us a glass of sherry.

"May I offer all of you a glass of sherry?" Jives asked half a second later. Somehow he'd produced a small round tray on which were balanced several elegant crystal glasses filled with clear golden liquid. He presented the tray to Betty, who helped herself to one of the glasses. Next he offered one to Winston, then headed over to me.

"Miss?" he asked, bowing toward me slightly.

"Uh, sure." I wasn't much of a drinker, aside from wine, champagne, and any beverage that was made in a blender and served with a paper umbrella. Still, it occurred to me that drinking anything *but* sherry in surroundings like these would seem as out of place as wolfing down a Big Mac.

I took a sip, surprised that the experience reminded me of those fire-eaters who used to be a part of sideshows.

Whoa! I thought. *Whatever type of sherry this is, it sure isn't something to trifle with!*

I was gearing up for a second sip when a tiny woman with a slender frame swept into the room. The first thing that struck me was that she moved with incredible grace even though she was wearing a floor-length skirt. It was made of black satin that matched the lapels of her short black velvet jacket. I'm no fashion expert, but even I recognized that her outfit was extremely tasteful, reflecting classic design and fine workmanship.

Her hairstyle was similarly timeless: a neat gray pageboy with a few strands in front that swooped elegantly beneath her chin. She had clearly been beautiful when she was young. In fact, she was still extremely pretty, thanks largely to her chiseled features—

especially her pronounced cheekbones, which gave her a patrician look. She wore very little makeup, just a hint of pink on her lips and a light dusting of blue on her lids that precisely duplicated the color of her eyes.

"Betty! Winston!" she cried as she crossed the room. "I'm so grateful to you both for coming!"

The three of us rose to our feet. I waited patiently while the others hugged and air-kissed, meanwhile murmuring all the right things about the sad occasion that had brought us here in the first place.

"Charlotte, I must introduce you to Jessica," Betty said once that was out of the way and she'd sat down again. "She's a dear, dear friend, and I'm sure the two of you will become friends, as well, even though of course I wish you'd met under different circumstances."

"Hello, Jessica. I'm Charlotte Merrywood." As she reached out to shake my hand, her smile was warm and friendly. But the look in those pale-blue eyes of hers struck me as much more calculating. I got the feeling she was evaluating me—not necessarily in a bad way, just as a means of trying to figure out what I was all about.

"I'm so sorry about your loss," I said.

"Thank you," she replied with a sad smile. "I can't tell you how much it means to me that Betty and Winston came at this terrible time to offer me support. If you being here, as well, helps them find the strength they need now, then I'm grateful to you for joining them."

What a gracious woman, I thought. I decided on

the spot that she had every right to evaluate me. After all, I was pretty much an intruder, a stranger who'd come at a time when Charlotte and the rest of her family would surely prefer to be with people they knew well.

Charlotte took the glass of sherry Jives offered from the tray and lowered herself onto an upholstered chair with legs carved like lion's paws. Glancing down at the two dogs still hovering nearby, she commented, "I see you've met Admiral and Corky."

Smiling, she added, "Corky—he's the smaller one—is a shih tzu and Lhasa apso cross. Admiral, the basset hound, is his much older brother. It's obvious that they've both taken a shine to you, but please let me know if they're bothering you."

"Not at all!" I assured her.

"Jessica's a veterinarian," Betty informed her, her voice bursting with pride. "She loves animals—and they love her."

"A veterinarian!" Charlotte exclaimed. "How fascinating. And how rewarding it must be to work with animals. Where is your office?"

"I have a mobile-services unit," I told her. "In other words, a clinic-on-wheels. I treat animals all over Long Island."

"She takes care of dogs, cats, even horses," Winston added proudly.

"In that case," Charlotte said, with a warm smile, "I can see why Admiral and Corky already adore you."

Returning her smile, I said, "They both seem like great dogs."

"They belonged to Linus." Suddenly Charlotte's face sagged, and all the light went out of her eyes, as if someone had flipped off a switch. "They were completely devoted to him. In fact, the two of them keep looking at me, as if they're asking where he is..."

Her voice trailed off, but not before I heard the beginnings of a sob. It was almost a relief that at that moment a booming clap of thunder set the entire house to shaking.

"My, this storm is turning out to be quite powerful," Charlotte commented, quickly regaining her composure. Glancing out the velvet-framed windows, she added, "I do hope we don't lose our electricity."

That's all I need, I thought morosely, being stuck in a haunted house on a remote island with no lights, no heat, and—worst of all—no coffeepot.

"Aw righty, that's done." A brash female voice, as abrasive as the screeching of a microphone, suddenly cut into the room. "Yer rooms are all ready for the loikes o' you. Even got fires burning, warmin' things oop a bit."

A wiry woman about my age had come rushing in, bearing an elegant silver tray piled high with cheese, crackers, and fruit. She was dressed in a dowdy dark dress that looked as if it had been designed by the same person who'd clothed the sour-faced souls hanging in the hallway. She wore a starched white apron over it, and on her large, pigeon-toed feet were boxy shoes with thick rubber soles. Her bright red-orange hair was pulled up into a loose topknot, with plenty of tendrils spilling over her face and neck. But her hairstyle looked haphazard, as if she simply couldn't be bothered to fuss with it—as opposed to going for a carefully calculated bed-head look.

The woman walked quickly and kept her head down, as if she was one of those people who's continually in a hurry. As she neared the sofa, I noticed a smudge on her cheek. At first I thought it was coal dust. At second glance, however, I decided it looked more like eyeliner gone awry.

"Blimey, the bunch o' you are wet as all get out!" she cried, setting the tray down on a table. She looked us up and down, meanwhile wiping her hands on a linen dish towel she'd pulled out of her apron pocket. "You'll catch yer death, every last one o' you. You'd be wise to do what that gentleman over there is doing, standing by the fire and warming 'is 'ands."

Eliza Doolittle, is that you? I thought, blinking.

"What a marvelous suggestion for combating the rawness of this chilly evening," Charlotte said kindly, even though none of us budged. "Thank you so much for your concern, Gwennie."

Ah, I thought. So this is the famous Gwennie, the maid who spends her free time hauling suitcases and posing for steroid ads.

"Come on, now, 'elp yerselves," Gwennie said, bustling around as she distributed forks and napkins. "Everybody 'oo comes off that ferry is always 'ungry. Shattered, too. Something about being out on the open seas makes everyone knackered. Sometimes even a bit dicky."

I deposited Frederick on the carpet, then stepped over to the tray the thoughtful Gwennie had brought and smeared a water cracker with Brie. She was right: I was famished. As for being a bit dicky, I couldn't say.

"Are the children back yet, Gwennie?" Charlotte asked.

"Not yet, Missus," Gwennie replied. "But I'm sure they'll be 'ome soon." Glancing toward the window, she added, "Cold, dark night like this—nobody in their roight mind should be out and about. Still, it's not as if they didn't have good reason."

Turning to us, Charlotte said, "I'm sorry my children aren't here to greet you. My two youngest went to the funeral home early today to make arrangements for Saturday and they're not back yet. I've decided to let them make all the difficult decisions, since at this point it's more than I can cope with."

Smiling wanly, she added, "Missy and Brock are taking such a load off my shoulders by dealing with all those details. As for my oldest, Taggart, he had some business to attend to in the city today, but he'll be back shortly." With a tired sigh, she added, "There's been so much to do, ever since..."

Once again, she let her voice trail off. It didn't matter, since we all knew exactly how she would have finished her sentence if she'd had the strength.

"The children were all at the house last night, weren't they?" Winston asked gently.

"That's right," Charlotte said. "We were all here

together, celebrating Linus's seventy-fifth birthday."
Her voice thickening, she added, "That's the one good
thing, I suppose. That poor Linus had one last night
with his entire family around him, I mean. His business
partner, Harry, too. He's in the city at the moment, but we expect him tomorrow. And his assistant,
of course. She was totally devoted to him—"

"Excuse me, Mrs. Merrywood," Jives interrupted,
stepping into the room abruptly. I'd forgotten about
him, mainly because he'd disappeared as soon as he
supplied everyone with a glass of that high-octane
sherry. Since I hadn't heard him approaching, he
seemed to materialize out of thin air. "Miss Scarlet has
arrived."

I blinked. Miss Scarlet? *Don't tell me,* I thought.
*She's the killer—and she did it in the kitchen with the
candlestick.*

"Wonderful," Charlotte said. "Please show her in,
Jives."

I braced myself for a pretty but flashy young
woman, someone with too much makeup and
platinum-blond hair worn in a 1930s style—a wavy
perm, maybe. And a startlingly bright red dress, of
course.

But while the woman who strode into the room a
couple of seconds later was indeed young, little else
about her bore any resemblance to my imagined version. In fact, she seemed determined to present herself
as far from flashy as possible, even venturing into the
realm of prudishness.

She didn't appear to be wearing any makeup at all,

although her thick tortoiseshell glasses made it difficult to get a good look at her eyes. She wore her dark-brown hair pulled back into a tight chignon, a style that struck me as strangely severe. It was consistent with her surprisingly stiff posture. She carried herself as if she wasn't quite comfortable in her own body. As for her outfit, it also seemed unusually prim for someone in her mid-twenties, consisting of a conservative black suit with a tailored jacket and a slim, hip-hugging skirt.

True, she wore a red scarf, but it was a tasteful shade of burgundy. In one hand she clutched a leather portfolio of the same color, which made her look efficient—and important.

"Miss Scarlet," Jives announced with great ceremony.

I couldn't help noticing that as he said her name, his lips curled disdainfully.

O-kay, I thought. So there's no love lost there.

But I turned my attention to the new arrival.

"Hello, Miss Scarlet," I greeted her. "I'm Jessica Popper."

She looked startled, then laughed. "Oh, heavens. That's just Jives's idea of a joke. My name is actually Miss Sandowsky. Scarlett Sandowsky—with two *T*s, like Scarlett O'Hara."

That's a relief, I thought as I shook her hand. *So I'm not living in a board game, after all.*

Still, I couldn't help wondering how long it would be before Professor Plum and Colonel Mustard joined us in the conservatory.

"Scarlett, I'd also like you to meet Winston and Betty Farnsworth," Charlotte said. "Winston and Linus were good friends. They knew each other from the club."

"Hello," she said politely, shaking their hands, as well. "I am—I *was*—Mr. Merrywood's personal assistant."

My eyebrows shot up. Why would a man in his seventies need a personal assistant who was so young? I wondered. Not to mention one who was so pretty, once you got past her attempts at concealing that fact.

I couldn't decide if I was being sexist or simply suspicious, the way a good investigator should be. I decided to hold off on forming any opinions until I got to know Miss Scarlet—uh, Scarlett—a little better. In the meantime, I headed back to that Brie.

"Scarlett is practically a member of the family," Charlotte commented. "She's been so helpful to Linus over the past two or three years."

Smiling shyly, Scarlett added, "I was so grateful to Mr. Merrywood for hiring me right out of college. I can't imagine working for anyone nicer."

"Scarlett was an economics major at Vassar," Charlotte explained.

"And I knew I could learn more working for Linus than anywhere else," she commented. Her forehead creased as she said, "But I interrupted you. I'm so sorry. Please go on with whatever you were saying."

"Where was I?" Charlotte asked, sounding distracted.

"You were telling us about Linus's birthday party,"

Betty reminded her. "And how nice it was that he had his whole family with him."

"That's right," Charlotte said breathlessly. "It was a lovely party. A real celebration. And the thought that's kept me going ever since is that at least Linus had a chance to see everyone one last time. It was an absolutely perfect evening and a wonderful dinner. Cook made it all herself, from soup to nuts."

Peeking over from the linen napkins she was folding, Gwennie added, "Quoite a spread, it was. All 'is favorite foods—including the ones that were bad for 'im."

She shook her head disapprovingly. "Lobster with melted butter, shrimp smothered in garlic and oil, even a fancy chocolate birthday cake almost as tall as I am. Imagine, a man 'is age, eating foods loike that."

"Now, Gwennie, none of that matters, does it?" Scarlett piped up. "Mr. Merrywood enjoyed his last meal, and that's what matters."

"Y'ask me, it was all that nasty saturated fat wot did 'im in," Gwennie grumbled.

As I sat back down, I glanced over at Charlotte, wondering how Linus's grieving widow felt about an argument on this particular subject. I was relieved that Gwennie's hands flew up in the air, as if she'd just noticed that something was missing, and she rushed out of the room to remedy the situation.

The sound of voices out in the hallway caught everyone's attention.

"Of course Mummy wouldn't start dinner without us," a woman exclaimed. "I wouldn't be surprised if she was doing something civilized right now like enjoying cocktail hour, the same way she would have if Daddy were still here—see, Townie? I was right! Some things never change, thank goodness!"

A woman in her mid-thirties strode into the room a few paces ahead of a man about the same age, pausing as she glanced at the tray of snacks and the glasses of sherry that everyone held. A look of satisfaction crossed her face.

"I'm sorry we're so late, Mummy," she said, leaning over to kiss Charlotte's cheek. As she nestled onto the couch next to me, all three dogs—Frederick, Corky, and Admiral—converged on her, wagging their tails and demanding attention.

"It's positively ghastly out there!" she moaned, reaching down to pat each of the dogs distractedly. "But at least we managed to accomplish what we set out to do, thanks largely to Townie. He's ever so organized!"

Ever so organized? I thought with amusement. I was beginning to think I'd truly been transported into a 1930s black-and-white movie.

I studied the woman I surmised was Charlotte and Linus's only daughter, Missy. Her glossy chestnut-brown hair, just long enough to brush her shoulders, was held in place by a brown-and-black-plaid headband. I recognized it immediately as the signature fabric of Saint Burberry, the patron of preppies.

But her choice in headgear wasn't the only thing about her that screamed preppie. Missy Merrywood wore a beige blazer with a pair of tailored wool pants that looked as if they had been custom-made to show off her fit figure. Tucked loosely around her neck was a patterned brown scarf I thought might be Hermès. Hanging from her shoulder was a quilted black purse on a gold chain. Even I recognized it as Chanel, thanks to the shiny gold logo on its front flap.

Next I checked out her husband. I thought I'd heard her call him Townie, but I figured I had to be mistaken.

He struck me as considerably more staid than his bubbly wife. And it wasn't just his conservative clothing—a dark sports jacket worn with gray slacks—or his closely cropped light-brown hair. It was more the way he held himself slightly apart, not only in the vibes he gave off but also physically. Rather than sitting with the women or standing at the fireplace with Winston, he chose to stand off to the side. It was almost as if he was watching rather than participating.

Charlotte would have none of it. "Townie, come sit with us," she insisted. "I must introduce you to our friends. Betty and Winston Farnsworth..."

Once again, the lady of the house made sure all her guests were properly introduced. When it was my turn, Townie stepped over and held out his hand.

As soon as I reached out, he seized my hand enthusiastically, clamping on to it with the tightest grip I'd ever experienced in the name of meeting someone new. I squeezed back as hard as I could, not wanting him to think I was a featherweight.

"Townsend Whitford the Third," he said through a clenched jaw. In fact, it looked as if his top teeth had been cemented to the bottom row with Krazy Glue. "But call me Townie. Everyone does."

"Jessica Popper the First," I said. "But call me Jessie. Same reason."

"Aha!" Townie chortled, still doing an impressive job of making sure his teeth remained pressed against one another. "So this one has a sense of humor! I like that in a woman!"

His open approval of *moi,* the only real outsider in the room, appeared to arouse some feelings of jealousy on wifey's part. Missy immediately stood up and rushed over to his side. She grabbed his arm as if an earthquake had suddenly begun rocking the room. She practically sent the man sprawling across the floor.

"Come sit with me, sweetie!" she cooed. "Over here, on the love seat. Don't you just adore love seats? It's the absolutely perfect name for a piece of furniture that's built for two, don't you think?"

Once Mr. and Mrs. Whitford had staked out their own part of the room, Townie pulled a carved wooden pipe out of his pocket.

"No one minds if I smoke, do you?" he drawled.

"Of course no one minds!" Missy exclaimed. "Goodness, Townie, it's not as if you smoke those nasty cigarettes. Your pipe has a delicious aroma. Cherries—like the ones we used to pick at our summerhouse on Nantucket. Remember, cupcake? At least, that's what the smell always reminds me of. There's something ever so romantic about it. Not that you and I need any *more* romance, angel pie, do we?"

Even though Townie looked as if he was basking in his wife's adoration, once again Missy grabbed his arm. She clutched it so fervently that I wondered if she feared he was about to bolt. I was curious to see how the poor man was going to manage to light that pipe of his, given the fact that he now had the use of only one of his hands.

Addressing the rest of us breathlessly, Missy said, "I think just about everything this man does is simply amazing. Don't I, sweet pea? As a matter of fact, I consider myself the luckiest woman in the world. If I ever sat down and made a list of all the qualities I wanted in a mate, I'd be able to put a big red checkmark next to every single one. Not that I've ever done that, of course. Why should I, when I already know I managed to find the one man on this planet who was custom-made for me . . . ?"

Missy's endless gushing was making my stomach turn even worse than the roiling waves of Peconic Bay had. I was zoning out when I noticed something moving near the door. A young man was lurking in the hallway, right outside the door. He kept glancing into the room furtively, as if he hadn't yet decided if he really wanted to come in.

"Oh, good," Charlotte said, interrupting her daughter's oration about the wonders of Townsend Whitford III. "Brock is here."

She rose from her seat and floated across the room. By the time she reached the doorway, the lurker had stepped in, probably having realized he no longer had any choice now that he'd been spotted.

"Hello, Mother," he greeted her. His expression softened as he kissed her lightly on the cheek, which told me that she wasn't the one he was ambivalent about.

Now that he was inside and I got a better look at him, I saw that Charlotte and Linus Merrywood's youngest offspring was tall, slightly built, and lean to the point of being bony. Brockton Merrywood, who looked as if he'd barely made it into his thirties, wore his dark-brown hair in a shaggy style that was more Yippie than yuppie. Perched at the end of his slender, almost delicate nose was a pair of wire-rimmed glasses similar in style to the ones John Lennon favored.

Given Brock's taste in eyewear, it wasn't surprising that his duds consisted of jeans that bordered on scruffy and a white tunic-style shirt embellished with tiny white beads and elaborate embroidery. And even though the calendar read November, his toes peeked out from the ends of a pair of well-worn Birkenstock sandals.

Charlotte beamed as she said, "Everyone, I'd like you to meet my baby—that is, my youngest. Brock, this is Winston Farnsworth and his wife, Betty..."

Once all the introductions were done, Brock lowered himself onto an ottoman. But it was Townie who got the conversation moving once again.

"Brock recently launched a new enterprise," he said, addressing Betty and me. "He just went into the bead business."

"It's a jewelry business, actually," Brock replied coldly.

"Yes, but it's beaded jewelry, right?" Missy countered. In a strained voice, she added, "My baby brother is one of those artsy-craftsy people. You know, the kind who like to *make* things."

"At least I work," Brock shot back.

"I don't have time to have a job!" Missy insisted. "I'm too busy with all my charity work, which I can assure you adds up to more hours than most people put in at their office!"

"What Missy meant to say is that Brock has always been extremely artistic," Charlotte explained, ignoring her children's bickering. There was pride in her voice as she added, "Brockton was never interested in the family business. He always found it so cold and dry. There's nothing the least bit creative about all those bits of metal being turned into such practical things, and Brock thrives on creativity."

"Much to Linus's dismay," Townie commented in a voice so soft I wondered if anyone besides Missy was meant to hear him.

"Poor Daddy," Missy said with a loud sigh. "We'll all miss him so much."

"Everyone misses him already," Townie added. "Not only was he phenomenally successful, he was also universally loved. Now, that's a pairing you don't see every day."

A silence fell over the room as all of us remembered why we were here. But I was already learning that silence was as rare in this house as a dust-free surface.

Once again, Gwennie's brash voice cut through the room like the proverbial fingernails on a chalkboard.

" 'Scuse me," she said, bustling into the room. "If y' don't moind, dinner is served. 'At's wot Cook told me to say."

"Oh, good," Charlotte said. "Gwennie, would you take the dogs into the mudroom and give them their dinner?"

Can I go with them? I thought mournfully as I stood up, along with everyone else in the room.

Here I'd been on Solitude Island for less than an hour, yet I was already pining for the one thing I suspected I'd get very little of while I was here: solitude.

Chapter 3

"We should look for someone to eat and drink with
before looking for something to eat and drink,
for dining alone is leading the life of a lion or wolf."
—Epicurus

Like every room I'd seen so far in the Merrywood
mansion, the large dining room was decorated in
a grand manner—at least by nineteenth-century
standards. The walls were covered in ornate dark-
green wallpaper that appeared to be made of silk. The
windows along one wall were framed by velvet drapes
in the same somber hue. Hanging on the walls were
more huge oil paintings of people who, from the expressions on their faces, looked as if whatever they'd
last eaten hadn't agreed with them.

Also like the rest of the house, this room was
shrouded in darkness. The rain beat mercilessly

against the windows, the slightly alarming sound punctuated by the occasional clap of thunder. Aside from periodic flashes of lightning, what little light there was came from another chandelier. It was just as big, fancy, and useless as the one in the front hallway.

Placed at either end of the long, narrow table was an elaborate candelabra. The dozen or so candles stuck into them emitted a pale, flickering light that cast eerie shadows across the dark walls but other than that did little besides drip wax onto the white linen tablecloth. I found myself wishing I'd packed a decent flashlight along with my travel alarm clock and my moisturizer.

The table was set for eight, with glistening crystal, snow-white plates, and silverware so shiny that someone in this household obviously knew their way around a polishing cloth. At each place was a salad that looked appetizing enough, along with a dinner roll on a plate with its own pat of butter molded into the shape of a rose.

As hungry as I was, I hovered near the doorway, not sure what the lady of the house had in mind in terms of seating arrangements. Charlotte immediately headed for the chair at the end of the table, the seat closest to the swinging door I assumed opened onto the kitchen. Betty sat down on her left, while Winston chose the chair to her right.

Townie and Missy, meanwhile, pulled out the two chairs next to Winston, while Brock and Scarlett took the two on Betty's side of the table. That left me with no place to sit but the other end of the table, opposite

Charlotte. I perched nervously on the edge of the high-backed wooden chair, hoping that being so visible wouldn't mean anyone would be looking to me for guidance in the area of table manners.

"Isn't this nice!" Missy gushed. "Doesn't the table look lovely, buttercup? I see Gwennie even took out the best china and silverware."

"It was already out," Brock noted, sounding a tad irritated. "We used it for Dad's birthday dinner, remember?"

"Of course I remember!" Missy shot back. "I was just commenting on how pretty everything is, that's all."

"I'd say we could all use a glass of wine," Townie interrupted heartily. He grabbed one of the bottles that had been strategically placed around the table. I surmised that when it came to setting the table properly in this house, making wine accessible was a top priority.

"Now, who's interested?" he asked, holding it up.

"I am," Missy said eagerly, wasting no time in handing her wineglass over to her husband.

"I'll have some, but just a small glass," Charlotte said. With an apologetic smile, she added, "The sherry has already gone to my head."

I had a feeling I'd be wise to have a little, as well. In fact, it seemed that everyone at the table agreed that a glass of wine was a good idea. That is, except for one lone voice.

"None for me," Brock announced loudly. "Our

bodies have enough toxins to fight off without adding to their burden by inflicting alcohol on them."

I couldn't help noticing the disdainful look Missy and Townie exchanged. I was relieved that just as Missy opened her mouth to react to her younger brother's comment, the swinging door behind Charlotte burst open.

Standing in the doorway was a plump woman in her sixties bearing a large round tray. Encircling her ruddy face was a cloud of blond hair topped by a starched white cap. It matched the starched white apron she wore over a plain gray dress that could best be described as matronly. At the bottom of two barrel-shaped calves was a pair of scruffy black flats, stretched to the limit by what looked like unusually wide feet.

If this woman's name is Mrs. White, I thought with alarm, *I'm taking the first ferry off this island.*

"Good evening, Cook," Charlotte greeted her with a warm smile.

Aha, I thought, as the woman nodded a silent greeting. *So she doesn't actually appear to have a real name.*

"I don't know about the rest of you, but I'm absolutely starving," Scarlett commented, smoothing the linen napkin in her lap.

"Me, too," Missy gurgled. "What have you prepared for us tonight, Cook?"

By this point I was much more interested in the food than in the cast of characters inhabiting this place. The wonderful smells wafting out of the kitchen were having a dramatic effect on my stomach, which was empty except for the Brie I'd managed to stuff into it.

Still, given my surroundings, I half-expected an Indiana Jones–type meal, complete with monkey brains and eyeball soup. So I was greatly relieved when Cook placed the tray on the sideboard and pulled the silver cover off the largest serving platter. A flock of tiny birds was arranged in a circle on a large dish, all of them facing the center as if they were enjoying a game of duck, duck, goose. Only in this game, there were clearly no winners.

"Rock Cornish hen," Cook announced. "Although I've always suspected they're no more Cornish than I am."

At last, I thought. *A servant whose accent is more Queens than Queen Elizabeth.*

"Oh, my," Brock said with dismay as he surveyed the plate being passed around the table. "I hope you also made plenty of veggies, Cook."

"Don't tell me you're still a vegetarian," Missy said, not even trying to hide her exasperation.

"Vegan, actually."

Missy rolled her eyes. "It's always something with you, Brock, isn't it?"

Glowering back at his sister, he replied, "I don't know that I'd classify a healthy and socially responsible way of eating as 'something.' "

"Personally, I couldn't live without meat," Townie interjected. As if to make his point, he plucked the largest Cornish hen off the platter.

"Personally, I couldn't live without planet earth," Brock countered. "And if everyone who lives on it doesn't start behaving more responsibly—and that includes *eating* more responsibly—there's not going to be much of a planet left. Then, of course, there are the obvious health benefits of giving up destructive practices like smoking and eating dead animals and torturing one's liver with alcohol—"

"Brock, Missy, I think we've had enough," Charlotte interrupted in a low, controlled voice. "I would appreciate it if you would all put your personal agendas aside at this extremely difficult time."

A heavy silence fell over the table, one that was interrupted only by the pinging of silverware as the serving platters continued to be passed around. I was relieved that one of them turned out to be piled high with carrots, broccoli, and several other vegetables that presumably qualified for Brock's A-list. Or V-list, in this instance.

"So what do you do, Jessie?" Townie finally asked in a congenial voice. He paused as he stuck a fork into the ill-fated bird on his plate. "Career-wise, I mean."

"I'm a veterinarian," I said.

"A vet!" Brock exclaimed. "Wow, that must be great. I considered going to vet school myself at one point."

Barely removing her lips from the edge of her wineglass, Missy muttered, "And architecture school and computer-graphics school and chiropractic school..."

"I've heard it's even harder to get into vet school

than medical school," Townie remarked, clearly impressed by my résumé. "Where did you attend?"

"Cornell."

"Ah. A fine school," Townie said with an approving nod. "Of course, I'm a Harvard man myself. At least, undergraduate. Got my MBA at Wharton." Reaching for the platter of veggies, he added, "Where's your office?"

"I don't have an office," I replied. "At least, not the usual kind. I actually work out of a—"

I was interrupted by a loud thumping that sounded as if it was coming from above. Automatically I looked up, afraid that something large and dangerous was about to fall on my head. But I saw nothing but a ceiling.

Confused, I glanced around the table. Yet with the exception of Betty and Winston, who both looked surprised, no one seemed to react.

Probably ancient plumbing, I decided. After all, that was something I had experience with myself, thanks to the more-than-a-century-old cottage that had formerly been my home.

Not wanting to be rude, I decided to forge ahead.

"Anyway, I work out of a van," I went on. "A clinic-on-wheels. I have everything I need right inside it, and I travel all over Long Island, making house calls—"

This time, it wasn't just the thumping that stopped me. It was the distinct sound of wailing.

It almost sounded like an animal. But I knew animals well enough to recognize that this was a human voice.

"What *is* that?" I demanded. "Is someone hurt?"

"It's nothing," Brock said, without bothering to look up from the potatoes he was shoveling into his mouth. "Ignore it."

It certainly didn't sound like nothing to me. Once again I looked over at Betty, who appeared to be as puzzled as I was. But I decided not to pursue it, since none of the Merrywoods seemed the least bit concerned.

"So tell me, Jessie," Townie said, once again focusing on me. "How well did you know the old man?"

He spoke in his usual tone, which I'd started to characterize as forced joviality with a side order of lockjaw. But I was pretty sure I detected an edge lurking underneath. I chalked it up to competitiveness over our respective educational pedigrees.

"Actually, I didn't know Linus at all," I replied. "But he was a good friend of Winston's, and he and Betty asked me to join them on this visit." I glanced at them both to make sure my answer met with their approval.

"That's right," Betty agreed. "Jessica is like a daughter to Winston and me, so we brought her along for moral support."

Just then, a particularly loud roll of thunder set the entire house to trembling. In fact, it sounded as if a bowling alley had moved in next door. Through the window, flashes of lightning continued to illuminate the sky.

Betty glanced around warily, then in a barely audible voice muttered, "And I think we're going to need all the support we can get."

"Each and every one of us needs whatever support we can get," Missy chimed in, clearly having heard what she hadn't been meant to hear. "Especially from one another. Dad's passing is such a terrible thing. And so unexpected! It's not as if any of us had any warning. The man had never been sick a day in his life—"

She was interrupted by more flashing lights and, a few seconds later, another round of booming thunder.

And then everything went dark. Or at least *darker*.

I glanced upward and saw that the tiny bulbs in the chandelier had gone out, leaving only the flickering candles to keep us from sitting in total blackness.

"Oh, no!" Charlotte cried. "Just as I feared. We've lost the electricity—again."

"Oooh!" Missy squealed. "This is kind of spooky!"

My thoughts exactly. Even though I don't think of myself as someone who scares easily, being stranded on Solitude Island in the dark with the Addams Family was enough to give anyone the heebie-jeebies.

"Darn!" Scarlett cried. "And my cellphone is about to die. I was planning to leave it on the charger overnight. Now I won't be able to get any calls!"

Or make any, I thought uneasily. Including those all-important 911 calls.

"Cell-phone service is bad enough on this island that it's not going to make much of a difference, anyway," Townie grumbled. "There's no Internet service, either. Coming to this island is like going back in time a hundred years."

"It's just as well," Brock interjected. "Cell phones and computers and BlackBerries are destroying civilization as we know it. People don't talk to the people they're with anymore. I can't tell you how many times I've seen two people sitting in a restaurant together, each of them talking to somebody else on a cell phone."

"I didn't know you went to restaurants," Missy shot back. "Aren't they simply tools of the proletariat?"

Brock pushed away his plate. "Now *I've* had enough." Glowering at his sister, he muttered, "And I'm not just talking about the food."

He stood up and started toward the door when Charlotte called after him, "What about dessert?"

"He said he was full, Mother," Missy said, her bottom lip protruding sullenly. "Let him go."

"Actually," Winston said, clearing his throat loudly, "if you don't mind, I think I'd like to go to my room, as well. It's been a long, stressful day, and I suspect that tomorrow will be just as demanding."

"Of course," Charlotte said. "Jessica, I've put you in a quiet room at the end of the north wing. You'll have that part of the house to yourself until Harry Foss arrives. His favorite room is just a few doors down from yours."

Turning to Betty and Winston, she added, "I've chosen a lovely room for you two. It's in the south wing and has a wonderful view of the bay, as well as its own bathroom. Scarlett is right across the hall if you need anything. As for the children, they're all staying in their old rooms. They're right near mine, in the east section of the house. I tried to spread everyone out so you can enjoy some privacy. I'll have Jives and Gwennie escort all of you to your rooms."

"I'm sure we can find them on our own," I assured her. I didn't see any reason to inconvenience either Jives or Gwennie, especially since I was pretty sure I could find my way around. "Just point us in the right direction."

Frankly, I was more than ready for a little downtime. And it wasn't just the complicated interactions that apparently went on in this household day and night making me feel that way.

I suddenly missed Nick and my animals terribly. I could picture Max trotting around Betty and Winston's house with his favorite rubber pink poodle in his mouth, looking for his favorite playmate, and Lou lying by the front door, making little whimpering noises that said he missed me as much as I missed him. I imagined Cat waiting for me on the softest cushion Betty owned, which she'd put in the corner near the fireplace, and Tinkerbell meowing unhappily....I wondered why I hadn't just thrown caution to the wind and tucked them all into my suitcase.

With the lack of electricity and spotty cell service, I wasn't even going to be able to call home and wish them all good night. At the moment, my regular life,

not to mention the rest of the world, seemed far, far
away.

• • •

Betty, Winston, and I tromped up a tremendous staircase that was covered in red carpeting and edged with
an ornate wood-carved banister. It reminded me of the
one in the mansion Scarlett O'Hara and Rhett Butler
moved into after they married. But then, according to
the directions we'd received, it was time for us to part
ways, with Betty and Winston heading off to the right
and me going to the left.

"Good night," I said, holding the candelabra I'd
brought along higher so they could see my face. "See
you tomorrow."

"Actually, I'm heading back over to Long Island
early in the morning," Winston said. "As we were getting up from the table just now, Charlotte told me her
lawyer, Oliver Withers, set up a meeting with someone
from the medical examiner's office in Riverton first
thing. She asked me to go with him."

"It's kind of you to be so helpful," Betty commented, squeezing his arm.

"I'm just glad there's something I can do," he
replied. "There aren't many people I've been friends
with for thirty years."

"And I was just getting to know him," Betty added.
"Good night, Jessica."

As we headed off in opposite directions, I found myself alone, shuffling through a long, shadowy hallway,

guided only by the dim candlelight. I realized that I was walking around with a potential weapon.

Dr. Popper did it in the hallway...with the candlestick, I thought with amusement. Or maybe that should be Dr. *Purple*.

When I heard the floor creak, I assumed it was simply because of the wind whipping around the house— It whooped and hollered so loudly that I decided it was what was responsible for the strange noises I'd heard during dinner.

This big old house really does feel haunted, I thought. *It's a good thing I don't believe in—*

"A-a-gh!" I yelled as something large jumped in front of me. I jerked backward, the sudden motion causing hot wax to drip onto my hand. That caused me to let out an even louder yelp.

"Ow!" I cried, not sure if the sound I'd just made was the result of fright or simply good old-fashioned pain.

Still, by that point, I'd realized that what had crossed my path so abruptly wasn't a demon or a spirit or any other creature that hailed from a world other than this one. It was a man.

Even though it was a dark, rainy night in November, he was dressed for cocktails on the terrace. He wore white linen pants that miraculously didn't have a single wrinkle in them, a phenomenon I didn't believe I'd ever witnessed before. His shirt was also white, but it appeared to be made of nubby raw silk. It looked as if Armani or someone of his caliber had designed it: It fit the man snugly in the torso yet had sleeves that were expertly cut to show off how nicely the fabric draped. His clothes also showed off his trim, muscular physique, no doubt the result of long, grueling hours at a gym.

As I held my candelabra up higher, I saw that he was quite handsome, with thick blond hair that even in the pale light reminded me of my favorite Crayola back in elementary school. Its unlikely shade made me suspect that the folks who made Lady Clairol had recently launched a Lord Clairol line. His eyes were also unusually rich in color. Even in the dim candlelight I could see they were a bright shade of turquoise.

Mother Nature—or Bausch & Lomb? I couldn't help wondering.

It was only after I noticed how good-looking he was that I became aware that, for some reason, he was gripping a tennis racket in one hand. The effect of his country-club-esque sports equipment, combined with his tennis whites, made him look like someone Jay Gatsby would invite to one of his parties.

"Did I startle you?" he asked, looking surprised.

"Heavens, no," I replied sarcastically. "I was totally anticipating that someone was going to leap out of the shadows at me."

He laughed, revealing a set of perfect white teeth that gleamed even more brightly than the fabrics he wore. "I like to keep people on their toes."

"You must be Taggart," I concluded. Which meant he was Linus and Charlotte's oldest child, according to what Winston had told me on the boat ride over. The son who already had one or two marriages under his belt, even though he was probably only a few years older than I was.

"One and the same." He grinned. "Call me Tag. The old man was the only one who ever called me Taggart. Which leads me to the obvious question: Who are you?"

"My name is Jessie Popper," I said. "I'm here with some friends, Betty and Winston Farnsworth. They're also friends of your parents. Your mother asked them to stay with her for a few days, and they asked me to join them."

"Same reason I'm stuck here, putting up with the entire Merrywood clan," Tag said breezily. "It's what's known as a command performance. First the old man's big birthday bash, and now this."

His comment startled me more than his abrupt appearance, since he sounded as if he didn't particularly want to be around his family, even for his own father's funeral.

Wanting to change the subject, I said, "Are you planning to play some tennis tonight?" I gestured toward his racket with the hand that wasn't getting an impromptu paraffin treatment.

"What, this?" He glanced at the racket with surprise, almost as if he'd forgotten he was carrying it. "I found this in that hall closet." He pointed to a closed door a few yards away. "When we were kids, we always cleaned our rooms by stashing most of our junk in there. I haven't looked in it in ages, so I figured I'd see if I'd left behind anything good. This was actually a decent racket at one time. I thought I'd bring it home with me when I finally get out of this godforsaken place."

Good thing he happens to be wearing his tennis whites, I thought wryly.

"Speaking of leaving, when did you arrive?" I asked. I realized I sounded as if I was giving him the third degree, so I fibbed, "You were missed at dinner."

"Ha! I sincerely doubt that, but thanks for saying so." Flashing his pearly whites at me once again, Tag added, "I had some pressing business in the city, and I just got here a few minutes ago. Good thing the ferry has enough room for my car, since there's no way I'd feel comfortable leaving it on the other side of the bay, completely unattended.

"See?" he added, gesturing toward a window at the end of the hall. "That's my little roadster, right out there."

Dutifully, I walked over and glanced outside. Despite the rain and fog, I could see a cluster of cars: Winston's Rolls, a shiny black BMW I suspected belonged to Missy and Townie, and a dilapidated clunker that had to be Brock's. But I got the feeling the one Tag wanted me to notice was the gleaming cherry-red Ferrari. I'm no car expert, but I was pretty sure that thing was the ultimate in boy toys.

I also had a sense that swooning over Tag's choice of transportation was the best way to rack up a few brownie points.

"Wow!" I exclaimed, doing my best to sound sincere, even though I could never get that excited about a vehicle that didn't come equipped with its own

X-ray machine. "That's some set of wheels! I bet you—"

I froze at the sound of the same wailing that had erupted during dinner. As if that wasn't enough to make my blood run cold, loud, gloomy organ music filled the hallway a couple of seconds later.

"What *is* that?" I demanded, hoping I'd get a more satisfying answer than last time.

Tag chuckled. "Don't worry, it's only Aunt Alvira."

I could feel my eyes growing as round as two tennis balls. "Elvira—as in Elvira, Mistress of the Dark? That creepy character from the horror movies?"

"Not quite." Grinning, Tag explained, "That's Alvira—with an *A*."

"You have an aunt living in the house?" I asked, surprised.

"Yup, up on the top floor," he replied. "She's my father's sister. She lives all alone up there, where she can't get into any trouble."

I blinked. "You keep your aunt locked away in an *attic*?"

He laughed again. "You'd have to meet her yourself to understand. But that's not likely to happen. Aunt Alvira is—well, let's just say she's not very sociable."

As if to drive his point home, the mournful wail from above cut through the house once more. Eerie organ music followed, this time a complicated melody in the same minor key.

Nervously, I said, "This strikes me as a bizarre new twist on the concept of mother-in-law apartments."

Tag looked deep into my eyes. "You'll find that a lot of things here on Solitude Island aren't the way they are anywhere else."

I was about to ask him what he meant when he gave his tennis racket a few swings. "I don't know about you, but I've had a very long day. I'm ready to hit the hay. Catch you later, Jessie."

With that, he turned. I watched him walk down the hall toward the stairs I'd just come up, still swinging his racket as he faded into the shadows.

As I continued toward my room, I realized for the first time that I, too, was wiped out. Still using nothing but flickering candles to light the way, I followed the directions Charlotte had given me, going all the way to the door at the very end of the hall.

I pushed it open, reassured that I'd found the right room when I spotted my suitcase on the floor. *Go, Gwennie,* I thought, as I held the candelabra up higher to get a better look.

The good-size room was outfitted with the same heavy, dust-covered antiques used to furnish the rest of the house. In here were a four-poster bed, an armoire, and a tall dresser covered with a lace doily. A fireplace still glowed with the last remaining embers of what had probably once been a decent fire but at this point didn't do a thing to make the room any warmer—either temperature-wise or ambience-wise.

The thick drapes had already been drawn so that they concealed the windows from view. The thick velvet fabric was a subdued shade of blue that in the dim light looked gray.

The wallpaper appeared to be the same color. At first, its busy pattern looked like an abstract design of squiggles and other odd shapes. But after staring at it for a few seconds, I realized that scattered across every few feet were two circles positioned side by side, with a dot in the middle of each.

They looked an awful lot like pairs of eyes.

That design seemed vaguely familiar. I racked my brain, snapping my fingers when I finally remembered where I'd seen it before.

The Haunting, a classic film made in the early 1960s and based on a scary novel by Shirley Jackson called *The Haunting of Hill House.* The wallpaper in one of the characters' bedrooms looked a lot like this, and at night those circles turned into glowing eyes accompanied by the sound of a child crying—

It was only a movie! I reminded myself. Still, I wished that when it came to watching DVDs, I'd stuck to comedies and romances.

I carefully placed the candelabra on the dresser, sat down on the bed, and began pulling off my shoes.

You're really letting your imagination run away with you, I scolded myself. *This is just an ordinary bedroom, one that happens to be in a big, old house that needs an interior designer almost as much as it needs a good cleaning service.*

But by that point I'd begun to wonder if the run-down look of the Merrywoods' mansion was simply the result of the family's affinity for shabby chic, a decorating style that was a favorite with the well-to-do. It was especially popular with "old money." It clearly stated, "Sure, I can afford whatever I want. But nothing I could buy would come close to these cherished old things that have been part of my family forever." In other words, "We've been rich for generations."

I glanced around one more time, testing my theory. It was then that I noticed the wooden bookshelf in one corner. It was tall, reaching nearly to the ceiling. I padded over to it in my socks, grabbing the candelabra off the dresser as I crossed the room.

I scanned the titles on the spines of the thick, dusty volumes, many of them bound in leather. They were classics, mostly—plays by the ancient Greeks Aeschylus and Sophocles, the works of Shakespeare, novels by Milton and Melville and the Brontë sisters.

Then I spotted a copy of *Frankenstein,* by Mary Wollstonecraft Shelley. I couldn't resist reaching for it, thinking it might be appropriate to skim through the first few pages before going to sleep.

As soon as I pulled it off the shelf, I heard a low, rumbling sound.

Earthquake? I thought with alarm.

Almost immediately, I realized where the noise was coming from. The entire bookshelf was moving to one side.

"Oh, my!" I cried out loud. "What have I done?"

My clouded brain assumed that somehow I had caused one of the walls to fall apart simply by removing a single book. But after only a few seconds, the noise stopped.

I blinked a few times, trying to decide if I was really seeing what I thought.

I was. The bookshelf had shifted a distance of five or six feet, revealing a door that up until now had been completely concealed.

My heart pounded violently as I stepped over to the door, wondering if I dared try to open it.

I couldn't resist.

The palm of my hand was moist as I grabbed the cold metal doorknob and tried to turn it.

It turned with surprising ease.

By this point, my heart felt as if it were getting ready to explode in my chest. But I wasn't about to let that stop me.

I pushed, holding the candelabra up so I could see what was on the other side.

The door wouldn't give.

Huh? I thought, not sure if I was relieved or dismayed.

It took me about three seconds to realize what the problem was.

Pull, don't push, an exasperated voice inside my head instructed.

I did. And it opened.

Once again, I thrust out the candelabra, blinking as I struggled to see in the dark and hoping my heart would hold out just a little longer before it broke into a thousand pieces. And then I saw what was on the other side.

A staircase. A hidden staircase.

Yikes!

I seemed to recall that somewhere along the line, Nancy Drew, one of my childhood idols, had encountered a hidden staircase.

But Nancy was a lot braver than I was.

In fact, now that I knew what was behind the door, I decided that that was enough. It was true that part of me was intrigued. But another part of me recognized that venturing up those stairs would be a foolhardy proposition at any time—and that doing it in the dark of night, without the aid of either electricity or a decent flashlight, was likely to be downright dangerous.

I could trip and fall! I told myself. *Or encounter bats or rats or—or even crazy Aunt Alvira!*

With all those solid rationalizations in mind, I closed the door firmly, hoping that whatever was at the top of the hidden staircase would stay put. After all, this wasn't exactly a hotel in which I could request a room with a better view—or fewer features from ghost stories and horror movies. I was a guest in the home of a woman who had just suffered a terrible loss, and the last thing she needed was one of her houseguests complaining about the accommodations.

I pushed *Frankenstein* back into place on the shelf. As I'd expected, the magic bookcase began to rumble again, this time moving in the opposite direction and settling itself with what sounded like a sigh of relief.

It was definitely time to go to bed. It had been a long day, one that included nutty aunts locked away in the attic, business associates named after characters in a board game, butlers who looked like walking cadavers, stuffed ravens and antique suits of armor covered in dust—and now this, a hidden staircase right in my bedroom.

I quickly changed into my flannel pj's and slid between the sheets. I expected to lie awake for hours, worrying about Aunt Alvira and conjuring up visions of ghosts and ghouls and who knew what else. I decided to give it five minutes. Then, if I was too overcome with the heebie-jeebies to fall asleep, I'd go ask Betty and Winston if I could sleep at the foot of their bed. Instead, in what seemed like mere seconds after my head hit the pillow, I was out, no doubt the result of having consumed both sherry and wine in the very same evening.

The last thing I remembered was listening to the sound of the rain pounding on the roof, hoping it would drown out any screams, organ music, or other assorted noises that threatened to keep me awake.

● ● ●

When I woke up the next morning, I lay in bed without moving, relishing the feeling of snuggling up in a warm, soft, surprisingly comfortable bed with my eyes closed. I listened for the sound of rain on the roof. When I couldn't hear any, I hoped that meant the sun had come out.

I finally opened my eyes, expecting to see bright sunlight streaming in. No such luck. Instead, my bedroom was shrouded in shadows. Pale shadows, but shadows nonetheless.

So much for a sunny day, I thought, groaning inwardly. I glanced at the windows and saw that hovering right outside was more of that dreadful fog and the endless rain.

And then a shock wave jolted through me, banishing any traces of sleepiness that still remained.

I can see the windows, I thought with alarm. *But when I went to sleep last night, the drapes were completely drawn.*

Which could mean only one of two things.

One was that I had walked in my sleep—something I'd never done in my life—and taken advantage of my mobility to do a little redecorating.

The other was that someone had come into my room in the middle of the night while I was in a deep sleep.

Impossible! I thought, instinctively pulling the covers up to my chin.

My eyes darted over to the bedroom door. It was closed, exactly the way I'd left it.

That didn't mean someone couldn't have opened it.

Gwennie? I thought. *Could she have gone traipsing through the house last night or early this morning, quietly opening the drapes in each room so the guests would wake up to views of this fine day?*

While it wasn't a great explanation, I decided it was the one I'd stick with.

I rolled over, figuring now that I'd solved that puzzle, I'd check my travel alarm clock to see if it was time to get up.

I was surprised to see it was later than I'd thought—almost nine. But the shock of the glowing red numbers was nothing compared to what else I saw on the night table beside me.

Someone had left me a present.

I reached for it, not sure what it was.

It wasn't until I held it close that I saw it was a little doll made out of yarn. It had yellow hair, cut about the same length as mine. And its clothes, fashioned from bits of fabric loosely sewn together with uneven stitches, were the same color as the ones I'd worn yesterday.

In other words, from the looks of things it was supposed to be me.

And around her neck, pulled tight, was a piece of cord made of black leather.

Chapter 4

"I know when it is necessary,
how to leave the skin of lion to take one of fox."
—Napoleon Bonaparte

Voodoo? I wondered, dropping the doll on my
pillow like the proverbial hot potato.

*And if someone is attempting to cast an evil
spell on me, who is it?*

I jumped out of bed, scarcely noticing how icy the
wooden floor felt beneath my bare feet. I was suddenly extremely motivated to figure out if Linus Merrywood really had been murdered—and, if so, who
was guilty.

I was equally interested in finding out if the killer
was the same person who had left me this souvenir.

Tentatively I switched on the lamp next to my bed,
curious about whether the electricity had come back

on during the night. Fortunately, it had. I dressed quickly, tucking the voodoo doll into my pants pocket, where it was out of sight but not out of mind.

While a shower would have been refreshing, I wasn't in the mood to wrestle with a plumbing system that I suspected would turn out to be as unreliable as the electricity. I was also desperate for coffee. While the little gift I'd found on my night table had done wonders to wake me up, I wasn't in the habit of facing a new day without the assistance of caffeine. Contemplating the idea of a morning without that all-powerful cup of coffee was a horror show all its own, one more reason I was ecstatic that the electricity had come to its senses.

In fact, it was the intoxicating smell of freshly brewed java that led me to the right spot. Breakfast was being served in the dining room, the same place in which we'd all had dinner the night before.

I thought daylight might make the dining room look cheerier, despite the relentless rain. It didn't. The grayness outside made for a gray atmosphere inside. Even in the light of day, the dour-faced men and women in the oil paintings stared down at me as if they were waiting around for something fun like another slew of witch trials.

However, I was much more interested in the food. Cook had set out quite a spread. Several silver chafing dishes, containing bacon, sausage, and hash browns, were lined up on a sideboard. Fresh croissants and bagels were piled high on a platter, while a fruit salad provided at least some color in the otherwise dreary room.

Yet despite the abundance of breakfast goodies there for the taking, only one other person was in the room.

Someone new.

The man appeared to be in his mid- to late forties, his dark hair flecked with silver and his forehead creased. His facial features were attractive enough, if not particularly memorable: hazel eyes, a straight nose, thin lips. He boasted a tan, as if he'd recently returned from someplace warm and sunny. He was also strikingly fit, with broad shoulders and a lean torso that were complemented by his well-cut suit jacket. I decided he was one of those incredibly self-disciplined individuals who, like Tag, routinely spent time at the gym.

Harry Foss, I guessed. Linus Merrywood's right-hand man.

"Goodness, are we the first ones up?" I asked, casting him a friendly smile as I made a beeline for the pair of matching silver urns on the sideboard, one for coffee and one for tea.

"More like the last ones," the man replied, sounding amused. "At least you are. As for me, I drove out from the city early this morning and was just delivered here by boat."

"In that case, I'm glad there's still food left," I said. "Quite a bit of it, too."

"I'd go for the croissants, if I were you," he suggested.

I followed his advice, then joined him at the table.

"Charlotte isn't here to make sure we're properly introduced," I told him, "so I'd better do the honors myself. I'm Jessie Popper."

"Pleased to meet you," he said politely. "I'm Harry Foss. I'm the CFO at Merrywood Industries. Linus's close friend, and as chief financial officer his number two man."

"I'm here visiting with friends of Linus and Charlotte," I explained. "Betty and Winston Farnsworth."

"Farnsworth, huh?" he repeated. "That name sounds familiar."

"Winston and Linus belonged to the same club in New York."

"Ah. That explains it," he said with a nod.

Noticing the folded copy of *The Wall Street Journal* on the table next to him, I commented, "I didn't mean to interrupt your reading. Please feel free to go right ahead."

"Nothing but bad news," he said with a wry smile. "I'd much rather converse."

I paused to sip my coffee, then took a moment to relish the miraculous sensation of that first swallow of the magic potion slipping down my throat.

"How are the employees at Merrywood Industries handling Linus's death?" I finally asked, sincerely curious.

Harry frowned. "Everyone is in shock, naturally. Even though the company is huge, Linus was unusually hands-on. Just about everyone knew him personally. Liked him, too. He was the type of person who made you feel as if you were the most important person in the room, even if you were only a waiter who worked for the caterer. He always had a smile and kind word for everyone.

"He also had an unbelievable memory for names," he continued, his admiration reflected in his tone of voice. "Once Linus met someone, he remembered that person's name forever. Whenever I walked through the corridors with him, he'd greet every employee we passed by name. He'd remember something about their lives, too, so he'd say, 'Good morning, Mary, how's the baby?' or 'Hey, Chuck, still enjoying that new Beemer?' The man was simply amazing."

"Linus certainly sounds like he was well loved by everyone who met him." I stared into my coffee cup, thinking, *Unless he was murdered—which means someone is out there who didn't share the love.*

"Don't get me wrong," Harry insisted, as if he'd guessed what I was thinking. "Linus had his share of enemies. No one can become that powerful without making quite a few of those along the way."

I quickly swallowed the sip of coffee I'd just taken. But before I had a chance to ask him to elaborate, he said, "You know, it's kind of strange that everybody is acting so surprised by Linus's death—especially that they're all saying the man was in such good health."

He glanced around, as if making sure we really were alone. Then, in a softer voice, he said, "I worked with the man day in and day out, and believe me, he was definitely showing signs of aging. After all, he'd just turned seventy-five."

Thoughtfully, I commented, "Seventy-five seems to be an age at which some people still seem young while others—well, not so much. I suppose it depends on genetics, as well as an individual's lifestyle and general health."

I was thinking of Betty. Winston, too. They were both around Linus's age, yet they seemed as sharp and as energetic as other people I knew who were in their fifties or even younger.

But, according to Harry, that wasn't the case with Linus.

"Was his performance at work starting to reflect his age?" I asked.

Harry frowned. "Let's just say it wasn't exactly helping."

The sound of someone clearing his throat prompted me to turn. Winston was standing in the doorway, the wet splatters on the shoulders of his bright yellow slicker telling me he'd returned to Solitude Island from the early-morning appointment on Long Island he'd mentioned after dinner.

Frankly, I would have liked another five minutes alone with Harry. But now that Winston had joined us, I looked up at him and smiled.

"Good morning, Winston," I greeted him. "Pull up a chair and—"

It was only then that I noticed his troubled expression.

"Is everything all right?" I asked, my smile fading.

"I wish it were," he replied.

Harry frowned. "What's going on?"

"I think I'd better talk to the entire family at once," Winston said somberly. Nodding toward Harry, he added, "You and Scarlett, as well."

"What's all this about?" Harry asked.

Winston took a deep breath before replying, "I just got back from that meeting with the medical examiner's office in Riverton. There have been some important developments surrounding Linus's death."

• • •

While Harry volunteered to find Scarlett, I took it upon myself to track down everyone else. Assembling the entire Merrywood clan in one room turned out to require nearly twenty minutes, since the members of the family were scattered all over the house.

I found Charlotte in the bedroom she and Linus must have shared. Like mine, it was decorated with old-fashioned, floral-patterned wallpaper, antique furniture, and thick drapes that looked as if they'd been designed to keep out the rest of the world.

She was sitting on the edge of the queen-sized bed, her expression forlorn as she gazed at an assortment of items strewn across the white bedspread. They looked as if they'd been dumped out of the wooden box pushed off to one side. While I didn't want to seem nosy, I made a quick survey, spotting a few black-and-white photographs, a stack of yellowing letters tied together with a frayed pink satin ribbon, and a dried rose, its flaking petals breaking up into confetti.

I hovered in the doorway, reluctant to interrupt. Instead, I watched silently as she picked up one item after another, stroking it lovingly as she examined it.

"Charlotte?" I finally said, my voice nearly a whisper.

Her head jerked up, and she blinked a few times as if she was confused.

"Jessica!" she cried after a second or two. "How nice to see you. I was just looking at some very old things." Smiling apologetically, she added, "At least that's how they must seem to you. To me, they're all wonderful memories."

"I'm sorry to bother you," I said, "but Winston is back from his meeting on Long Island. He asked me to gather everyone into the conservatory so he can talk to the whole family about something he found out."

Alarm crossed her face. But sounding as calm as usual, she said, "Of course. I'll be there in a minute."

She'd already turned back to the item in her hand. From where I stood, it appeared to be a wedding photograph.

Still feeling terrible about having intruded on such a private moment, I turned and headed down the hallway, continuing my search.

Brock was also alone. He had sequestered himself in his bedroom, which from the way it was decorated looked as if no one had touched it since he was a teenager. The wallpaper in here was cheerful blue-and-white stripes, and a shaggy throw rug that picked up the same shade of blue covered most of the floor.

A half dozen shelves were stuck up against the wall. Most were crowded with books, their bindings worn as if they'd been handled almost to the point of falling apart. A few of the shelves were cluttered with action figures and video games that looked comically out of date. From their surprisingly pristine condition, I got the feeling he hadn't gotten much use out of them during his youth.

Brock lay stretched out on the single bed, fully clothed—including his sandals—with an open book resting on his chest. I tried to peek at the cover, but the angle at which he held it made it impossible for me to see.

Probably the ramblings of some obscure philosopher, I mused. Or maybe a book of broccoli recipes.

Then I noticed that he wasn't completely alone. He had brought the two dogs upstairs with him. They lay next to the bed, Admiral snoring a bit as he indulged in a nap and Corky panting away as if he was waiting for someone to pull out a Frisbee. I knew how badly they were hurting now that their longtime master was suddenly gone, so I was glad they'd found someone else to keep them company.

I cleared my throat. "Winston has asked that the family meet downstairs in the conservatory," I said when Brock glanced up. "He has something he wants to talk to everyone about."

Without a word, he clamped his book closed and started to rise from the bed. But I noticed he held the book to one side, as if to prevent me from seeing the cover.

Interesting, I thought. *So Brock may have a few secrets. Either that or he's simply embarrassed by his choice of reading matter.*

I found Missy in what I surmised had been her father's study, running her fingers along a shelf of leather-bound books. They looked as if they'd been in that exact same spot for so long that they were part of the building's structure.

Scarlett was on the other side of the room, settled into a chair with a stack of papers in her lap. From the three or four piles on the floor around her, she appeared to be sorting through them one by one, probably trying to figure out a way to handle whatever unfinished paperwork Linus had left behind.

Since this was the first glimpse I'd gotten of Linus's study, I hovered in the doorway for a few seconds, looking around eagerly while trying not to be too obvious. Two entire walls were lined with the floor-to-ceiling bookshelves that at the moment held Missy's interest. A huge desk dominated the back half of the room. Manila folders and stacks of papers covered the desk completely, leaving room only for an ornate brass lamp with a stained-glass Tiffany-style shade. Centered on the floor in front of the desk was a large, lush Oriental carpet with an intricate pattern, the varying shades of red probably once brilliant but now faded.

A series of framed black-and-white photographs hung on one of the bare walls. Even from where I stood, I could see that they were shots of Solitude Island taken back in the estate's glory days. The mansion looked stately, rather than decaying. The manicured front lawn and well-tended gardens bursting with blossoms also helped. I spotted a photograph of an elegant glass greenhouse that didn't seem to exist anymore. Yet the narrow wooden dock was the same one at which our ferry had landed when we'd arrived, with the same tiny boathouse jutting up at the far end.

"I don't see how Mummy will ever have the heart to go through his things," Missy was saying. With a sigh, she added, "Daddy was the center of her universe. Of course, I'm the same way with Townie. I think seeing what a wonderful marriage my parents had served as a model for my—oh, hello, Jessie!"

Even as she smiled at me brightly, her brown eyes clouded. I wondered if she was trying to figure out how much I'd overheard—and what she'd been saying before I walked into the room.

Or maybe you're just reading too much into things, I warned myself.

"Hello," I said with an awkward little wave. "Sorry to interrupt, but Winston wants everyone to meet in the conservatory. He just came back from Riverton, and he has some news he wants to share."

Missy and Scarlett exchanged a look of dismay, then immediately rose and headed for the door.

"I'll get Townie," Missy said breathlessly. "Tell everyone I'll be there in two minutes."

"And I'll find Tag," Scarlett volunteered. "The last

time I saw him, he said he planned to spend the morning working out in the rec room."

Once I managed to round everyone up in the conservatory, most people pretty much drifted toward the same spot in which they'd positioned themselves the previous evening, right before dinner. This morning, Tag and Harry, the two more recent arrivals, stood near the windows, with Townie joining them.

The dogs acted as if they thought getting everyone together in one room like this was a great idea. Corky lay in front of the fireplace, happily ripping a rawhide chew to shreds. Admiral plunked himself in front of Charlotte, who distractedly stroked his head with the same affection she'd exhibited around her collection of keepsakes. As for Frederick, he'd insisted on curling up in Betty's lap. I supposed even he preferred seeking out the familiar when the air was so thick with tension.

Winston waited in silence as the small talk died down. Meanwhile, he stared into the flames in the fireplace. The seriousness of the expression on his face was causing a knot to form in my stomach.

Apparently I wasn't the only one who was anxious.

"So what's the news?" Tag finally asked impatiently. "Whatever it is, I have a feeling it's going to seem anticlimactic after all this drama."

"Be quiet, Tag," Missy scolded. "I'm sure Winston has something important to tell us. I can tell just by looking at him that there's something on his mind."

"It is quite important," Winston said, finally turning away from the fire to address the group. Speaking in his usual impeccable English accent, he continued, "Last night, right before we all headed upstairs to bed, Charlotte asked me to join Oliver Withers at a meeting he'd arranged with the medical examiner's office. So first thing this morning I took the ferry over to Long Island and drove to Riverton."

A stricken look crossed Scarlett's face. In a thick voice, she asked, "Have they already gotten the results of the autopsy? I thought it took much longer."

"You're right, it usually does take longer," Winston agreed. "But this time they made an exception."

"Probably because Linus was so important," Townie commented.

"Or because he was so rich," Brock muttered.

"Whatever the reason," Winston said impatiently, "the results of the autopsy are quite... devastating."

A heavy silence fell over the room as we all waited for him to continue. Every pair of eyes was fixed on him as he said, "It appears that Linus died from an allergic reaction."

Linus had a severe allergy? I thought.

But I'd barely had a chance to form the question in my mind before Missy cried, "Daddy ate *eggs?*"

"But that's impossible!" Brock exclaimed. "Eggs haven't been allowed on this island for decades!"

Eggs? I thought, not sure I'd heard correctly.

But then a lightbulb went off in my head as I pictured the breakfast buffet. It had included sausage, bacon, and hash browns—but no eggs. It wasn't until this moment that the significance of the omission struck me.

"Eggs have always been treated like hand grenades around here," Tag muttered. "Who would have had the audacity to sneak any onto the island?"

"Obviously the person who wanted to kill him," Scarlett said. She immediately turned the same color as her name, as if it had just occurred to her that she might have said something she shouldn't have.

"That's certainly what it looks like," Winston agreed softly.

"Wait, go back to the beginning," Townie insisted. "Tell us exactly what they found during the autopsy."

Winston took a deep breath. "A lot of this terminology is new to me, so forgive me if I get some things wrong. But basically the medical examiner's conclusion is that Linus suffered from the symptoms of anaphylaxis, which is most commonly associated with a serious food allergy."

"It's something we've all worried about for years," Charlotte said in a strained voice. The color had drained from her face, making me glad that the ladies happened to be sitting down, after all.

Scarlett still looked confused. "It seems as if the rest of you are familiar with this ana . . . ana—"

"Anaphylaxis," I said, unable to resist jumping in. "The term refers to an allergic reaction that's severe enough to be life-threatening. When certain people ingest a food they're allergic to, the airways in their lungs become constricted, their blood pressure drops dramatically, and their tongue and throat swell to the point of causing suffocation.

"It's not all that common," I added, "at least not to

such a serious degree. I seem to remember reading that the number of Americans who die from food allergies every year is about one hundred fifty."

"And the old man was one of them," Brock said, sounding amazed.

"I don't know much about this," Betty interjected, "but isn't there some kind of injection people with allergies can give themselves—something they always keep with them?"

"EpiPens," I said with a nod. "People who know they have serious allergies generally carry one with them at all times. It's the size and shape of an ordinary pen, but it's actually a shot of epinephrine, the antidote to allergic reactions."

Automatically I glanced over at Charlotte.

"Of course we have EpiPens," she said, still looking as if she was in shock. "Dozens of them, all over the house, in the cars, even on the ferry. I can't imagine why Linus couldn't get to one any more than I can imagine who allowed a food that he was so horribly allergic to onto this island."

Turning to his mother, Brock demanded, "Tell us exactly what happened that night. After dinner, I mean, when you were with him. How was Dad acting right before he died?"

"I—I don't know," Charlotte replied, twisting her hands in her lap. "You see, I wasn't actually with him. I left him alone after we finished dinner and all of you went your separate ways throughout the house. He told me he was tired and wanted to rest. He went up to our bedroom, and I stayed down here to read by the fire. When I went upstairs a while later, I found him..."

Once again, her voice trailed off before she finished her sentence.

Tag let out a low whistle. "So the old man was murdered."

"But couldn't it have been an accident?" Missy protested. "After all, everyone loved Daddy!"

"Apparently not," Tag observed dryly.

"It seems unlikely that it was accidental," Brock said. "Mother is right. Everyone in this house, including the staff, was fully aware of how terribly allergic Dad was to eggs. The possibility that an egg—or something made with eggs—was served to him without someone fully intending to do him harm seems pretty remote."

"According to the medical examiner, allergic reactions occur quickly," Winston noted. "That means that whatever food contained the eggs had to have been ingested shortly before he died."

"This is horrible!" Scarlett cried, looking stricken. "What you're saying is that he probably died because of something he ate at his birthday dinner!"

"Given the contents of Linus's stomach at the autopsy," Winston added somberly, "the medical examiner believes the cake was the culprit."

"Not his birthday cake!" Scarlett exclaimed. "That's too horrible to imagine!"

"Death by chocolate," Tag said under his breath. "Literally."

"It makes sense," Brock mused. "I'm not what

you'd call a great cook, but even I know that nothing else served at that meal was likely to have contained eggs. A birthday cake could not only contain them, they would be impossible to detect."

"Cook is the one who prepared Linus's last meal, including his birthday cake," Townie pointed out, his forehead furrowing. "Doesn't that make her the most likely suspect?"

"I'm sure the police will do everything they can to find out if she knows anything about this," Betty said.

"It couldn't have been Cook," Brock scoffed. "She's been with our family for close to forty years. Not only did she make all the meals at our place in the city, she also came out here on weekends and vacations whenever we did. She's practically a member of the family."

"She certainly kept us well fed," Missy piped up.

"She did more than that," Brock insisted. "The woman practically raised the three of us. I remember all those times she made us fudge or some other sweet that didn't require eggs, then decorated whatever goodies she'd whipped up with little jack-o'-lanterns or Christmas trees—"

"She taught me how to bake," Missy said wistfully. "In fact, I remember bringing my entire Brownie troop here to the house so she could teach us how to make a cake. I even remember her telling us all about food allergies and talking about how to substitute the ingredients in a recipe."

"I remember one Thanksgiving when each of us insisted we simply had to have a different kind of pie,"

Brock added. "I wanted apple, Tag insisted on pump-
kin, Missy wanted pecan...Anyway, I remember
Cook staying up half the night making three different
kinds." With a deep sigh, he added, "That woman has
been dedicated to this family for practically her entire
life."

"But she's hardly the sole suspect," Tag observed.
"After all, Cook isn't the only person who could have
interfered with the old man's last meal."

While I didn't feel it was my place to chime in with
my opinion, I couldn't have agreed more. In fact, I'd
come to that exact conclusion while Missy and Brock
were reminiscing about the role Cook had played in
their family's life while they were growing up.

Tag continued, "I can't resist pointing out that
there's room on the suspect list for almost everyone in
this room right now, as well as Jives and Gwennie—
anyone who was in this house that night.

"Besides," he went on in a jeering tone, "either that
day or the day before, every one of us was on Long
Island, where eggs are as easy to find as...as traffic.
Missy, Townie, Brock, and I all showed up here at the
house that afternoon, a few hours before Dad's dinner.
So did Harry and Scarlett. Any one of us could have
stopped somewhere on the trip over and picked up a
dozen ticking time bombs.

"As for Mom and the servants, they were no doubt
traveling back and forth between Solitude Island and
Long Island for days, shopping and running errands
and doing whatever else they needed to do to get
ready for the big birthday bash. They had as much op-

portunity to sneak eggs or something made with eggs onto the island as we did—which means that any one of us could have added the magic ingredient to the old man's food."

"Tag, that's a vile thing to say!" his sister protested.

"Even for you," Brock added in a snide voice.

"We can count out Winston and Betty and Jessica, of course, but let's face it," Tag went on breezily. "Every other person who's in the house had something to gain from the old man's death—which makes each and every one of us a suspect."

"Tag, please stop!" Charlotte protested. "This is hardly the time and place—"

"Why not be honest for a change?" Tag interrupted. "True, it's something this family has never been very good at. Owning up to the truth is simply not an area in which the Merrywoods have ever excelled."

"And for some reason you've decided this is a good time to turn all that around?" Brock sneered.

"I'd say this is the *best* time," Tag replied archly. "Our father is dead. Wouldn't it be nice to figure out who was responsible?"

"Of course it would," Missy said, her voice wavering. "But the idea that any one of us could have done such a horrible thing is absolutely despicable!"

"And Tag's claim that each one of us had something to gain is simply wrong," Brock declared.

"Is it?" Tag asked, his eyes glinting as he cocked his head provocatively. "In fact, we can't leave Harry and

Scarlett off the list of people who stood to benefit from the old man's death, either."

Scarlett gasped. At the same time, Harry said through gritted teeth, "I think you'd better watch yourself, Tag."

"My feelings exactly!" Missy seconded, her cheeks turning pink. "Besides, poor Scarlett had something to *lose*! Daddy's death means she's now out of a job."

"That's true," Tag agreed. Pointedly ignoring Scarlett, even though she was only a few feet away, he added, "But there could have been some other reason she wanted him dead."

"Like what?" Missy challenged, wrapping her arm around Scarlett protectively.

"Revenge, anger—who knows? It's even possible he was about to fire her, and none of us was aware of it." Tag's overly blue eyes narrowed as he added, "Or maybe the two of them had a relationship that went beyond employer and employee, and she was losing patience because he refused to leave Mom—"

Scarlett let out a cry. "That's ridiculous! You have no idea what you're saying!"

"Taggart Merrywood, you have an evil mind!" Missy cried.

She'd barely gotten the words out before Charlotte interjected, "That's enough, Taggart. If you weren't my son, I'd order you out of my house right now for saying such horrid things."

"But what I'm saying is true," he insisted, glancing around the room. "And you all know it. Let's face it, our father was an extremely powerful man. He could have made an enemy of any one of us. Any one of us could have killed the old man—and for a hundred different reasons, from getting revenge to silencing him."

Don't forget money, I was tempted to say, for the first time wondering about the provisions of Linus's will.

For the next few seconds, the room remained eerily silent. The only sound was the rain slapping against the windows and the wind whipping tree branches around outside. It was as if everyone was starting to grasp the magnitude of what they had just learned.

It was Charlotte who finally spoke.

"I don't care what the medical examiner's office says," she said, her voice low and controlled. One by one, she looked at Tag, Missy, and Brock. "I find it impossible to believe that one of you was responsible for Linus's death. You three are his children, and I know you all loved him. There's absolutely no way any of you could have wanted something bad to happen to your own father.

"The same goes for Scarlett and Harry," she continued, glancing at them. "You both thought the world of Linus. Even if you sometimes had differences of opinion about the way he ran the business, I'm convinced that neither of you would have ever wanted to hurt him.

"I also believe that Cook, Gwennie, and Jives are innocent," Charlotte added. "Brock is right about the fact that Cook has spent nearly her entire life working for us, and she's practically a member of our family. I can't imagine a more dedicated employee. As for

Gwennie and Jives, even though they came to us only recently, I never *ever* questioned their loyalty to the man."

"You left out one person," Tag commented.

Charlotte frowned. "But Winston and Betty—and of course Jessica—weren't even here the night of Linus's birthday party."

"No, but you were," he replied simply.

"Taggart!" Missy cried. "Now you've really gone too far!"

He shrugged. "I'm just making an observation. If somebody poisoned the old man the night of his birthday, we have to consider every single person who was in the house."

"You're despicable," Missy seethed.

"That's putting it mildly," Brock seconded.

"I hate seeing my children argue," Charlotte said, shaking her head tiredly, "and I hate having any of you suspect such a terrible thing of family members. Taggart, I'm going to do everything I can to forgive you for what you just said." She sighed before adding, "If it were up to me, I'd put all these horrible accusations behind us so we could do our best to move on."

"Unfortunately, that probably won't be possible," Winston said.

"For goodness' sake, why not?" Charlotte asked.

"Because Linus's death has now become a criminal matter," Winston replied somberly. "In fact, we should all brace ourselves for a visit from a homicide detective."

Missy gasped. "A homicide detective?"

"That's right," Winston said with a nod. "I was told that the Norfolk County Chief of Homicide, Lieutenant Anthony Falcone, will be paying us a visit shortly."

While every member of the Merrywood household seemed horrified, their reaction didn't come close to mine. I'd dealt with this particular individual once or twice before.

Great, I thought. *It's not bad enough that I'm stuck on a creepy island. Now I'm going to have to deal with a genuine creep.*

Chapter 5

"An army of asses led by a lion
is better than an army of lions led by an ass."
—George Washington

The Merrywoods had barely had a chance to digest the fact that a real live homicide detective would be paying them a visit before Jives appeared in the doorway.

"I'm sorry to interrupt," he drawled in his thick English accent, "but a visitor has arrived. A Lieutenant Anthony Falcone."

As the members of the family exchanged looks of alarm, I jumped from my seat.

"I'll bring him inside," I offered. By way of explanation, I added, "He and I already know each other."

"Thank you, Jessie," Charlotte said, sounding

grateful. "I think we all need a moment to compose ourselves."

I was already rushing out of the room and into the hallway. I immediately spotted Falcone standing in the foyer, his black raincoat dripping water all over the marble floor. His sopping wet coat, combined with his small stature, reminded me of a little black dog someone had left outside during a rainstorm. One of those yappy dogs that drive even me crazy. In fact, I half-expected him to shake himself, splattering the dour old crones in the oil paintings so that they ended up looking as if they had tears streaming down their cheeks.

Instead, his beady dark-brown eyes darted around as he took in his new surroundings.

"*Madon'!*" he muttered. "This place looks like the haunted house at Disney World! And didn't anybody around here ever hear of dusting?"

His eyes drifted over to me. A shocked look passed over his face, but only for a second. Then his tight lips relaxed into a sardonic smile.

"Docta Poppa. We meet again."

Thanks to Falcone's classic New York accent, the man acted as if the letter *R* was silent, like the *H* in rhapsody—or the *K* in knucklehead.

"So it seems," I replied.

"You're the last person I woulda expected to find here," he went on. "Then again, maybe I should have anticipated this, since it's not the first time you butted your nose into somebody else's business. What's your excuse this time?"

As always, it didn't take more than ten seconds in the man's presence to get my blood boiling.

And, as always, I did my best not to show it.

"Linus Merrywood was a close friend of Winston Farnsworth's," I said evenly. "And Winston is the husband of one of my closest friends, Betty Vandervoort. I'm keeping the two of them company while they pay a condolence call to Linus's widow."

"Uh-huh." Falcone knit his bushy black eyebrows together in a way that implied he wasn't sure whether or not to buy my story.

"What about you?" I asked him. "Are you here by yourself?"

"Not quite. I got a coupla uniformed cops outside, lookin' around."

"But why you?" I persisted. "Couldn't someone else from homicide conduct this investigation?"

He cast me a look of surprise. "Do you have any idea how big this is? A guy as important—not to mention rich—as Linus Merrywood, the victim of what looks like murder?"

He shook his head slowly. "I guess you've been outta the loop, stuck out here on this island and all. But believe me, this case has graduated to major news. Now that word is out that Linus Merrywood was murdered, the press is all over this. I'm talkin' the *national* press. Those vultures descended faster than you could say the word 'headline.' In fact, I got a buncha guys guarding the shoreline to keep the reporters and photographers who are suddenly swarming the area from comin' over here in a canoe or a raft or whatever they can get hold of. Fuhget about this stormy weather. Even as we speak there are guys standing out there twenty-four seven with telephoto lenses, hopin' to get a shot of one of the family members."

With a sly grin, he added, "I spotted your buddy from *Newsday* out there, Forrester Sloan. But even he doesn't have the connections to get onto this crazy island."

Just as well, I thought.

Forrester and I had what could be characterized as a love–hate relationship—meaning he fancied himself in love with me while I hated being anywhere near him. At least that was how I liked to think about our association, which from the start had been complicated by the sparks that flew whenever we were together.

Having Falcone on this island was bad enough.

Distractedly, he smoothed his shiny, greased blue-black hair, adding, "To keep 'em happy and away from the Merrywood family, I scheduled a press conference for this afternoon. Everybody's gonna be there—CNN, CNBC, Court TV, you name it."

Oh, boy! I thought. Another chance for Anthony Falcone to get his name—and his picture—splashed across TV screens and in newspapers all over the country. No wonder he broke out the Matrix Men styling gel this morning.

"But are you even sure it's murder?" I asked. "After all, people die of allergic reactions all the time."

He eyed me suspiciously. "Surely Mr. Farnsworth

told you about the phone call, since the two of you are so close and all."

My mouth dropped open. So Winston had finally told the police about Linus's assertion that someone was trying to kill him. And I was certain that, while he was at it, he'd mentioned that Linus had claimed it was someone close to him.

"I figured you knew about that," Falcone continued, obviously reading my reaction. "Mr. Farnsworth told me about the phone call at our meeting with the medical examiner this morning."

"Winston didn't mention that you were there, too," I observed.

"I was," Falcone said with a nod. "And the phone call came up while we were discussing the results of the autopsy. Needless to say, the information we have makes Mr. Merrywood's death suspicious enough that we're considering it a homicide."

Glancing around, he added in a much lower voice, "However, the call from the deceased is something we intend to keep from the family and everybody else in the household at the moment, if you catch my meaning."

"Got it," I assured him.

A hundred questions about what Falcone and the rest of his team had uncovered so far whirled around inside my head. But before I had a chance to wrest any more information from him, he stepped over to the ceramic urn and ran a finger along the surface.

"So what is it with the dust in this place?" he asked,

glancing at his darkened finger with a scowl. "I feel like I'm in a tomb."

"I think the Merrywoods have had problems finding top-notch cleaning people," I replied. I couldn't resist adding, "You know how hard it is to find good help these days."

I was about to try to steer the conversation back to Linus's murder when Charlotte came bustling into the hallway.

"You must be Detective Falcone," she greeted him.

"That's Lieutenant Falcone," he corrected her. "And you are..."

"Charlotte Merrywood. Linus's wife." Smiling as warmly as if she was hosting a dinner party instead of an investigation, she extended her hand. "I'm so pleased to meet you."

As they shook hands, Falcone said, "Sorry about your loss, Mrs. Merrywood. I can promise you that the Norfolk County Homicide Department is doin' everything in our power to find whoever committed this heinous crime."

That's hay-nous, I thought irritably. *Not hee-nous.*

Beyond his embarrassing mispronunciation, I got the feeling his little speech was something he'd been told to say, rather than a reflection of some innate sensitivity I'd never witnessed before. And when he'd memorized it, it was probably in writing.

Yet I couldn't help noticing that, even as he expressed his condolences, he was eyeing Charlotte suspiciously. No doubt he was taking in her expensive jewelry, her well-made designer clothes, and her patrician demeanor. He also looked closely into her eyes, trying to read whatever he could in them.

"I'd like to speak to everyone who was in the house the night Mr. Merrywood passed away, one at a time," he told her, suddenly all business. "According to the medical examiner's report, the victim died from an allergic reaction to a food substance he ingested a few hours earlier, most likely at dinner. It's possible that it was an accident, of course, but right now we're actin' on the presumption that it wasn't. What can you tell me about the last meal Mr. Merrywood consumed?"

"Wednesday was his birthday," Charlotte replied sadly. "His seventy-fifth. The whole family was here. We'd also invited two business associates who were close to him. And the servants, of course..."

As Charlotte filled Falcone in on the details of that evening, he jotted down names and other pertinent information. I stood by quietly, hoping no one would notice me hovering behind the two of them and ask what I was doing there. Fortunately, they both seemed too wrapped up in their own conversation to bother with me.

Falcone finally clicked his pen closed. "Give me a few minutes to get organized here, Mrs. Merrywood. Then I'd like to speak to each of these individuals, someplace private. And for now, at least, I'd like everybody to stay here on the island."

"Of course," she agreed with a curt nod. "I'll go tell them all what to expect."

When she was gone, Falcone turned to me and said, "So whaddya think?"

I blinked. "What do *I* think?"

"That's right. After all, you've already been here awhile, right?"

"I only got here last night," I explained, "so I haven't really—"

"Yeah, but I know you, Docta Poppa," he interrupted. "And I'd bet the farm you already got the lowdown on each one of these people." His mouth stretched into a grin that actually bordered on playful as he added, "So d'you think the butler did it?"

Before I had a chance to reply, he laughed. "Y'know, I always wanted to say that. But this is the first chance I ever got."

"Actually, it's possible the butler *did* do it," I said.

"Really?" He looked pleased. "Tell me more."

For a second or two, I was too shocked to speak. Was it possible that Lieutenant Falcone was asking my opinion? I was tempted to look out a window to see if pigs had started to fly.

But that impulse passed as I realized I did have a lot to say. Even though I had, indeed, been on Solitude Island for less than twenty-four hours, I'd already learned quite a bit about the intrigues of the Merrywood household. Falcone added to his notes as I filled him in on what I'd observed so far: Missy and Tag's disdain for their little brother, Charlotte's protectiveness of Brock and her general role of peacemaker, Tag's reputation as a playboy, Missy's over-the-top adoration of her husband, Scarlett's devotion to her boss, Harry's concern that Linus had begun showing signs of aging, even the quirks of the hired help.

I didn't say a word about Aunt Alvira. I was so intrigued by the notion of a crazy aunt locked in the attic that I wanted to explore it on my own before I sicced the chief of homicide on her.

When I'd finished, Falcone actually looked impressed. Grateful, too.

"Thanks, Docta Poppa," he said. "Now, if you'll excuse me, I think I'll talk to every one of those people myself." Checking his notebook, he added, "Starting with the cook."

"That's Cook," I corrected him, "not *the* cook."

"Whatever." He waved his hand in the air dismissively. "She's the one who made all the food around here, right? Including that last dinner the victim ate Wednesday night? She was also perfectly aware that Mr. Merrywood had a serious allergy to eggs. So if anybody tampered with the cuisine that night, it was most likely her."

He was right; she was the most obvious suspect. Which was precisely why I would have bet *my* farm that she wasn't the guilty party.

But I wasn't the one in charge.

"Maybe you can point me in the direction of the kitchen so I can get started," Falcone said. Glancing around, he muttered, "Jeez, ya practically need a map to get around in this place!"

"Go down this hallway and turn left," I advised. "And I'll be around after you've finished, if you need me."

• • •

Even though I was doing my best to act nonchalant, I was dying to know what Falcone found out during his interviews with Cook, the other two servants, Harry, Scarlett, and of course the entire Merrywood clan. I spent the next couple of hours in the front sitting room, pretending I was catching up on back issues of *Town & Country*. In reality, I was doing little besides watching the clock.

I also did plenty of fidgeting, squirming around in a comfortable upholstered chair. From my behavior, you would have thought I was a dog whose owner had tied his leash to a parking meter while he dashed into Starbucks. In fact, I did more wiggling around than did Corky and Admiral, who were lying on the floor next to me, as still as a pair of bookends.

When I finally spotted Falcone again, he was making a beeline for the front door. I jumped out of my chair, sending a cloud of dust flying. The two dogs looked up in surprise but were apparently too comfortable to budge.

"Well?" I demanded as I dashed into the front hallway.

"Well, what?" Falcone countered. He seemed to have forgotten all about his initial interest in my assessment of the situation. Instead, he was back to looking irritated, as if he found my mere existence on the planet a source of distress.

"Did you talk to everyone?" I asked anxiously. "What did you find out? Did the butler do it? Or

Linus's pretty young assistant? How about one of his children?"

He cast me a stony look. "I'm still workin' on it."

"What about Cook?" I demanded, just in case the most obvious suspect did turn out to be the killer. "She knew as well as anybody that Linus was allergic to eggs, and as you pointed out she's the one who made the meal—"

Falcone shook his head. "First of all, it turns out the cook has a real name: Margaret Reilly. Second of all, she doesn't appear to be the perp." With a smirk, he explained, "And that's mainly because one important *ingredient* is missing."

I wasn't nearly as impressed by his cleverness as he was. "What's that?" I demanded.

"A motive." Frowning, Falcone added, "From the looksa things, she thought the worlda the guy. She worked for him and the rest of this family for almost forty years. She even followed them back and forth between this horror show of a weekend house and their place in the city while the kids were growing up and goin' to school in Manhattan. Then she moved out here full time when Linus and Charlotte started spendin' most of their time on the island. Not that I won't be keepin' an eye on her. But at the moment I got nothin' solid on her or anybody else.

"Speaking of horror shows," he continued, glancing around, "this place really creeps me out. What about you?"

"Actually," I said with a little shrug, "I've kind of gotten used to it."

His face flushed. "Not only do I have a problem with this freakin' house, I also don't like the fact that it's on an island. See, I also have, uh, kind of a problem with, uh, seasickness."

He looked around as if he wanted to make sure we were still alone before adding, "Comin' over here on that boat, I thought I was gonna hurl."

"How awful!" I said, doing my best to sound sympathetic without admitting that I'd had a similar experience myself.

Suddenly a strange smile crossed his face. "Y'know, I just had an idea."

"Really?" I said, fighting the temptation to express my surprise over something that I suspected was a pretty rare event.

"Maybe you could do me a favor."

"Ye-e-e-s?" I asked suspiciously.

"This is not a case I'm gonna solve instantaneously," he said. "Since you're gonna be spending the next couple days here anyway, I'm thinkin' maybe you could keep your eyes and ears open. Both of us know that buttin' your nose into other people's business is something you're pretty good at. So maybe you could see if you pick up on any information that could turn out to be relevant."

In other words, conduct an investigation.

I was floored by Falcone's request—even though it was couched in an extremely backhanded compliment. After all, up to this point, all I'd ever gotten from him concerning my interest in poking around murders was complaints. So I didn't know whether to throw his offer back in his face like an unwanted gift—or run with it.

I chose option B.

"Sure," I replied casually. "I could do that."

"Good." He shrugged his shoulders a couple of times, meanwhile straightening his tie. "This'll help cut down on the amount of time I gotta spend here. Bein' stranded on this island is startin' to make me claustrophobic. Even if these people are richer than creases."

Uh, I believe that's richer than Croesus, I was tempted to say. I also found it hard to resist explaining that, despite the similar pronunciations, the expression he was attempting to use referred to an ancient Greek whose wealth became legendary—not a dry cleaner who wasn't very good with a steam iron.

But I was too taken aback by Falcone's invitation to worry about the man's tendency to mangle the English language—as well as the Greek language. Not only was I astonished by what he'd just asked of me, I was positively tickled.

Even though the main reason Betty and Winston had brought me here had been to look into who might have wanted Linus dead, my role as an ad hoc investigator in the case of Linus Merrywood's murder was now official.

• • •

I stood at one of the narrow stained-glass windows that framed the front door, watching Falcone's silhouette disappear into the fog, still marveling over what had just transpired. But the sound of someone clearing his throat behind me caused me to turn.

I saw that Winston had wandered into the front hallway, probably not noticing me because of the dim light. He had stopped in front of one of the portraits hanging on the wall at the back of the house—one of a somber-faced woman who looked physically incapable of cracking a smile. From the expression on his face, his thoughts were a million miles away.

"Are you all right, Winston?" I asked, going over to him and linking my arm in his.

"I suppose I am, all things considered," he replied, patting my arm and forcing a smile. "Having to address the entire household this morning, delivering such bad news, was a disquieting experience. I never expected that I'd be forced to tell anyone something so terrible. Especially with respect to a man who's been such a close friend for so many years, not to mention a member of such a distinguished family."

His eyes returned to the woman in the picture. "The Merrywoods go way back," he said. "They've been prominent in this area for nearly four hundred years." With a sigh, he added, "How very sad that one of them met with such a tragic end."

"It is sad," I agreed. "I'm sure everyone who knew Linus feels that way and is anxious for the truth about what happened to come out."

"Hopefully Lieutenant Falcone's involvement will help make that happen," he said.

Lowering my voice, I said, "As a matter of fact, I just talked to him. He's already questioned everyone who was here the night Linus died." I hesitated before adding, "But I plan to do the same, since it's the best way for me to figure out who might be the culprit."

Winston frowned. "Is it still necessary for you to worry about any of this, Jessica? When Betty and I asked you to accompany us here to see what you could find out about Linus's death, we were motivated by nothing more than mere suspicion. But it no longer seems necessary for you to be involved now that the police have launched a full-scale investigation."

"Actually," I said, glancing around to make sure no one was lurking nearby, "Lieutenant Falcone asked for my help."

"Really!" Winston exclaimed, his eyebrows shooting up to the sky.

From the way he reacted, I couldn't tell if he was horrified by the idea—or simply surprised that Falcone had asked me. "Isn't that rather...unusual?" he said.

"I'm sure Falcone will put as much effort into this case as he would into any other," I assured him. "But he felt that since I was staying here at the Merrywoods' house, I might have access to some information, or even come up with some insights, that someone on the outside wouldn't be privy to.

"Besides," I added, "he's well aware that I have a bit of a track record when it comes to solving murders."

What I didn't mention was how much my interest in Linus Merrywood's murder had been piqued. Now that I'd gotten to know the members of his immediate circle, I was intrigued. I found them to be a fascinating group, not only because of their individual quirks but also because of the way they interacted with one another. In less than a day I'd become completely absorbed in the puzzle of which of them might have wanted the man dead.

Then there was Linus himself. As the CEO of a Fortune 500 company, he was one of the wealthiest and most powerful industrialists in the nation. Yet from all accounts he had earned the respect, admiration, and even love of many of the people who had known him. That unlikely combination made the fact that he had been murdered all the more provocative.

Besides, there was something about a murder occurring in a big, creepy old house that made investigating it irresistible.

I suddenly remembered a thought that had popped into my head as I'd sat with the other members of the household, watching them react to Winston's report.

"Winston," I said, lowering my voice even further, "has anyone mentioned Linus's will?"

He looked surprised by my question. "No. And to be perfectly honest, ever since Linus's phone call I've been so dumbstruck by everything that's happened that it hasn't even occurred to me to think of anything that practical."

"Do you know anything about the provisions he made?" I asked.

As I expected, he shook his head. "There was never any reason for him and me to discuss something like that. But I do know that the man's personal fortune was somewhere in the millions. It's very possible that his money played a role in all this."

With money generally being considered the root of all evil, that wouldn't surprise me in the least. But given the diversity of murder suspects, along with Tag's speculations, I had a feeling there were plenty of other possible motivations, as well.

The challenge before me was finding out what they were.

• • •

Now that I'd been officially charged with conducting my own murder investigation, I knew exactly what I was going to do next—climb the hidden staircase I'd stumbled upon in my bedroom, which I suspected would lead me to the mysterious Aunt Alvira.

It sounded like a good idea until I went into my bedroom, locked the door, and pulled *Frankenstein* off the shelf. As the shelf began to move, just as it had the night before, I suddenly got a bad case of the heebie-jeebies.

Who knows what I'll find up there? I thought nervously, staring at the door that had just emerged and picturing the shadowy staircase I now knew was on the other side. Chances were, there was a good reason why the Merrywoods kept Aunt Alvira locked away.

That the woman was dangerous, for example.

Now that I was contemplating paying her a visit, an image of the woman began forming in my mind. It was based on every horror movie I'd ever seen, every Grimm's fairy tale I'd ever read, every haunted house

I'd ever visited at an amusement park. That meant that, in my head, Aunt Alvira resembled one of the three witches in *Macbeth*, complete with a crazed expression, a cackling voice, and wild gray hair that could have benefited from some of Falcone's hair product.

You can do this, I told myself.

And then: *Look, you* know *you're going to do it, no matter what, so why not just get it over with?*

I took a deep breath, flung open the door, and began to climb the stairs. Astonishingly, they didn't creak. But I decided that was because the gigantic dust bunnies scattered over each one acted as soundproofing.

My heart thudded loudly in my chest as I continued up the steps. Once again I wished I'd brought a flashlight along on this trip. It was so dark that I kept both palms pressed against the walls on either side to keep from tripping and falling.

As I neared the closed door looming at the top, I imagined that on the other side I'd find a gloomy dungeon-type room with craggy gray stone walls and a couple of porthole-size windows. Maybe even some chains embedded in the wall.

It occurred to me that the door was likely to be locked, since if you were going to lock someone in an attic, that was pretty much the way it worked.

Then again, Aunt Alvira had to have a way of getting out. After all, I suspected she was the one who sneaked into my room in the middle of the night to leave the voodoo doll.

Not knowing what to expect, I tentatively put my hand on the knob. It moved easily, enabling me to push open the door gently. And while I'd been expecting more dungeonlike darkness, I was instead nearly blinded by brilliant light.

I blinked a few times, trying to adjust to the unexpected brightness. As I did, I became aware of the sound of a human voice talking softly.

A familiar voice.

A voice that sounded like... Oprah's?

Sure enough, what I heard was the talk-show host introducing a guest who wondrously had lost fifty-five pounds by making just a few important changes to her lifestyle.

Not surprisingly, the voice was coming from a TV. A very large flat-screen TV that hung on the wall above a low wooden bookshelf I was nearly positive I'd seen in the latest Crate & Barrel catalog.

I surveyed the room, noting that this jarring juxtaposition of new over old pervaded the entire room. The off-white couch and lounge chairs looked as spanking new as the television set. By contrast, the well-worn Oriental rug looked as if it had been someone's souvenir from the Crusades, along with that sword hanging in the front hallway. The pictures on the walls were surrounded by ornate gilt frames that screamed nineteenth century. But the artwork inside them consisted of prints of cuddly kittens and bouquets of wildflowers.

There were also a few whimsical touches, like the serious-looking bust of Beethoven that had been decorated with a French beret. Around his neck was draped a white silk scarf that made him look a lot more debonair than the great composer was reputed to be.

Pushed against one wall was an electric organ, which accounted for at least some of the weird noises I'd heard coming from this place.

But even more startling than the décor were the cats. From where I stood, I counted four. A gray-and-black-striped tabby lounged on a small rectangular Oriental rug in front of the organ, while a white long-haired beauty stretched across a windowsill, napping. A Maine coon with thick, fluffy orange fur and amazingly expressive green eyes blinked at me from a couch. And a black cat with glowing green eyes chose that particular moment to dash across the room, right in front of me.

"Four cats!" I cried without thinking.

"Five, actually," a scratchy female voice corrected me. "But Muffin is kind of shy. He hides most of the time, even from me."

This voice belonged to someone other than Oprah.

A second later, the speaker emerged from behind an upholstered chair so huge that it looked as if it had formerly belonged to Papa Bear.

Yet the woman who was now standing in front of me was roughly the size of Baby Bear. The septuagenarian couldn't have stood more than four feet ten, and she looked as if she weighed about as much as my Dalmatian, Lou. Coincidentally, the short puff of hair that encircled her head like a giant cotton ball was the same color as the fur of my Westie, Max: snow white.

Not that her diminutive stature made her look the least bit frail. Of course, that was largely because she was clenching two hot-pink ten-pound dumbbells.

Her weights weren't the only thing bursting with color. She wore a tracksuit the color of raspberry sherbet, and neon-orange laces crisscrossed her white Nikes, which were almost as puffy as her hair.

Just as the room at the top of the hidden staircase hadn't turned out to be what I'd expected, neither did its occupant. Here I'd been picturing Aunt Alvira as a wild-eyed lunatic with a tangled mane of hair who was dressed in rags, flailing about the room as she ranted and raved. Instead, I was face-to-face with someone who looked like a cast member from the television show *The Golden Girls*.

"You're Aunt Alvira?" I asked in amazement.

She narrowed her eyes suspiciously. "Who should I say is looking for her?"

"But you must be Aunt Alvira!" I exclaimed. "Who else would be locked in the attic?"

"I'm not locked in!" she replied indignantly. "I like it up here! Y'think I want to be downstairs with all those crazy relatives of mine?"

I blinked. "But aren't you lonely up here?"

"Me? Nah." Shrugging, she said, "I keep busy, believe me. I've always been a doer. Y'know, always doing something like playing cards or scrapbooking. And I used to volunteer at a senior center." Earnestly, she added, "I'm very good with old people."

"Then why are you up here all alone?"

She sighed. "After Billy died—he was my husband— it just wasn't the same, living in that condo in Boca. So I came back up here from Florida to live with my brother."

Grimacing, she added, "Seemed like a good idea at the time. That was before I realized those kids of his would be coming around all the time. A bunch of other people, too, like that floozy he called his assistant. Ha! I bet I can guess what she assisted him with. And that business partner of his, Harry Whatever. Hmph. I don't trust that man as far as I can hit a Ping-Pong ball."

"Besides," Aunt Alvira continued, "I like it up here. Why wouldn't I? I've got everything I need: a minifridge, a microwave, satellite TV, a DVD player, Netflix . . . I've even got TiVo!"

"And it looks as if you get all the exercise you need," I observed, gesturing toward her weights.

"Sure do. Y'get to be my age, y'start worrying about osteoporosis." To demonstrate, she lifted one of the dumbbells and gave it a few pumps. When one of them suddenly slipped out of her hand and fell to the floor with a loud bump, I understood the source of the banging sounds I'd been hearing.

"I guess making dolls is another one of your hobbies," I commented.

She brightened. "Did y'like it? I wanted to surprise you. I expected you to wake up, but you were sleeping pretty soundly when I came into your bedroom to leave it for you."

I vowed then and there to keep away from that deadly sherry. Especially when I was staying in a house that was also occupied by a murderer.

"I know I got the hair right," Alvira added, "but I'm not so good with the other details. Especially since I get a lot of my information by sneaking around the house when it's dark so nobody will catch me. I've gotten pretty good at hiding in the shadows!"

So the walls in this place really did have eyes, I thought. But they weren't in the wallpaper. They were in the nosy relatives who stole through the rooms like cat burglars.

I pulled the doll out of my pocket. "I was actually a little...confused by the black-leather, uh, accessory."

"Y'mean the bow?" she asked, peering at it. "I thought it was kinda pretty. Don't y'think so?"

"Uh, yes." *Especially now that I know it was supposed to be decorative,* I thought, *and not threatening.*

In fact, I was more than a little relieved at having finally met the relative who lived in the attic. Not only did she appear harmless, but the longer I talked to her, the more charming I found her.

"Since you're here," Aunt Alvira said abruptly, "how about a game of cards?"

"Excuse me?" I asked, not sure I'd heard her right.

"Rummy five hundred. A penny a point." With a sly wink, she added, "But I should warn you that I'm probably gonna beat the pants off ya."

"Sure," I agreed. I figured that even if I lost the whole five hundred pennies, having the opportunity to talk to Linus's sister for the entire length of the game was well worth it.

She switched off the TV and we sat down in the living-room area, me on the couch and Alvira on a chair opposite me. As I nestled into the soft cushions, the Maine coon, still draped across a couch cushion, glared at me, the look in his green eyes telling me he was annoyed that I'd invaded his space. But there were clearly no hard feelings on the part of the sleek black cat, who came over and began rubbing against my leg, purring loudly. I responded by reaching down to pet his silky fur.

All the movement prompted the white long-haired cat to wake up from his nap. He leaped off the windowsill and wandered over to plop down on a large flat pillow that looked as if it had been placed on the floor expressly for that purpose. I got the feeling that now that a card game was about to start, he wanted to be closer to the action.

Even Muffin came out of hiding. She was a pretty gray-and-white kitty who was so shy she hovered behind Alvira's chair, all but hidden. She poked her head around the corner just enough to watch both of us and the rest of the cats from afar, acting like the kid nobody wanted to hang out with on the playground.

Meanwhile, the gray-and-black-striped tabby marched right past all the others and jumped into Alvira's lap. She moved with surprising energy, given the fact that she was a bit overweight.

"Don't tell the others, but Madeira is my favorite," Alvira confessed, lovingly stroking the cat who had just curled up in her lap. "She thinks she's better than the rest of 'em. Still acts like a kitten, too. Or a puppy, to be more accurate. Loves to play, chews up everything in sight...She's a real snuggler, too."

"You're lucky you have such a loving family," I commented, gesturing toward her entourage.

"Darn right," she agreed. "They don't talk, either."

Picking up the deck of the cards resting on the table, she said, "I'll deal." She began tossing cards at me with the adeptness of a dealer at Monte Carlo—or at least someone who'd spent a lot of time racking up pennies at the Boca Raton Senior Center.

I waited until she'd scored 312 points to my meager 108 before cutting to the chase.

"I haven't had a chance to tell you how sorry I am about your brother's death," I said, watching for her reaction.

Alvira's face crumpled. "Terrible, isn't it?" she said, lowering her freshly dealt hand of seven cards. "The poor man went way before his time. Linus was only a couple of years older than I am. That brother of mine was the picture of health. At least, that was what I thought."

"One consolation is that he no doubt enjoyed his last night," I commented, "being surrounded by so many of the people he was close to. I understand his birthday dinner was a lovely event."

"I wouldn't know," she mumbled. "I skipped it. Linus came up for a glass of champagne beforehand so he and I could have a little celebration all our own. There was no way I going to force myself to sit through dinner with those insufferable relatives of mine."

I realized with a jolt that Alvira had no idea her brother had been murdered. How could she? No one had thought to invite her when Winston revealed what he'd learned at the medical examiner's office. And while the news was quickly becoming common knowledge to anyone who owned a television, she'd apparently been watching *Oprah* broadcasts she'd recorded with TiVo rather than the news.

Hesitantly, I said, "Alvira, what do you think of the idea that there might have been foul play involved in Linus's death?"

She didn't miss a beat before asking, "Y'mean the possibility that somebody bumped him off?"

Startled by her bluntness, I replied, "Yes. That's exactly what I mean."

"It's possible," she said thoughtfully. "Maybe even likely."

I was equally startled by her immediate acceptance of the idea that her brother had been murdered. "Why would you think that?"

Keeping her eyes fixed on the cards she clutched in her hands, Alvira replied, "Like I said, Linus was in pretty good health, so he wasn't supposed to die. Not yet, anyway. But it sounds as if you know something."

I took a deep breath, then as gently as I could told her about Linus's phone call to Winston, the results of the autopsy, and the chief of homicide's conclusion that her brother had been murdered.

I braced myself for her reaction, expecting rage or

tears or some other explosion of emotions. Instead, her eyes misted over and her cheeks reddened.

After a few seconds of silence, she said in a choked voice, "I guess that doesn't surprise me. Not when there were plenty of people who had something to gain by my brother kicking the bucket."

"Who?" I blurted out.

She raised her eyebrows but didn't say a word as she studied me for a few seconds. Finally she cocked her head and said, "You look like a pretty smart lady. I bet you can figure that out all by yourself."

"But you're part of Linus's family," I pointed out. "You've known Charlotte and his children and all the other people who were close to him for years. I only met them yesterday."

I also suspected that Alvira was someone who knew pretty much everything that went on in this house—and that she was someone I could trust to be straight with me. I made a mental note to ask Betty and Winston what they knew about Linus's eccentric sister, the first chance I got.

"I'd love to see the monster get caught," Alvira said, her voice tinged with bitterness. "Even if it turns out to be somebody I'm related to."

"I would, too," I told her. "But I can use all the help I can get."

"In that case," she said with an odd little smile, "I'll give you a clue."

"Great!" I cried. "What is it?"

She hesitated. "On second thought, I think I'll wait."

I felt like a balloon that had just had a close encounter with a cactus. "Why?"

"Because I like you," she replied, her chin jutting in the air defensively. "You're spunky, like me. I like spunky. And I want you to come back to visit. We can even play another game of rummy, if you want. I need to check my calendar, but I believe I'm available tomorrow."

"I'll come visit you anytime you'd like!" I insisted. "I promise! You don't have to lure me up here with promises of information."

"Aw, I know how it is," she said, waving her hand in the air dismissively. "People get busy and they forget about things they intended to do. This way I know you'll be back.

"Besides," she added mysteriously, "who knows what you'll find out between now and then? You might not even need my help."

Suddenly her face lit up. "Hey, if you're coming back to visit me tomorrow, how about doing me a favor?"

I hesitated before asking, "What kind of favor?"

"Bring me some of Cook's homemade fudge. Every once in a while she makes a batch and sends some up with my dinner. I'm supposed to watch the sugar, but lately I've been craving that stuff like you wouldn't believe."

Everybody has their price, I thought. I supposed that in the grand scheme of things, buying information with fudge wasn't such a bad deal.

Especially since it wouldn't pave the way only with

Alvira. Securing a batch of homemade fudge would also give me an excuse to talk to the woman who'd prepared Linus Merrywood's final meal, the one that had apparently done him in. And while Falcone had been quick to take Margaret Reilly off his list of suspects, I didn't see why I needed to be in such a hurry to remove her from mine.

• • •

Just as Aunt Alvira had promised, by the time I went back downstairs to the part of the house where the really quirky people hung out, I was out eighty-three cents. But instead of agonizing over my newfound vice, I was mulling over what to do next.

I yearned for the chance to sit down with each member of the household, one at a time, to see what I could find out—just as Falcone had. But the chief of homicide possessed credentials I lacked, which meant I was going to have to come up with a more creative strategy.

I was still pondering possible ways of accomplishing my goal when I wandered into the sitting room in the front of the house, right off the front hallway. I'd hoped to have it all to myself. Instead, I found Charlotte, Missy, and Scarlett standing at the window, peering out into the fog that still surrounded the house.

"This *never* happens!" Missy cried. "People just *know* better!"

"Goodness, I hope it's not someone from the press," Charlotte added. "That nice Lieutenant Falcone warned me that reporters and photographers were doing everything they could to sneak across the bay."

"It couldn't be a member of the press!" Scarlett insisted. "The cops would stop them—wouldn't they?"

"What's going on?" I demanded.

"A boat just pulled up at the dock," Missy replied. "Someone's coming onto the island! A man—someone the family hasn't authorized."

I didn't know if her explanation for why the three of them were in such a tizzy was good news or bad news. From the way the three of them were acting, it sounded as if Attila was lining up outside with all his other Hun buddies. Instead, one lone soul had ventured across the stormy seas to Solitude Island, someone who was either very brave or very foolhardy.

When the knocker sounded, I realized we were all about to find out which of those characteristics the individual in question possessed.

"I'll get it!" Missy cried, dashing toward the front door with such speed I suspected Jives would be no match for her, even if he'd been capable of mustering up the energy to try.

I followed, with Charlotte and Scarlett close behind. So I had an excellent view as Missy flung open the door, revealing a hunched-over figure, his face covered by the hood of his dripping-wet raincoat.

He wasn't readily recognizable. But I couldn't say the same for the two friends he'd brought along, both of them even wetter and more miserable than he appeared to be. And I couldn't remember having ever been so happy to see anyone in my life.

Chapter 6

"An optimist is someone who gets treed by a lion but enjoys the scenery."

—Walter Winchell

Nick!" I cried, resisting the urge to hug someone so wet. "You're here!"

"I missed you," he replied. He gave a little shrug, and the lock of dark-brown hair that's always falling into his eyes did exactly that. "And I decided that even second-year law students are entitled to the occasional weekend in the country. Or, in this case, a remote island."

"Definitely," I agreed. Glancing down, I added, "And I'm so glad you brought Max and Lou!"

Nick's eyes were shining as he came toward me, and he was wearing that smile that always makes me feel as if my internal organs are melting. As soon as he peeled off his sopping jacket, he took me in his arms. Then he gave me exactly the kind of kiss you'd expect from someone who's been married to you for only five months.

But our romantic reunion did not go uninterrupted. My Westie and my Dalmatian kept jumping up and down, pressing their paws against our legs as if they were saying, "Pay attention to *us*!" I didn't know which of the new arrivals seemed happier to see me, my husband or my two dogs.

And as delicious as kissing Nick was, I couldn't say no to my beloved canines.

"I think you'd better show them how happy you are to see them, too," he said, as I pulled away from him reluctantly. Grinning, he added, "You and I will have plenty of time to catch up later."

I crouched down so that I was at eye level with Lou, who was wagging his tail so hard I was glad there were no valuable antiques close by.

"Hey, Lou!" I cooed, pressing my face against his. "How's the best doggie in the world?"

The other contender for that highly coveted role wasn't about to take that comment lying down. Max, being a terrier, is the more energetic of the two— which is just a polite way of saying he's pushier. Terriers are known for their tenacity, which means they have absolutely no qualms about shouldering their way to the front of the line whenever something of value is being doled out. And that includes affection.

"Hell-o, Maxie-Max!" I cried, turning to him. He was jumping up and down, panting and waggling his nearly tailless butt. I scratched both his ears and rubbed my nose against his wet, pulsating snout. "I missed you, too! I'm so happy to see my favorite Westie in the entire universe!"

"I left the cats and Prometheus with Suzanne," Nick told me as he stood by, watching us luxuriate in our joyful reunion. "And Leilani will be fine in her tank for the next few days."

Suzanne Fox is a veterinarian, too, which meant she'd undoubtedly taken adding two felines and a blue-and-gold macaw to her household in stride. At the moment, her only other animal resident was Skittles, who partnered with her boyfriend and roommate, Trooper Kieran O'Malley, on the New York State Canine Unit. I had a feeling Tinkerbell and Cat would be bossing that German shepherd around in no time.

I suddenly remembered that we weren't alone—there were witnesses to the humiliating behavior I always indulge in around my beloved doggies.

I stood up and made some quick introductions, relieved to see that Charlotte, Missy, and Scarlett looked a tad sheepish, too, even though they hadn't just reverted to baby talk and goofy conduct. I supposed that their embarrassment was rooted in their panicked reaction to the arrival of someone who turned out to be interested in their houseguest rather than them.

"It's lovely to meet you, Nick," Charlotte greeted my husband warmly, shaking his hand. "And you're more than welcome to stay as long as you like—now that we know who you are, of course."

"We should probably leave you two alone," Missy

said, leading her mother and Scarlett away. "Or I suppose I should say you *four*."

"I'm really glad you found the time to come," I told Nick after the others were gone and we'd done some more catching up in the kissing department.

"Me, too." His grin faded. "It wasn't easy, though. You should see the madhouse on the other side of the bay!"

"Paparazzi?"

Nick nodded. "The entire coastline is packed with photographers and reporters and vans from all the TV stations. Even the snakes from the tabloids are standing out there in the rain."

"It serves them right," I said, chuckling.

"I'll say," Nick agreed. "You should see the sound bites they're coming up with, Jess. *Billionaire Bites the Dust—Literally. Captain of Industry's Death Is No Yolk.* It's really horrible."

"I can't believe how quickly word spread," I said, grimacing. "It sounds as if those reporters found all this out even before the family did. It's just as well that the Merrywoods are keeping away from all the craziness out there. Speaking of which, how did you manage to get over to the island?"

"Turns out I know a couple of the cops on duty," he replied, "from before law school, back when I was still a private investigator."

Turning back to my doggies and giving them both an even more vigorous ear-scratching, I gushed, "You sweet little doggies are going to love it here! There are lots of long hallways to run down, lots of corners to sniff, Frederick is here—and you're going to make two terrific new doggie friends named Admiral and Corky!"

"What about me?" Nick asked teasingly. "Am I going to love it here, too?"

I stood up. My eyes widened as I breathlessly told him in a near whisper, "Nick, you're not going to believe this place!"

Glancing around, he replied in a soft voice, "I already don't believe it. Have I just walked onto the set of a horror movie?"

"Trust me, the way this place looks is the least of it," I assured him. "Wait until you get to know the Merrywoods and everyone else who's associated with Solitude Island. As far as I can tell, everyone who's in this house right now is a suspect."

Nick grimaced. "In that case, maybe I should pack up Max and Lou and get the heck out of here."

"Don't you dare!" I cried. "I need you. In fact, I can't wait to get you upstairs in my bedroom—alone."

He sidled up to me, wearing a big, sloppy grin. "Because you so desperately missed my hot, irresistible body?"

"Not exactly," I told him. "It's more like I missed your hot, irresistible analytical mind."

He looked so crestfallen that I couldn't help laughing.

"Okay, I need you because of that other reason, too," I told him, wrapping my arms around his neck. Leaning closer, I whispered, "But not until I've filled you in on what's been going on around here."

• • •

As Nick lugged his suitcase and his black nylon back-pack through the door of the bedroom, with Max and Lou following right behind, he let out a low whistle.

"Whoa!" he exclaimed as he dropped his suitcase onto the floor. "Talk about a haunted-house motif! Are those *eyes* in that wallpaper?"

"Quite a design, isn't it?" I replied with a grin. "Wait until you see that hidden staircase I mentioned."

His eyes widened. "I thought you were joking!"

"This is not a place you joke about," I assured him, lowering my voice so Aunt Alvira—or anyone else—wouldn't overhear me. "There's even a crazy aunt locked up in the attic. Except that she's not actually locked up. She's not crazy, either. It's more like she's quirky. One heck of a rummy player, too.

"But there are plenty of other weird things going on here," I continued. "At first I was taken aback by the house and all the bizarre things in it: a stuffed raven, the dusty suits of armor in the front hallway, the creepy portraits hanging all over the house...Then there's the hidden staircase. It's behind a door that opens when you take a copy of *Frankenstein* off that shelf over there."

Looking at my face, Nick said, "You're really not kidding, are you?"

I shook my head. "But I realized this house is only the tip of the iceberg as soon as I met the Merrywoods and all the other people who were here the night Linus died," I told him. "Believe it or not, they're even more intriguing than all that other stuff."

"We have a lot to catch up on, don't we?" Nick

commented. After kicking off his shoes, he dropped onto the bed, crossed his legs at the ankle, and folded his arms behind his head. "So let's hear it, Detective Popper."

I lay down on the bed with my head resting on his shoulder. Max immediately jumped up to snuggle with us, nestling next to my hip. Lou must have decided the climb was too demanding, since he sat on the floor and rested his head on the edge of the mattress, gazing at me with his soulful brown eye. I got the feeling he wanted to make sure he was within petting distance—and that I knew it.

"I'll start with Taggart, the Merrywoods' oldest," I began, reaching over to stroke Lou's smooth head. "After Winston met with all of us to reveal the medical examiner's conclusion, Tag came right out and said he believes that every single person who was in the house the night Linus died could be the murderer. He insisted that the old man's death would have benefited each one of them in some way."

"Such as?" Nick prompted.

"All the usual reasons," I replied. "Tag feels the motive could have been jealousy, revenge, or even wanting to silence him. Then there's the obvious angle: getting at Linus's fortune."

"Whoa. I guess that about covers it." Nick reached over to scratch Max's neck. My hedonistic Westie sighed in ecstasy. "But I'm shocked that Tag thinks the members of his own family could be capable of killing Linus."

"Including his brother and sister," I agreed. "Which

brings the concept of sibling rivalry to an entirely new level. Then again, he also named his own mother as someone who couldn't be left off the list of suspects."

"And what do you think, now that you've had a chance to meet all of them?"

"I'm afraid I have to agree that it's not out of the question," I said, "though I haven't had a chance to find out enough to pin a motive on any one of them."

"Wait a minute." I could feel Nick's entire body tense. "I thought you were here to keep Betty and Winston company while they paid a condolence call."

"I am!" I insisted. "But in addition they asked me if, as a favor to them..."

Nick let out a loud sigh. "I think I know where you're going with this."

Abruptly, I turned on my side so that I faced him. "This whole thing is so fascinating, Nick! This huge spooky house, which you said yourself looks like something out of a horror movie, is absolutely crawling with suspects! Besides, it really seemed to mean a lot to Betty and Winston that I was willing to help figure out the truth behind Linus's death. They were suspicious even before the results of the autopsy came in, since Linus had called Winston shortly before he died and said he thought someone close to him was trying to kill him."

"Are you serious?" Nick cried. "That's something that hasn't even made it onto the Internet."

"Winston didn't say anything about it to the police until this morning," I explained. "But it just makes the people in this house look more suspicious. And makes the case more difficult to solve. Lieutenant Falcone told me—"

"Falcone?" Nick repeated, looking surprised.

I could feel my cheeks burning. "I guess I forgot to mention that he showed up here this morning. After all, this is the highest-profile case that's come up around here in a long time, and he is the head guy. He questioned every member of the household. But he admitted that even he feels that Linus's murder will be a tough case to crack. Believe it or not, on his way out he asked me to help!"

From the skeptical look on Nick's face, I could tell he wasn't quite buying this.

"It's true!" I insisted. "He said something about becoming claustrophobic on islands—and apparently he gets seasick. Besides, he's sharp enough to see that I can get an inside look at the goings-on in this house, which gives me a real edge."

"Okay," Nick said with an air of resignation. "So tell me exactly who's in the house and what their motive might have been for wanting Linus Merrywood dead."

Suppressing the urge to grin, I said, "Nick, each person in this place is a real character in his—or *her*—own way. For example, Tag seems like someone whose whole life is devoted to living extravagantly. He even has the car to go along with that image."

Nick let out a low whistle. "If you're talking about that red Ferrari that's parked near Winston's Rolls, I have to agree."

"That's the one," I said. "Interestingly, Tag's little brother, Brock, the youngest of the three, couldn't be more different. He seems to be stuck in 1967." To drive home the point, I added, "He makes beaded jewelry for a living."

"Ah. So Brock isn't quite the high-powered industrialist his father was," Nick observed.

"Neither is Tag," I said. "No one's mentioned what he does for a living, but I wonder if he does anything at all. Maybe Brock or Tag could have been anxious to get their hands on their inheritance sooner rather than later.

"Linus and Charlotte's daughter, Missy, doesn't have a career, either," I went on. "That is, aside from doing charity work—and being the reigning queen of preppydom. She has every accessory that goes along with it, from a Burberry headband and a Chanel purse to a self-important Wall Street–type husband who's really good at slipping into the conversation the fact that he went to Harvard."

"What about ambition as a motive?" Nick asked. "Are any of the three in line to take over Merrywood Industries now that Linus has passed away?"

"No," I replied. "According to Winston, Linus was pretty disappointed that none of his children possessed the qualities he thought were required to fill his shoes. In fact, he hired Harry Foss to be his right-hand man in the hopes that he'd do the job when the time came."

Thoughtfully, I added, "Harry was here Wednesday night, which makes him a suspect, too. Especially if you factor in ambition as a possible motive. But I noticed something interesting about him: While everyone keeps talking about how Linus was the picture of health, he's the only one who said Linus was showing signs of aging."

"Maybe he simply wasn't in denial about Linus getting older, even though the members of the immediate family were," Nick suggested.

"Could be," I agreed. "But his comment also made me wonder if he was concerned about the way Linus was running Merrywood Industries. It's possible that could have led him to want Linus out of the picture."

At this point, Lou must have decided I wasn't doing a good enough job of petting him, because he went over to the other side and placed his chin next to Nick's hand. I took over Westie duty, while Nick automatically switched from Max's neck to Lou's.

"But the one thing everyone seems to agree on is that Linus was a truly wonderful person," I continued. "His assistant, Scarlett, for example, seems to have worshipped him."

Nick blinked. "Wait—go back. Did you just tell me there's someone named Miss Scarlet in this house?"

"Actually, it's Miss Sandowsky. But if you forget about her having a last name, then yes, there's a Miss Scarlett."

"And is there a lead pipe somewhere in the house?" Nick asked, grinning. "Or maybe a candlestick?"

I rolled my eyes. By this point, the Clue comparisons had become old hat. "Both, I'm sure. But despite Tag's rather crass speculation about what the real dynamics might have been between Linus and Scarlett, I have yet to come up with a motive."

"What about Linus's wife?" Nick asked.

"Charlotte?" I stopped short. "I suppose I have to consider her, too. After all, the spouse is always one of the first people real murder investigators look at. And her own son didn't rule her out. Still, it's difficult to imagine her being the killer."

"Because she's such a sweet person?"

"No, even though she seems to be exactly that," I replied. "It's because she seems to think the sun rose and set on Linus. Still, you're absolutely right. As the victim's wife, Charlotte definitely has to occupy a prime place on our list of suspects.

"So do the three servants, since they were all here that night," I went on. "Margaret Reilly, who's the cook and also happens to be called Cook, seems unlikely. She's been working for the Merrywoods for practically her entire adult life. She seems extremely committed to this family."

Nick rubbed his chin. "Something could have happened lately to make her a lot less committed."

"You're right," I agreed. "We can't rule that possibility out, though she seems to have won Falcone over. There are two other servants, as well: a creepy butler, who's not very good at buttling, and a maid named Gwennie, who doesn't appear to be much better at her job. In fact, I doubt the woman has ever even heard of a dust rag, not to mention a vacuum cleaner."

"Still, being lazy doesn't mean someone is a murderer," Nick commented.

"No," I agreed. "But the simple fact that they were here that night means they're suspects. Which means I need to find out more about their relationship with Linus."

"Wow," Nick said with a deep sigh. "It sounds as if you and I really have our work cut out for us."

Gesturing toward the overstuffed nylon backpack he'd lugged into the bedroom and dropped into a corner, he added, "Or *you* have cut out for you. After all, you're the one who agreed to help figure this thing out. As for me, I've got exams coming up in a couple of weeks. That bag over there is filled with law books, and I intend to use this weekend to get some serious work done."

"As long as you can study by candlelight," I said. "The electricity in this place seems to go out at will."

"Oh, yeah?" Gently, he pulled me down so that we were both lying across the bed. "I could get used to that. Candlelight sounds pretty romantic."

He slipped his hand under my shirt.

"Got any plans for the next half hour?" he asked, his voice suddenly low and husky.

"I do now," I replied, wrapping my arms around his neck.

I only hoped that Aunt Alvira would stay put, at least for a little while.

• • •

Nick and I wasted no time in making it clear just how glad we were to see each other—even though we'd been apart for only one night. But then he reminded me of the pact he'd made with himself before coming to the island: that he'd do the same amount of study- ing he would have done if he'd stayed home.

I was only too happy to leave him with his law books. I also left Max and Lou behind to keep him company as I headed downstairs to do some more nosing around.

Given the long list of suspects—and the fact that I'd barely had the chance to get any one of them alone— I hoped I'd find at least one member of the Merry- wood household who was willing to sit down and have a chat. So I was pleased when I wandered into the conservatory and found Brock sprawled across the couch, in front of the roaring fire.

Both Admiral and Corky lay beside him, stretched out on the floor and basking in the warmth of the flames. It seemed that, at least for now, they had both decided that Brock was the next best thing to their ab- sent lord and master, Linus.

"Mind if I join the three of you?" I asked.

I offered Brock a friendly smile as I settled into an armchair that gave me a good view of both him and the fireplace. By that point the two dogs had come over to greet the newcomer. Corky's fluffy, curved tail wagged excitedly, while Admiral's was more like a windshield wiper on its lowest setting.

"Not at all," Brock said, barely glancing up. "But this gray weather is sapping all my energy, so I can't promise any scintillating conversation."

"It is pretty dreary out there," I agreed. "But that just makes sitting in front of a roaring fire that much nicer."

I reached down to pat both Admiral and Corky on the head. That, of course, increased the rate of tail-wagging, which in turn prompted me to give both dogs a vigorous neck-scratching.

I froze when my fingers made contact with something hard on Admiral's neck.

Frowning, I asked, "What's this bump on Admiral?" I was talking to myself, rather than to Brock.

But he pulled himself up and bent over the basset hound to get a better look. "I don't know what you mean."

"This lump, over here," I said, pushing back Admiral's fur so Brock could see.

"I don't know," he said, sounding concerned. "I don't spend enough time around here to know anything about his health. Aside from the fact that he's getting on in years and that he could afford to lose a few pounds."

"Let me see if I can get a better look," I said.

Admiral patiently allowed me to drag him across the floor until he was underneath a lamp. Fortunately, it turned out to be one of the few in that house that had decent wattage.

I examined the small bump, wishing I'd brought my medical equipment to the island. There are probably fifty different causes for the lumps and bumps that frequently show up on dogs' skin. They can be as innocuous as a wart or a callus—or as dangerous as a melanoma or some other type of cancerous growth that requires surgery.

"What is it?" Brock asked anxiously.

"It's not easy to make a quick diagnosis," I told him. "Admiral should really have a biopsy, just to be safe. But don't get too concerned, since it's probably something that's not too worrisome."

I certainly hoped so. The Merrywoods might have their quirks, but they had enough to deal with at the moment. They didn't need an ailing house pet on top of everything else.

"Maybe you could get Admiral to a vet," I suggested. "I know you're not familiar with the area since you haven't spent much time here since you were a kid, but I can give you a few names."

"Thanks," Brock said.

I turned back to Admiral, wrapping my arms around his neck. It was hard not to hug a lovable, sweet-natured dog like a basset. "I think you'll be fine, Admiral," I told him. "But it's too bad I didn't bring my clinic-on-wheels."

"That's right, you mentioned that you have one of those mobile units," Brock commented. His concern over Admiral's health, however limited, had at least infused him with enough energy that he'd apparently come out of his catatonic state.

"Yup," I replied. "It has everything a regular vet's office has."

Thoughtfully, I added, "Almost everything. There are a couple of labs I work with that do some of the more complicated testing, and if I need special equipment— for a difficult surgery, for example—I have friends who make their facilities available to me."

"Cool," Brock said, nodding. "So you get to be on the move all day."

"That's right," I said. "Even though I live on the North Shore, in Joshua's Hollow, I travel all over Long Island, making house calls. My business is called Reigning Cats and Dogs. My practice is primarily for small animals, but I also treat horses."

"That sounds fantastic," Brock said, looking impressed. "Running your own business like that. I mean, you seem to be pretty successful."

I shrugged. "I've done well enough. But the main thing, at least the way I see it, is that I really love what I do."

"That's my definition of success, too," Brock agreed. "Doing what you love—and being able to make money at it."

"We actually have quite a bit in common, don't we?" I observed, still scratching Admiral's neck. "The most obvious thing is that we're both in business for ourselves. I run my veterinary practice and you have a jewelry business."

"True," he said, nodding.

"And I bet you're like me in that you'd rather concentrate on the part you love instead of worrying about keeping track of finances and marketing and filing taxes." With a rueful smile, I added, "That's the problem with pursuing your passion. There are a whole bunch of other tasks that go along with it that aren't nearly as much fun."

"But if you're good enough at the thing that's your passion," Brock noted, "you can make enough money to hire people to do the stuff you'd rather not waste your time on."

"Point taken," I agreed. "Actually, I hired an assistant just a few months ago. She doesn't have any training in veterinary medicine, but sometimes it's helpful simply to have an extra pair of hands—especially if they're attached to a really good brain. She's great at organization, like keeping track of my finances and laying them out on spreadsheets so they look impressive. But she's also terrific at tasks like re-doing my schedule whenever some kind of crisis comes up. Somehow she manages to explain things to my clients without them feeling shortchanged." I sighed before concluding, "Overall, Sunny has turned out to be worth her weight in gold."

"Sunny?" Brock asked. "That's her name?"

"It's actually Sunflower," I said, chuckling. "But that name suits her parents' lifestyle much more than it fits who she is, so she came up with her own version."

"Sounds like the kind of people I'm surrounded with in Massachusetts," he commented with a smile.

"Is that where you live?" I asked.

He nodded. "Amherst. Up there I'm surrounded by tons of New England charm, not to mention so many colleges and universities I couldn't begin to name them all."

"So you don't live in the New York area," I said, remembering that Betty had mentioned that one of the three Merrywood offspring lived elsewhere.

"Nope. Missy and Tag both still live in Manhattan, on the Upper East Side not far from our parents' place. But I've been living in Amherst since I was eighteen. I went to college there, then decided to stay after I graduated."

"What school?"

"Hampshire."

His choice of colleges seemed like a good match. Hampshire College was as well known for its freestyle atmosphere as it was for its slightly offbeat curriculum. In fact, that entire section of Massachusetts struck me as a place where Brock would fit right in. As he'd mentioned, it was chock-full of first-rate colleges, including Amherst, Smith, and Mount Holyoke, along with an accompanying population of intellectuals ranging from nerds to free spirits.

"Hampshire turned out to be the perfect place for me, since it truly helped me find myself," Brock continued, almost as if he'd guessed what I was thinking. "The school specializes in interdisciplinary majors, instead of just offering single-subject majors the way most colleges do. I was in the School of Humanities, Arts and Cultural Studies. The students all design their own curriculum, so I was able to take a lot of studio art courses along with classes in philosophy and psychology and a bunch of other fields that interested me."

"It must have been great to tailor your courses to your personality," I observed.

"It was," he said. "I really appreciate having had those four years to get to know myself better. And since then I've been lucky enough to find a group of similar-minded people to live with."

"Other Hampshire graduates?"

"No," he replied, "but people who are also motivated more by a search for fulfillment than by chasing the almighty dollar."

He hesitated before adding, "I live in kind of an experimental community called Cold Spring Farm." His tone had suddenly changed. I was pretty sure I detected an edge of defensiveness. "A bunch of us live cooperatively, meaning we split up a lot of the chores. We prepare and eat most of our meals together, we focus on living green, and we generally try to be supportive of one another rather than competitive. Quite a few of the people who live there are also artists, so we can bounce around ideas and just generally feed off one another's creative processes. All in all, I'm really happy with my living situation."

"It sounds as if a lot of that makes sense," I commented. "Especially the part about sharing dinner every night. It must be fun to eat with a big crowd. Sharing the cleanup isn't a bad concept, either."

Brock smiled, as if he was pleased by my approval of his chosen lifestyle.

"It's not only the practical stuff that appeals to me," he went on. "What matters even more is how good it feels to be part of a community. We're all pretty like-minded, so we focus on things that matter. The whole place is solar-powered, and we generate hardly any garbage at all, between composting and recycling and just shopping carefully. We also grow a lot of our own fruits and vegetables. That saves energy by cutting down on trips to the store."

At this point, Corky wandered back to him, probably because he feared Admiral was getting the bulk of my attention. Reaching down to pet him, Brock added wistfully, "But I'd still love to do something I really care about and make enough money to hire somebody like your assistant. I hate doing all the accounting and the day-to-day business stuff as much as you seem to. It would be so great to be free to spend all my time doing what I care about—which at this point is making jewelry."

I hesitated before saying, "This may not be any of my business, but it seems to me that your family is in a position to help you out a bit." Quickly, I added, "At least during the beginning stages of your new endeavor. I'd think your parents would have been happy to extend a loan—or even become investors."

Brock's lip curled. "You'd think, right? Unfortunately, neither of them ever had much faith in me."

"But your mother seems to think the world of you!" I exclaimed.

Still wearing a look of disdain, he said, "She does—but only in my role as the baby of the family. Since I'm her youngest, Mom seems to think I'm eight years old. But when it comes to believing in my ability to make a go of things... Well, that's an entirely different story."

"What about your father?" I asked gently. "From everything I've heard about him, he seems to have been exceptionally generous."

"Ha!" Brock cried. "With other people, maybe. Not with his own kids. He believed we should learn to make our own way in the world. He was one of those parents who made us work for every nickel. If one of us wanted to buy a book or a CD—or even go to a movie with a bunch of friends—we had to do extra chores to get the cash.

"And not simple jobs like taking out the trash, either," he continued, his tone becoming increasingly bitter. "More like heavy yard work or even construction. One summer, when I was a teenager, I ended up building a new shed all by myself so I could make enough money to buy gas for my car—which of course I'd bought myself. Dad paid for the basics like food, clothing, and shelter. But we had to earn money for everything else we wanted—or needed." Scornfully, he added, "Dad called it teaching us the value of a dollar."

"But didn't that change once you all grew up?" I was thinking about Missy's love of designer duds. Since she'd mentioned herself that she was too busy doing charity work to bring in a salary of her own, I'd assumed that her ability to look as if she'd just stepped out of an ad was the result of her father's indulgence. Then again, it was possible that her husband was the one who footed the bills. He certainly looked the part of someone who was extremely successful.

As for Tag, I didn't know where he got the money to subsidize his hobbies. That car, for example.

"You'd think, right?" Brock replied. "Instead, my parents got even stingier. Especially with me. That was mainly because they never really 'got' me."

Sneering, he added, "My father used to say, 'Brock, you may be the youngest, but that doesn't mean you

have to act young for the rest of your life.' Hearing
that always made my blood boil. Even last weekend,
when he and I had the same argument, we—"

He stopped suddenly, all the blood draining from
his face.

"Not that that little fight of ours was any different
from the ones we've been having since I was a kid," he
said, visibly flustered. "It was nothing more than the
two of us going at each other like most fathers and
sons, rehashing the same old script."

But maybe this time, I thought, *you improvised a
different ending.*

"The same goes for my brother and sister," Brock
went on, speaking quickly, as if he was anxious to
move on to a different topic. "My beloved siblings
have the same attitude, in case you haven't noticed.
Missy and Tag both think I'm totally flaky."

"I did notice that Missy made a comment or two
about your lifestyle," I agreed.

"Ha! She thinks everything I do is worthless." By
this point, Brock's tone was scathing. "She always
thought she was better than me, even back when we
were kids. Now that we're adults, she makes fun of
the way I eat, the way I dress, the fact that I choose to
live in harmony with a bunch of other people of like
mind...She doesn't get that I'm on a quest to find
meaning in my life instead of...of frittering away my
time shopping or pretending to be a do-gooder or
whatever she does all day.

"And Tag isn't any better," he went on, still practically spitting out his words. "His spiritual side is zilch.

The only thing he cares about is picking up flashy women and buying the latest car and ... and partying, preferably somewhere in the world that's bursting with yachts and champagne and who knows what else. Lately he's been talking about buying his own plane. Do you have any idea how selfish and decadent that is? It would never even occur to the guy to try to minimize his carbon footprint. He acts as if indulging in whatever suits his fancy at the moment is what life is all about."

Suddenly Brock leaned back against the couch, closing his eyes and noisily letting out a puff of air. I got the feeling that expounding on the topic of his siblings' wastefulness had drained him of all energy. In fact, he was pretty much back to the state in which I'd found him.

Interesting guy, I thought, studying him. *Brock clearly has a disdain for money—or at least the ways in which most people choose to spend it, especially those with a lot of it. And that includes his sister and his brother.*

Yet he yearns for money of his own, mainly to subsidize a lifestyle of spending every waking minute doing only what he loves.

I was certainly sympathetic to that, since I was someone who had also made sure I found a meaningful career. But given all the feeling behind his words, I couldn't help wondering just how far Brock would go in order to make that happen.

Chapter 7

"Even a hare will insult a dead lion."
                                    —Latin Proverb

After Brock dragged himself off the couch and retreated to his bedroom, with Corky and Admiral padding happily after him, I checked my watch. I was surprised to see that it was already mid-afternoon.

That explained why my stomach was growling. I realized that Nick hadn't had any lunch, either. So I decided to put together a picnic that he and I could enjoy in the privacy of our own room, without any Merrywoods around.

I wandered into the kitchen. At first, I was disappointed that Cook was nowhere in sight. While Falcone had already talked to her, I was anxious to do a little questioning of my own.

But I quickly realized that the fact that no one else was in the kitchen left me free to do some poking around. I opened cabinets and checked both the restaurant-sized stainless-steel refrigerator and the pantry, which was practically a room in itself.

As I looked for the ingredients for a romantic meal for two, I also tried to get a sense of the room's layout. After all, since Linus's demise was believed to have been caused by his own birthday cake, the kitchen had played a key role on the night of his death.

The kitchen was huge, with lots of assorted counters and cabinets. Even more important, the room had no fewer than four different entrances. The most obvious was the doorway from the main hall, the way I'd come in. The second was the swinging door that led to the dining room. Cook had used that one the night before while serving the family dinner.

But there were two more ways to enter and exit the kitchen. One was a back door that led outside. Looking out through the glass panels set into it, I saw a walkway that appeared to curve around the house, leading in the direction of the dock. It occurred to me that if someone had switched the birthday cakes, that person could have used any one of these doors, with the one leading outside the house the best bet.

The fourth was an arched opening that led directly to a staircase. I suspected it connected with the section of the house that contained the servants' quarters.

On impulse, I decided this was a good time to find out.

I quickly piled an assortment of picnic goodies onto

a tray: a hunk of cheese, the leftover croissants and fruit salad from breakfast, and, for the main course, the remaining Rock Cornish hens from last night's dinner. My booty provided me with a good cover. If I ran into anyone, I'd simply say I got lost while looking for a more direct route from the kitchen to my bedroom.

Clutching my tray, I tromped up the stairs confidently. When I reached a landing, I saw that I'd been correct about the layout of this part of the house. A short carpeted hallway jutted off to one side. Four closed doors led off it, two on each side. Given the fact that these doors were considerably closer to each other than those in the main part of the house, I surmised that these smaller bedrooms were occupied by Jives, Gwennie, and Cook.

As for the staircase, it kept going up. But it got narrower, as did the walls surrounding it.

Those walls also became curved, and instead of being made of plaster that was painted white, they were composed of craggy gray stone. I suspected that this particular staircase led up into one of the house's towers.

As I continued up the stairs, still clutching my tray, I realized that my palms were damp and my mouth was dry.

Calm down, I scolded myself. *You've read too many fairy tales. Chances are there are no ogres locked up in this tower.*

In fact, there's probably no one up here at all, except maybe some mice. And definitely a few spiders, I thought, as I veered away from a web the size of a café curtain.

This tower turned out to be much higher than the one Aunt Alvira called home. I was out of breath by the time I reached the top. By this point, the stairs were so tiny that I had to walk up them on tiptoe. And simply holding on to the tray became a challenge, since I would have much preferred to use my hands to brace myself against the cold stone walls.

A handrail would be nice, I thought grimly. *So would a light.*

Once again, I cursed myself for not carrying a flashlight as standard procedure. Of course, like the tray piled with food that was starting to seem more burdensome than tempting, it would have been difficult to hold, anyway.

Still, at least I'd made it all the way up. In front of me was a wooden door with a curved top, the kind that's usually featured in gnomes' huts. It was also only as tall as your usual gnome—without his gnome hat.

There was probably nothing up here but an empty room, I decided. After all, this place was too inaccessible for anyone to have turned it into living space. It wouldn't even be useful for storage, since it would be impossible to drag up anything bigger than a shoebox.

I decided it must have been built as a lookout. Either that or the architect thought it would look cool for his castlelike structure to have a tower. At any rate, I intended to find out, no matter how creepy it was.

Balancing my tray on my forearm, I placed my free hand on the tarnished metal doorknob. My palm was so sweaty that I was afraid I wouldn't get enough traction to open it even if it wasn't locked.

So I was surprised when it turned easily in my hand.

I pushed open the door, immediately coughing as a cloud of dust puffed in my face. The hinges creaked loudly, making screeching sounds that were almost eerie enough to send me running back down those stairs.

But I'd come this far. Besides, by this point I was convinced that I'd find nothing but an empty room.

Sure enough, that was pretty much what I saw once I stepped inside. But while there was little light in the small round room, there was just enough that I could make out some shadowy shapes along the back wall. While they weren't readily identifiable, I was glad that none of them appeared to be shaped like the hunchback of Notre Dame.

But while Quasimodo might not have been up here, I got the feeling someone else was.

At first I thought I was imagining it. But as I stood inside the doorway, I could definitely hear something that sounded like short, quick breaths.

There was someone up here.

Or maybe some*thing*.

My heart was beating as loudly as the telltale version immortalized by Edgar Allan Poe as I squinted in an effort to adjust to the dim light, meanwhile bracing myself for whatever I might see. Some supernatural being, perhaps, or some grotesque soul who for some horrific reason was forced to live his or her life hidden away from the rest of the world.

And then something moved. One of the shadows rose from the floor and began moving toward me, into the light . . .

"Tag?" I cried, blinking.

As he emerged from the shadows, I could see a look of terror in his eyes. "Jessie?" he asked in a strained voice. "Is that you?"

"Of course it's me," I replied crossly, nearly collapsing as a wave of relief washed over me. Now that I'd discovered that the ghoul hiding at the top of this tower was only Tag Merrywood, I felt like a complete fool. "What are you *doing* up here?"

"Uh, just looking through some old things."

By now I was able to see quite well, and I glanced around the small room. I immediately realized that he couldn't possibly be telling the truth. The entire space was empty, aside from an impressive number of dust bunnies that had grown to the size of tumbleweeds.

Which could mean only one thing: Tag was hiding out up here.

"I was so pleased to find that old tennis racket," he babbled on, "that I figured I'd poke around the house to see if there was anything else I could bring back home with me."

"In that case," I said dryly, "wouldn't it help to have some light?" Or, even better, something to actually look *at*?

Sheepishly, he said, "I thought I might find some

stuff from my childhood up here. I was particularly interested in, uh, my old baseball-card collection. But I realize now that nothing's stored here anymore. I guess somebody cleaned this place out since the last time I came up."

"That would explain it," I agreed, still puzzling over what all this was about.

"So, uh, who came to the island just now?" Tag's voice was strangely thick as he added, "I saw someone sneak over here on a little boat a while ago. A man. Who was he?"

It took me a couple of seconds to figure out what he was referring to.

"Nick," I finally replied. "My husband. He's a busy law student, but he decided he could get just as much studying done here as at home. So he found someone to bring him over."

Tag let out a deep, relieved sigh. "Is *that* all," he said breathlessly.

He really is *hiding,* I thought, startled. *And not from his family, either.*

There's someone out there he's afraid of.

That realization led to another: Tag was in some sort of trouble. And from the deer-in-the-headlights expression on his face, I got the feeling it was rooted in something a lot more serious than an angry ex-wife or ex-girlfriend.

"What about you?" he asked in an accusing tone. "What brought you all the way up here?"

Now it was my turn to do some quick thinking. My

tale about getting lost en route to my bedroom wasn't going to fly.

"I was searching for a good place to have a picnic," I explained, holding up the tray of food as proof.

"By yourself?" he asked suspiciously. "That seems like an awful lot of food."

"I'm starving," I said with a shrug. "It's way past lunch. I lost track of the time, since I got involved in looking at a bump I found on Admiral's neck. Brock and I started to talk, and—"

"Ah, yes, Brock," Tag said coldly. "I've been thinking about him myself. In fact, now that we all know that somebody did our poor father in, I've been thinking about little *besides* Brock."

"What do you mean?" I asked, even though I was pretty sure I knew exactly what he meant.

His unnervingly blue eyes glittering coldly, Tag said, "I'm convinced my brother is the one who did the old man in."

I just stared at him, too astonished to speak. "Why would he do such a thing?" I finally demanded.

"The oldest reason in the book," he replied with an icy smile. "Money. That is, the money he's bound to inherit now that the old man is gone."

I guess my expression showed my surprise, since he added, "I know it looks as if I'm the spendthrift of the family. And it's true that I like fine things. The Ferrari, the yacht, the houses in Cap d'Antibes and St. Bart's..." With a boyish grin, Tag added, "Nothing wrong with living the good life, is there?"

"Not if you can pay for it," I muttered, wondering

how he managed to do so—especially since he'd just told me his high-priced car was only the beginning. While all along I'd simply assumed that all three of Linus's children benefited from trust funds or some other form of family money, I now knew otherwise, thanks to my conversation with Brock.

"And Brock isn't good with money?" I asked.

Tag laughed. "My brother may pretend he's a non-materialistic hippie, but don't believe it for a second."

"Really? He certainly had me convinced."

"He doesn't crave things like cars and nice clothes," Tag said. "But he wants the means to support his current obsession. Sometimes it's a cause, like saving the planet. And other times it's something that sounds as if it could turn into an actual career. But he never follows through."

"Missy did make a comment about that over dinner last night," I noted. "She mentioned that he'd expressed interest in architecture and computer graphics and some other fields at different times."

"Exactly," Tag said. "He's gone through one phase after another. He'll find some path he's convinced is right for him, and it's all he talks about. A few weeks later he's moved on to something else. Of course, he never actually does anything about pursuing his passion-of-the-month, like applying to programs in whatever he's so focused on. He's simply unable to stick with anything."

"And it sounds as if his current passion is making beaded jewelry," I observed. "But it doesn't seem as if you think this new business of his is going to fly."

"Ha!" Tag said with a snort. "I find it hard to believe Brock would ever be capable of running a business, even on a small scale. Not when he's always been such a disaster when it comes to money."

Winston's words about Linus Merrywood's disappointment in his children's potential for running the business that had prospered under his leadership echoed in my head.

"And not only does Brock lack any business sense," Tag went on. "He also lacks *common* sense. He's spent his entire life trying to find some get-rich scheme that will set him up for life. Since he never had any money of his own, he was always trying to get our father to lend him money to invest."

"Did he?"

Tag scoffed. "The old man was much too smart for that. So he'd turn him down, and then Brock would throw a temper tantrum. Eventually he'd find out what a bad investment it would have been anyway." Shaking his head in disgust, he said, "You wouldn't believe some of the crazy stuff Brock wanted to waste money on."

"Try me."

"One of my favorites was a biodegradable lunch bag some guy up in Vermont had invented," Tag said. "The idea was to keep schoolkids from generating garbage. The problem was that its revolutionary 'green' material biodegraded too fast—in just a few hours. The poor kids who were testing it ended up with apples and peanut butter sandwiches flying around their backpacks about ten minutes after they got to school."

He laughed coldly. "Then there were the dot-com guys who claimed they were going to create the next Google."

"They weren't up to it?" I asked, even though I already knew the answer. After all, if a search engine that was better than Google was out there, I had a feeling I would have heard about it. Switched to it, in fact.

"No one ever found out," Tag said, "since they skipped the country with everyone's money before you could hit *enter*."

"Okay, so your brother doesn't exactly have a nose for running a business or making worthwhile investments," I said. "That doesn't mean he's capable of murdering someone. Especially his own father!"

Tag's eyes narrowed. "There's more to it. You don't know Brock, so you have no way of knowing how competitive he is."

"Do you mean he felt competitive toward your father?" I asked.

"No. Toward me." Tag stood up a little straighter, as if being the object of his younger brother's competitiveness was something to be proud of. And that was apparently the exact message he was trying to communicate, since he added, "I must admit, I'm a pretty hard act to follow. Living with the pressure of being the younger brother of Taggart Merrywood wouldn't be easy for anyone."

Maybe that's your *take on the family dynamic*, I

thought, *but according to Winston, all three of Linus's children disappointed him—including you.*

"Brock's spent his whole life trying to show me up," Tag continued. "And my father had no qualms about letting him know what a disappointment he was."

I took a deep breath before asking the $64,000 question. "What about you?" I asked. "What do you do, Tag?"

He froze. It took several seconds for the stricken expression on his face to soften into one that was more natural. "I...dabble," he finally said. "Investments, real estate...I'm involved in all kinds of things."

O-kay, I thought.

But before I had a chance to ask him to expand upon what "all kinds of things" might include, Tag made a big show of checking his watch. "Hey, we're getting close to cocktail hour," he observed. "That means it's time for me to get out of this creepy tower."

At the moment, however, what interested me most about the man was not the lifestyle he apparently felt so entitled to—or even that he had tried to convince me that his baby brother had murdered their father.

What I was more curious about was the fact that the arrival of a stranger on Solitude Island had immediately sent Tag into hiding.

Who could he have been hiding from, I wondered, this cocky young man who didn't seem to be afraid of anything or anyone? While he appeared committed to living a carefree lifestyle that included every manifestation of the good life on the entire planet, he clearly had something more troublesome going on.

In fact, the more time I spent at the Merrywoods' estate, the more convinced I became that pretty much everyone on Solitude Island had something to hide.

• • •

I was heading back to my room—so poor Nick could finally get something to eat—when I was waylaid again. Only this time it wasn't by one of the Merrywoods or their entourage.

I bumped into Betty and Winston—literally. They were strolling out of one of the sitting rooms on the main floor, and I careened around a corner, my picnic lunch sliding around on the tray. As I gently collided with Betty, I heard a yelp, which I instantly realized came from Frederick. She was carrying the cute little ball of fur in her arms—although given the wirehaired dachshund's shape, he looked more like a baseball bat than a ball.

"Jessica!" she cried, looking pleased to see me even though I'd nearly knocked her and her dog over.

"Betty and I were just talking about you," added Winston, who had deftly stepped aside in time to avoid the collision.

She nodded. "Rumor has it that somebody else has joined us here on the island," she said, her blue eyes twinkling. "In fact, I heard *three* somebodies have arrived!"

"That's right. Nick decided to come for the weekend," I explained. "And Max and Lou insisted on tagging along."

"That's wonderful," Winston said warmly. "We're so pleased they were able to join you."

"Especially Nick," Betty agreed. "Newlyweds shouldn't be apart. In fact, I thought of suggesting it myself but assumed he was too busy with law school."

"*Busy* is definitely the word," I agreed. Gesturing toward the staircase with my tray, I noted, "He's up in our room right now, working his butt off. The poor guy didn't get any lunch, so I thought we could have a picnic."

"What a lovely idea." Betty leaned forward and in a much softer voice said, "But before you run off, I'd love to get an idea of how things are going with . . . you know. Winston told me that even though that horrid Falcone person is on the case, he asked for your help."

"That's right," I said, still scarcely able to believe it myself.

Stroking Frederick's head, Betty glanced around to make sure no one else was listening. "Any theories yet?"

"Not yet," I told her. "But one thing I'm sure of is that this place is absolutely crawling with suspects!"

I immediately regretted sharing such a harsh characterization of the Merrywood household with her—even though it was honestly what I thought. But Betty grimaced in a way that told me she knew exactly what I was talking about.

"I know what you mean," she replied in that same soft, conspiratorial tone. "From what I've seen so far, anyone in this house could have killed poor Linus. The servants, his business partner, his assistant— and, as much as I hate to say it, even his children."

"At least he had Charlotte," Winston commented. "The two of them were inseparable."

Betty sighed. "It's true. In fact, I don't know how she's going to go on without him."

I didn't say anything. That was mainly because I couldn't bring myself to tell Betty and Winston that, while I found it difficult to believe that Charlotte could be guilty, I couldn't completely eliminate her from suspicion. But that was only because I still had so much to learn about everyone on Solitude Island— including the mistress of the house.

Speaking of which, I remembered that there was another woman in said house about whom I was curious.

"By the way, do either of you know Linus's sister, Alvira?" I asked.

The puzzled look on Betty's face gave me her answer. As for Winston, he looked chagrined.

"I've never met her, but Linus did talk to me about her," he said. "Actually, he was quite concerned about her. It seems Alvira is a bit...off center."

"That sounds like a good way to describe her," I agreed.

For some reason, Frederick had suddenly focused on me. He was looking into my eyes and wagging his tail, as if he'd decided I wasn't paying enough attention to him. Naturally, I reached over and petted him, running my fingers along his wonderfully silky ears.

"Are you saying that *you* know Linus's sister?" Betty asked, looking more confused than ever.

"We've met," I replied. "She lives right here in the house." Not wanting to make Alvira sound any more eccentric, I diplomatically added, "In a fairly private room that's located on the top floor. In fact, she's the one we heard making those strange noises during dinner."

"I do remember Linus saying something about her preference for living in isolation," Winston said thoughtfully. "She apparently chooses to have as little contact with the rest of the family as possible. When Alvira lost her husband a few years ago, Linus invited her to come live with him. She agreed, but somehow she never managed to fit in with the rest of the family."

"That's been my impression, too," I said. "But what I'm wondering about is how credible she is."

The muscles in Winston's face tightened. "To be honest, from what Linus told me about her, I got the impression that she's not particularly...stable."

Off center. Not particularly stable. In other words, I thought as I stroked the velvety fur on Frederick's head, *Winston's conclusion about Alvira's state of mind, based on her brother's comments, was that she really was a nutty relative who kept herself hidden away in the attic.*

And here I'd been hoping that whatever clue she was planning to feed me—as soon as I supplied her with fudge—would help me wrap my head around the question of who had killed Linus. Now I was beginning to wonder if, to use a phrase inspired by Frederick, I was barking up the wrong tree.

Chapter 8

"It is all right for the lion and the lamb to lie
down together if they are both asleep, but if
one of them begins to get active, it is dangerous."
—Crystal Eastman

Nick and I lingered over our picnic, which by this
point was more of an afternoon snack than
something that could qualify as lunch. Eagerly,
we wolfed down the leftovers I'd scored in the
kitchen, camping out on our soft bed. Not only was
picnicking in our bedroom considerably more comfortable than sitting on the ground, we didn't have to
worry about ants.

The rain was still tapping against the windowpanes, but we'd made the room feel extra cozy by
lighting a fire in the fireplace and putting candles on
the mantelpiece, the night tables, and the dresser. Max

and Lou sat on the floor, watching us with eagle eyes and no doubt hoping that gravity would send a few crumbs their way.

After we'd stuffed ourselves, Nick admitted that he still wasn't ready to go back to work. Instead, we wandered downstairs to see if we could learn anything new.

We were strolling down the front hallway, nearing the small parlor in the back, when we both heard several different voices trying to talk over one another. That told me the members of the Merrywood clan had gathered once again to enjoy one another's company. Either that or Charlotte had insisted that her children come out of their rooms to spend some time together.

"Nonsense!" I heard Missy exclaim. "I think it's the perfect way to keep ourselves entertained on a dismal afternoon like this one. Townie, sweetie, don't you agree?"

I cast Nick a nervous look. What now? I wondered. Charades? Scrabble? Truth or dare?

"Maybe we'll get lucky and the electricity will go out again," Tag muttered as Nick and I walked through the doorway.

That takes charades and the other games out of the running, I thought, *since they can all be played by candlelight.*

"What are all of you up to?" I asked, glancing around the room.

Sure enough, the entire household was there. Harry Foss sat apart from everyone in a big overstuffed chair that had been pushed into the corner, nursing a snifter of what looked like brandy. Scarlett sat next to Missy on the couch. Even Betty and Winston were cuddling on a loveseat. The only ones missing were the three servants, who I suspected wanted to spend the few hours they had off doing anything but interacting with the Merrywoods.

"Missy just came up with an interesting idea," Charlotte told Nick and me. "She suggested pulling our family's home movies out of storage and watching them together."

"First step, first day of kindergarten," Brock said, sounding wistful.

"First fistfight, first time thrown out of boarding school," Tag added with his usual smirk.

Missy made a point of ignoring her brothers. "We even have some really old ones," she gushed. "They were originally eight-millimeter home movies, but we had them transferred to a DVD ages ago. They're mostly of Mummy and Daddy, and they go all the way back to when they were first married."

I looked back at Charlotte with alarm, wondering if she, too, agreed that taking a trip down Memory Lane at this particular time was such a fun idea.

Apparently she did, since she was smiling and a faraway look had come into her eyes. "Oh, yes!" she cried. "I'd love to see those. Brock, would you set everything up? You're so good at that type of thing."

"Right," Tag mumbled. "Turning on a DVD player with a remote is the next best thing to rocket science."

Getting geared up for showtime took Brock, Tag, and Townie almost ten minutes, two pieces of electronic equipment, and three remotes. So much for the convenience of modern technology.

"Okay, we're ready," Townie finally announced. "We'll start at the beginning."

"They're actually not chronological," Missy said with a frown. "Whoever put all our old videotapes and the eight-millimeter rolls onto a DVD didn't follow our instructions about the order."

"They'll be fun to look at, anyway," Scarlett insisted, pushing her glasses farther up the bridge of her nose. "I've never seen these."

"I have," Tag grumbled. "Believe me, they're not about to replace *Citizen Kane*."

"Shhhh," Missy scolded. "They're starting!"

Everyone in the room focused on the television screen as an image of three young children bearing lunch boxes and big smiles appeared.

"My first day at West Knolls!" Brock cried. "I was five!"

"I was starting third grade," Missy said with a smile. "I remember that dress. I loved it. We got it at Saks. Remember, Mother?"

"I remember," Charlotte said, her voice a near whisper.

I looked over and saw that she was wearing the same dreamy smile as before.

This is turning out to be a really good idea, I thought. *Reminding the Merrywoods of all the good times they had together is helping everyone feel better. Maybe it will even smooth over some of their wounds from the past.*

My theory pretty much fell apart when the next segment came on. Brock and Tag were standing in front of a bicycle, clowning around for the camera. It looked like a sweet moment, until Brock turned and started to climb onto the bike. Tag, probably about twelve, immediately became incensed. He pushed his brother, knocking over both him and the bike. Suddenly everything went black.

Charlotte sighed. "The two of you were always at each other's throats," she observed sadly. "You were so competitive, even back then!"

I was relieved when a new image appeared on the screen. However, this footage turned out to have been taken more than a decade earlier, during the 1970s, from the look of the clothes everyone was wearing: fabrics with big flowers and paisley designs in bright oranges and hot pinks for the women, wide neckties for the men. The hairstyles were similarly dated.

Not so with Charlotte. While her hair was longer and her dress definitely styled to reflect the period, it was clear that she'd never been one to blindly follow the latest trends. She held herself with the same dignity and pride she exhibited today, even though her flawless skin made it obvious she was barely into her twenties.

"These were taken back when Linus and I first got engaged," she said, filling in the silence that accompanied these early films, made before home movies included sound. Her voice was soft; yet, rather than being filled with sadness, she sounded almost exuberant. "Right after he popped the question, we had a huge party for all our friends. It was in the backyard, right here at the house. Everyone came over for the entire weekend. We had a barbecue, and for dessert there was the biggest cake I'd ever seen in my life.... It was such fun!"

Everyone in the room, including her three children, had grown quiet. It was as if we were all equally nervous about her reaction to seeing herself and her recently deceased husband together, back at a time when it had no doubt been impossible to imagine that they'd ever be where they were now: Linus gone, Charlotte alone.

Only she seemed immune to the sadness of it all. "Oh, look!" she cried. "Our wedding day! This was long before video cameras, of course, but one of our friends brought along his eight-millimeter movie camera. Goodness, look how young we were!"

And how happy, I thought, examining the exultant looks on both their faces. The younger version of Charlotte I'd seen before floated down the steps of a gray stone church. She held up the skirt of her long white dress with the same hand in which she clutched a bouquet of white roses interspersed with delicate baby's breath. At her side was a young man in a tux. While he wasn't exactly handsome, his eyes were intelligent, his smile was wide and genuine, and it was clear that he absolutely adored the woman whose arm he held onto as if he intended never to let go of her again.

"You look beautiful," Missy said breathlessly.

"And so happy," Scarlett added.

"We were both incredibly happy," Charlotte said, her eyes still fixed on the screen. Her voice even softer than before, she added, "That's the one thing that's gotten me through all this: the fact that Linus and I had so many wonderful years together. Even at this terrible time, I can't let myself forget that my marriage to Linus made me the luckiest woman in the world."

• • •

For more than an hour we sat in front of the TV, watching the Merrywoods' entire history unfold. There were only a few short reels of Linus and Charlotte, so we quickly moved back to the age of video cameras.

Frankly, I saw more of Tag's, Missy's, and Brock's graduations, awards ceremonies, birthday parties, sporting events, and summer vacations at the family's house on Nantucket than I really needed to. Still, the more I saw, the more I understood that the dynamic that existed among Charlotte and the next generation of Merrywoods had been pretty much the same all along.

But the next person on the list of murder suspects I wanted to interview wasn't a Merrywood. It was one of the Merrywoods' servants.

While Falcone had already questioned Cook, aka Margaret Reilly, I was still anxious to speak with her myself. True, Falcone had decided that the Merrywoods' longtime employee wasn't a very likely suspect. Yet when it came to reading between the lines, the man struck me as someone who moved his lips when he read. I couldn't ignore the fact that Margaret Reilly was the one who reigned over the kitchen, handling all the food in this house—including the birthday cake that appeared to have been the murder weapon.

And even if Falcone was right and she was a long shot, there was another good reason for me to talk to Margaret. While I certainly didn't have much experience with servants, I'd watched enough British television to realize that when it came to knowing everything that went on within a household, there was no better source. So I was glad that Alvira's request for some of Margaret's homemade fudge had provided me with the perfect means of getting my foot in the door—in this case, the kitchen door.

I waited until late that evening, when the Merrywoods and their entourage were beginning to drift into their bedrooms and out of the way. Even Nick was holed up in our room. After dinner, he'd headed right back upstairs for another session, bringing Max and Lou to keep him company. After walking through all the rooms on the first floor to make sure no one else was around, I wandered into the kitchen.

Margaret was still cleaning up from dinner, both her hands hidden inside puffy oven mitts as she pulled dinner plates out of a steaming dishwasher. Yet while her uniform looked as perky as if it was just starting a new day, I couldn't say the same about her face: Her eyes were watery, the corners of her mouth sagged, and her skin looked as if it were begging for a facial. I knew that she'd put in a long day, which had begun early that morning with breakfast preparations.

"I hope I'm not disturbing you," I said, suddenly feeling guilty about asking her to extend her day even further. "I couldn't resist coming down here and looking for a snack."

"In that case," she said with an authoritative nod, "I've got just the thing. When it comes to comfort food, I'm a real expert."

"Milk and cookies?" I asked.

Margaret cast me a strange look. "I was thinking of scotch."

So much for the comfort foods Mother used to make, I thought with amusement.

"Actually," I said, "I've heard great things about your fudge. I was wondering if I could get you to make a batch."

"It's true," she said, nodding. "I'm famous for my fudge. I'd be happy to introduce you to it."

"Thanks," I said. Offering her an apologetic smile, I added, "Sorry that I'm making you work overtime."

"Me?" She shrugged. "I don't expect that I'll be getting much sleep tonight, either—even with the help of this." She picked up a glass that I hadn't noticed before, mainly because it was tucked behind the electric mixer. Frowning, she added, "Talking to that Lieutenant Falcone earlier today is enough to keep anybody awake nights." She raised the glass in a silent toast, then downed a good third of its contents without coming up for air.

"I'm pretty sure Anthony Falcone has that effect on just about everybody he talks to," I commented.

"He wasn't treating me like everybody," she corrected me grimly, setting her glass down firmly on the table. Her voice wavering, she added, "It's hard enough coming to grips with the fact that poor Mr. M. was murdered. But the idea that I could possibly have had anything to do with it is preposterous. Nobody was more loyal to that man than I was!"

With agitated movements, she began to assemble ingredients: milk and butter from the refrigerator, sugar and squares of unsweetened chocolate from the pantry. She slammed each item down on the granite counter, making it clear just how upset she was over being considered a suspect in Linus's murder.

"What do you think happened that night, Margaret?" I asked gently.

"Like I told that Falcone," she said, "I agree with the theory that the eggs Mr. M. ingested had to have been in the birthday cake. That's the only thing on the menu that could possibly have been prepared with them. We had all his favorites: lobster with melted butter, shrimp in a garlic-and-oil sauce, plenty of veggies... There's no way to incorporate eggs into any of those. So it had to be the cake."

She grabbed a large knife from the block on the counter and began chopping up the chocolate with swift, angry strokes.

I was afraid to ask the obvious question but had no choice. "But didn't *you* make his birthday cake?"

"I made *a* birthday cake," she replied. Frowning,

176 • Cynthia Baxter

she reached into a drawer under the stove and noisily rifled through the pots and pans, finally pulling out a saucepan. "But somebody evidently substituted one that was made with eggs without me knowing."

She turned to me, wearing an agonized expression and still grasping the metal pan in one hand. "I should have paid closer attention," she told me, her voice a near whisper.

"How could you have anticipated that something like that would happen?" I asked. "Especially since someone clearly went to great pains to make the switch."

"Whoever it was certainly knew how things work in this house," Margaret mused.

"What exactly happened Wednesday evening?" I asked gently. "In terms of getting the cake ready for Linus's birthday?"

Margaret took a deep breath. "After I made the two chocolate cake layers, I left them on the counter. If you've ever baked a cake, you know it takes a while for it to cool down. You can't frost the layers until they're at room temperature or the frosting will slip right off. So I put the cake layers on a cooling rack and went about my business, getting other things ready and leaving the kitchen a few times to do some other errands.

"When it came time to frost the cake, I thought I noticed they looked a little different," she went on. "But I was in a hurry, and my mind was in a hundred different places... My theory is that while I was away from the kitchen, somebody sneaked inside and substituted two chocolate layers that they'd gotten some-where else. I went ahead and frosted the cake, then served it to the entire family."

I blinked, not sure whether to believe her version of what had happened. After all, she was the one who had control over the kitchen, spending more time here than anyone else. It wasn't impossible that someone had sneaked in and switched the cakes, of course. But it was at least as likely that she had put eggs in the cake herself.

Still, for the sake of questioning her, I intended to act as if I accepted her explanation without question.

"Who knew that you were making a chocolate cake for Linus's birthday," I asked, "and that you'd be making two layers that were that particular size?"

"Just about everyone who's familiar with this household," she replied matter-of-factly. "It's a Merrywood family tradition to serve a two-layer cake at everyone's birthday celebration. I always make two nine-inch layers, in whatever flavor the person likes best. That's a pretty standard size." Shrugging, she added, "As for the flavor, Mr. M. loved chocolate. So anyone who knew we were gearing up for a birthday celebration would have known it was guaranteed to include a chocolate birthday cake."

I hesitated for a few seconds before asking the next question that came to mind. "Margaret, who do you think might have substituted their cake for yours?"

She didn't look at me, instead pretending to be ab-sorbed in dropping chunks of chocolate into the milk she was heating on the stove.

"I'm not one to go around making accusations," she said evenly, her eyes still fixed on the saucepan, "especially when it involves something this important. But I've observed some things that not everybody in this house may know about."

My heartbeat quickened and my ears pricked up like Max's whenever he hears the refrigerator door open. "Like what?"

She cast me a wary look. "Like the fact that there was somebody in the house that night who I suspect had been trying to come between Mr. M. and his wife."

My eyebrows shot up as she continued, "Maybe that person finally got fed up that her plan wasn't going the way she wanted. Or maybe there was something else going on between the two of them."

I remained silent, mentally going through the list of people who were at the party the night before last. Aside from Linus's daughter and his wife, the only females in the house were Scarlett and Gwennie.

Margaret clearly thought one of them was pursuing Linus, motivated by a desire for either his love or his money. But, frankly, I found it difficult to picture either of them engaging in a flirtation with Linus, no matter what their motivation. Scarlett Sandowsky was as prim as they come. Repression appeared to be her middle name. As for Gwennie—well, it was difficult to imagine her in any role aside from an extra in *Mary Poppins*.

"Not that I blame her, of course," Margaret went on, still staring intently into the saucepan and steadily stirring the delicious-smelling chocolate mixture. "After all, what woman in her right mind wouldn't develop a strong affection for Mr. M., once she got to know him? The man was a prince. He was intelligent, sensitive, as polished as all get-out...I mean, how many men who'd achieved as much as he did would still care so much about using his fortune to help so many others?"

A sudden realization hit me like a lightning bolt.

Oh, my gosh! I thought. *Margaret was in love with him!*

I tried to wrap my mind around the fact that the family's loyal longtime employee obviously had feelings for Linus. Given that revelation, it was no wonder she was convinced, rightly or wrongly, that another woman in the household had also set her sights on him.

As she continued singing Linus's praises, meanwhile stirring more and more forcefully, my mind drifted to the two possibilities, Scarlett and Gwennie. If one of them did, indeed, have feelings for Linus, she could have become frustrated by his lack of interest in returning her affections and murdered him. Or, if money was her motivation, it was possible that she'd managed to get him to write her into his will, and she saw a quick inheritance as the next best thing to replacing Charlotte in the role of Mrs. Merrywood.

Either way, all the secrets cloistered within the walls of this creaky old mansion made this puzzle much more difficult to solve than one in a board game.

• • •

I didn't know how I'd ever fall asleep that night, even though I'd have the comfort of Nick beside me. There were too many thoughts whirling around inside my brain.

Still, it was late, the house was quiet, and the rooms were getting colder. It was definitely time to go to bed. With a pan of freshly made, foil-wrapped fudge in hand, I opened the bedroom door quietly, encountering darkness and hearing low, even breathing that told me Nick was already asleep. Darkness and his low, even breathing.

Enough light filtered in from the hallway that I could see he was sharing the mattress with Max and Lou. Both of my doggies woke up long enough to wag their tails—in Max's case, the stub on his butt—and gaze up at me adoringly through bleary eyes. After stashing the fudge in a drawer in case Alvira decided to pay another midnight call, I petted each of them for a minute or two before squeezing into the limited space that remained. I was glad that at least I now had Nick and the dogs to help ward off the chilly air that held the entire house in its grip after night fell.

But I'd been right about how elusive restfulness was going to be. As I stared up at the ceiling, one scenario after another played in my head. They were like a series of movie trailers, each with a different star: Brock, Tag, Cook, and just about everyone else in the household. In addition, the jumble of random clips never quite told a satisfying story.

They certainly didn't give any clues about what the ending would be.

I lay in the dark, trying to think up a good way of questioning Scarlett, Townie, Harry, and the two servants from across the pond without appearing to be interrogating them. But I froze when I suddenly heard a loud squeak. It sounded like one of the wooden floorboards out in the hallway—one that was right outside my room.

You're imagining things, I told myself, turning over on my side and resolutely closing my eyes.

Sque-e-eak!

This time there was no mistaking what I'd heard. Where it had come from, either.

Someone is out there, I thought with alarm. And since the only other person who had a room in this part of the house was Harry, it wasn't exactly a high-traffic area.

My heart had already gone into its jackhammer mode, and I could feel the adrenaline shooting through every nerve of my body.

It's probably nothing, I insisted to myself. *Just someone going to the bathroom—or down to the kitchen because they smelled Cook's fudge.*

Instinctively, I glanced over my shoulder at Nick. But he was sleeping so soundly that I couldn't bring myself to wake him. Certainly not over something like this, since the logical part of me knew it would most likely turn out to be nothing. My two "watchdogs" didn't even bat an eyelash.

Then again, there was something about this house

that wasn't like anyplace I'd ever been before. A noise in the dark of night that I assumed was nothing could turn out to be *anything*.

Sque-e-e-e-ak! I heard it again, this time a little farther away.

By this point, I knew there was no way I'd ever get to sleep without checking it out. So even though the room was icy cold, and even though I knew the floor was going to feel like a glacier beneath my bare feet, I pulled back the covers, climbed out of bed, and tiptoed over to the door. I opened it gently, sure it would turn out to be nothing more onerous than someone moving innocently through the house.

So I was unprepared for the sight of something white and diaphanous floating at the other end of the hallway. As I stared at it, blinking, a gust of cold air hit me, sending a horrible chill through my bones.

A ghost!

My chest was doing that telltale-heart thing again. I tried to find relief in the fact that, whatever it was, it appeared to be moving away from me.

Wait a minute, I suddenly thought. *You don't believe in ghosts! You're just imagining things—all because of this creepy house with its hidden staircases and eerie portraits and all this thunder and lightning*... As for that blast of cold air, it was probably a draft from an open window somewhere.

By that point, the ghost, or whatever it was, had disappeared. And I was feeling like an idiot.

I ordered myself back to bed, talking to myself as if

I were a naughty child suffering from the aftereffects of too much sugar.

Just because this house is creepy doesn't mean you have to start believing every horror movie you've ever seen, I scolded myself. I got back into bed, marveling over how quickly the sheets on my side had gone from toasty warm to freezing cold.

I was just beginning to warm up again when I heard a low moan.

A moan that sounded exactly like the kind of noise a ghost would make.

But there is *no ghost!* I reminded myself. *Not here or anywhere else!*

"Oh-h-h!" I heard again.

Okay, something was definitely going on. Either there was a ghost up here—or someone was trying to make me *believe* there was a ghost up here.

Either way, I decided it was time to get to the bottom of this.

Once again, I threw back the covers and was immediately assaulted by cold air. Cursing myself for not having thought to pack a bathrobe, I grabbed my Polarfleece jacket, the next best thing. Even though my feet felt like two giant ice cubes, I didn't put on my shoes. Maybe ghosts aren't sensitive to noise, but real live people are. And I was growing increasingly convinced that that was what I was dealing with.

I opened the bedroom door again, moving cautiously since I still wasn't certain what I'd find waiting for me on the other side. I was almost disappointed that this time there was absolutely nothing there—not even any Casper-like apparitions waving around.

I crept down the hallway, trying to be as quiet as possible—not only so whoever or whatever was making that noise wouldn't hear me, but also so I could get a better idea of where it was coming from.

"Oh-h-h!"

There it was again—and this time I was nearly certain the low moaning sound was coming from the other end of the hall.

The same place where I'd seen the wavy white apparition.

I was back to wondering *what* to believe. I moved across the cold wooden floor as stealthily as a member of a SWAT team, albeit one dressed in a pair of flannel pajamas, a coat, and bare feet. With no weapon, either, aside from my overactive imagination—which, I had to admit, in the past had generally done more harm to me than to anyone else.

The low moaning had stopped, but I'd almost reached the end of the hall when I heard another sound. It was a soft rustling I couldn't quite identify.

And it seemed to be coming from behind a closed door. The one that led to the bedroom I was pretty sure Harry Foss was staying in.

I went over to the door and stood outside it, hoping that whatever was on the other side couldn't hear my heart pounding as if it were demanding to be let in.

And then I heard something I was instantly able to identify: a giggle.

"Harry, *stop* that!" a shrill female voice insisted,

her tone indicating she didn't really want him to stop at all.

I knew that voice. And it didn't belong to any ghost.

It belonged to Missy, a woman who in less enlightened times would have been referred to as Mrs. Townsend Whitford III. The same woman who'd acted as if she put her husband on a pedestal so high, she practically needed a crane to kiss him good night.

Yet if my ears didn't deceive me, she was rustling around in the sheets with her father's business partner, no doubt after removing that diaphanous white nightgown she'd been wearing only minutes before.

As for the moaning I'd heard, that wasn't the least bit mysterious. It turned out to have more to do with passion than poltergeists.

•   •   •

So Missy and Harry are having a secret fling, I thought as I stole back to my room. I slid into bed, so amazed at what I'd discovered that I felt as if I would burst.

I'd barely had a chance to pull the covers up to my chin before I heard Nick mumble, "Jess?"

"Go back to sleep," I insisted.

"I'm trying," he replied sleepily, "but you seem to be running a relay race over there."

"I'm sorry," I told him. "Please, ignore me."

He let out a loud sigh. "I'm awake. So tell me."

"Tell you what?"

"Why you keep getting out of bed."

I took a deep breath. "Nick, you're not going to

believe this. I just found out that Missy and Harry are having an affair!"

"Wow!" Nick cried, sitting up abruptly. From the looks of things, he was now as awake as I was. "Talk about juicy! Are you sure? How did you find out?"

I glanced at him warily across the pillows. "Don't ask. Let's say it falls into the too-much-information category. But I'm wondering if you might have time to do me a favor."

"Now?"

"Tomorrow is fine," I assured him. "Whenever you've gotten far enough along in your studying that you feel you can take off your law-student hat and put on your sleuth hat."

He sighed. "Sure. The Fourth Amendment is pretty interesting, but even I can get tired of everything you ever wanted to know about search and seizure."

"In that case," I said, "your mission is to find out whatever you can about what Missy and Harry's secret liaison might mean—especially if there was anything about Linus's death that might have made it more convenient for the two of them."

"One obvious possibility is that Linus wouldn't have approved," Nick mused.

"And another is that they wanted his money—and his business," I observed. Teasingly, I added, "Figuring all this out sounds like the perfect job for someone with a law degree."

"I don't have one of those yet," he reminded me.

"No, but you have something even better."

"What's that?" he asked.

"The old Burby charm," I replied, grinning. "And that's the deadliest and most foolproof weapon of them all."

"You think I'm charming, huh?" Nick murmured, snuggling up closer.

I snuggled right back. "I'd say you fit into the charming category."

"I think you're pretty charming, too."

We forgot all about Linus and the rest of the Merrywood household as we got busy showing each other just how charming we could be.

Chapter 9

"The whisper of a pretty girl can be heard
further than the roar of a lion."
                                        —Arabian Proverb

The next morning, I woke up to find Nick curled around me like a giant bathrobe. Lou, meanwhile, was stretched out in front of me, while Max had somehow managed to find a comfortable spot between our feet.

I was amazed by how much less creepy the Merrywoods' mansion felt now that I had two dogs and—even better—a living, breathing teddy bear in my bed to cuddle with. In fact, the bedroom didn't feel the least bit haunted anymore, despite the wallpaper with eyes, the hidden staircase, and the quirky, if not actually scary, aunt living upstairs.

Yet once I fully reached consciousness, I realized

that there was still a dark cloud hanging over the day. A few seconds later I remembered why: Today was Saturday. Linus's memorial service was being held this morning, which meant it was going to be a difficult day for everyone.

I climbed out of bed in slow motion, taking care not to wake Nick. I managed to get dressed quietly enough that he was still asleep when I slipped out the door, with Max and Lou trotting beside me. The three of us headed downstairs, where I let them out for a quick pit stop. I stood in the front doorway, noting that there was still a nasty chill in the air and that a thick, smothering fog still hugged the entire island.

The dogs didn't want to stay out there any longer than they had to. As soon as they raced back inside, I led them to the kitchen to supply them with food and water.

They were still lapping away thirstily as I went into the dining room. The large room was set up the same way it had been yesterday, with an elaborate eggless breakfast buffet laid out on a side table.

Even though the ridiculously long dining-room table was set for the entire Roman army, only two people were seated. Townie was at one end of the table, with Missy sitting catty-corner to his right. At the moment, they were both sipping their coffee politely, with Missy somehow managing to keep her hands to herself.

"Good morning," I greeted them with a big smile. Meanwhile, I studied them, trying to pick up on any tensions or subtexts that might be lurking behind those coffee cups of theirs.

"Good morning, Jessie," Missy replied. "You're up nice and early."

Was I just imagining things, or was some of her usual chirpiness missing?

"How did you sleep?" she added, her cup clanging against the saucer as she put it down.

"Not that well, actually," I replied.

"That's too bad," she said. "What was the problem?"

How about things that go bump in the night? I thought wryly.

Aloud, I said, "I kept hearing strange noises." I watched her even more closely, searching for some indication of whether she'd spotted me last night—in other words, a sign that *she* knew that *I* knew.

But her expression remained blank as she nodded. "Whatever you heard was probably the result of this horrible storm," she commented. With a sigh, she added, "Goodness, I'm beginning to think it's *never* going to let up!"

Townie reached across the table and took his wife's hand. "You didn't sleep well last night, either, did you, honey?"

A startled look crossed Missy's face.

"I didn't, as a matter of fact. I even got up for a while." She gave his hand a squeeze. "I was tossing and turning so much I was afraid I was keeping you up, cupcake. So I went into one of the other rooms for a while and lay down."

Such a considerate wife, I thought dryly. *She can't sleep, so rather than disturb her husband, she finds another bed. One that happens to have another man in it.*

"You're so considerate, sweetums," Townie said.

I nearly gagged as I watched him lean over and plant a kiss on Missy's cheek. *If only you knew what I knew,* I thought.

But what mattered even more was the fact that Missy didn't seem to be aware that I'd spotted her sneaking off to Harry's room late last night. Which meant she'd have less reason to be guarded with me.

I decided to take advantage of her ignorance by finding out more about the allegedly happy couple.

"The two of you seem so happy," I said casually. "How long have you been married?" I bit into a blueberry muffin. Not only was it still warm, it was moist and flavorful and just sweet enough. I instantly concluded that Cook was at least as good with baked goods as she was reputed to be with fudge.

"Gosh, it's been almost eight years," Missy replied. Giggling, she added, "But it feels as if we're still newlyweds." She suddenly grasped Townie's arm, not seeming to notice that it kept him from smearing onto his croissant the orange marmalade he'd scooped up.

"I'm a newlywed myself," I told them. "Nick and I got married in June."

Missy's eyes widened. "Gee, you two really are newlyweds!"

Yes, I thought, *and our wedding vows are still fresh enough in my mind that I remember them.*

But enough about me. "How did you two meet?" I asked.

"Believe it or not, it was at a wedding, of all places." For some reason, Missy seemed to feel that statement warranted more giggling.

Townie jumped in, perhaps to give her a chance to catch her breath. "That's right," he drawled in his usual lockjaw style. "We were both in the wedding party. I was a friend of the groom, and Missy was a friend of the bride."

"Binky and I went to college together," she explained. "So of course I said yes when she asked if I wanted to be a bridesmaid. And the dresses were ever so pretty! Pale yellow, with full skirts and low necklines and ribbons and ruffles everywhere.... We even had big straw hats with long satin ribbons the exact same color!"

The image was chilling. As an antidote, I took another bite of Cook's blueberry muffin.

"And I was the best man," Townie continued. "Gates and I worked together back in the day. Our first job, right out of Harvard."

Oh, yes, the Harvard thing again, I thought as I chewed. *It's amazing how Harvard grads are so good at working the name of their alma mater into the conversation. Maybe the school offers a special seminar in how to do exactly that.*

"That was at Waterston Peabody," Townie added.

I guess my expression reflected my cluelessness, because Missy quickly explained, "Waterston Peabody is one of the most highly respected venture-capital firms in the country."

"And venture-capital firms do what exactly?" By this point, I figured there was no reason to try to hide my ignorance about the workings of the business world.

"They invest," Missy said with a dismissive little shrug.

"In new ventures," Townie added, patting his wife's hand. That is, the one that wasn't still glommed on to his arm as if the two of them were walking across a rickety bridge. "Entrepreneurs who want to start a business go to a firm like Waterston Peabody and present their business plan. If they have what sounds like a great idea, the venture capitalists invest their stockholders' money in the new venture they've proposed. In other words, they give them the money to turn their idea into reality. Then, if the new company is a success, the venture capitalists—and their stockholders—get a piece of the profits."

"It's kind of like buying stock, except you do it in advance, before the company has been formed," Missy added.

"I see." Maybe the workings of the business world weren't that complicated after all. "Is that what you do now, Townie?"

He hesitated a second or two, stroking that jaw of his that he kept in such tight control. "I'm actually involved in a few different things," he finally replied.

"Townie is ever so clever!" Missy chirped, her eyes shining. "He's one of those people who are incredibly creative when it comes to finding ways to make money."

Then maybe he *should have been the next in line to run Merrywood Industries,* I thought.

While that idea had popped into my mind all by itself, I realized that I might have just stumbled upon a possible motive for Townie. Perhaps Linus and Townie had indeed been talking about the possibility of him taking over the family empire. After all, he was a member of the family—and Harry, Linus's most obvious successor, wasn't. And if Townie really was as good at business as Missy claimed . . .

As if on cue, Linus's right-hand man came wandering into the dining room, appearing to be only half awake. Harry's hair was slightly mussed and his eyes were rimmed in red. He also looked as if he'd gotten dressed by pulling on the same pants and shirt he'd tossed onto a chair last night.

"Tough night?" I couldn't help asking the other half of the deceptive duo as he headed straight for the coffeepot.

"Yes, as a matter of fact." After grabbing a cup and filling it to the brim, he glanced up at me. "Why, does it show?"

"We all had a difficult night," Missy piped up. "We were just talking about that very subject. I think it's a combination of this awful weather and the fact that Daddy's funeral is today."

"That would explain it," Harry agreed.

I noticed that he didn't look at Missy—or Townie, for that matter—as he sat down at the table, as far away from his lady friend as possible. Instead, he focused on his cup, seemingly intent on ingesting as much coffee as he could.

While both Missy and Harry were highly skilled at acting as if nothing was going on, I wasn't nearly as good at it. So I was relieved when Nick came bursting through the doorway, as energetic as a talk-show host who was making his entrance.

"Good morning, everybody," he cheerfully greeted the four of us. "Looks like we're in for more rain."

Thank goodness for weather, I thought as everyone mumbled their agreement. How would any of us get through life without being able to bring it up whenever there was nothing else to say?

"It's going to be pretty uncomfortable, crossing the bay this morning," Townie observed. "The water will probably be rough enough to make all of us seasick. Fortunately, it's a short trip."

"Actually," Missy said, "it occurred to me that it might be a good idea for someone to stay behind while the rest of us are at the funeral. I expect most of those dreadful reporters and photographers on the other side of the bay to follow us to the funeral, but some might stay behind to try to sneak over to the island. I can imagine them snapping pictures and peering through our windows and heaven only knows what else. If that happened, we'd need someone to alert the police."

"Won't Alvira be here?" Harry asked.

"Aunt Alvira has already made it clear that she has no intention of accompanying the rest of us anywhere," Missy replied curtly. "True to form, she pooh-poohed the very idea of a memorial service for her brother. She intends to stay up in the attic, the way she always does."

Focusing on Nick and me, she added, "I wondered if the two of you would be willing to remain here at the house while the rest of us go to the service and then on to the funeral home. Since neither of you knew my father and all."

"Of course," I replied immediately.

"Whatever you want," Nick agreed.

Inwardly, I was rejoicing. Being asked to stay behind with Nick was more than I could have asked for. And it had nothing to do with my charming husband— but plenty to do with having just been handed the opportunity to do some high-quality snooping.

• • •

The first thing on the day's agenda was paying a second visit to Alvira. Ever since she'd promised to share a tidbit of information she referred to as a clue, I'd been counting the minutes until I had the chance to find out what it was. Since I'd soon have the house practically to myself, I decided to be patient.

After breakfast, Nick headed back up to our room to immerse himself in the principles of law. Max and Lou trotted after him happily. I, meanwhile, went into the sitting room that was closest to the front door to wait for everyone to leave. Since I figured I should at least try to look as if I had a reason for being there, I grabbed one of the thick volumes off the shelf. Fortunately, the gesture didn't set any shelving units or other pieces of furniture into motion.

I plopped into an overstuffed chair and opened the heavy book in my lap. But I was much more interested in the sounds of the Merrywoods and the rest of their household getting ready to travel across the bay together for the funeral.

When someone walked into the room, I automatically looked over to see who it was—then immediately did a double take.

At first glance I'd thought it was Scarlett, but I had to make sure I was seeing what I thought I was seeing.

I was, but this was a whole new Scarlett. The other one could best be described as *prim*. This one, on the other hand, could best be described as *va-va-voom*.

Instead of wearing her hair pulled back in a severe bun, today she had a lush mane cascading over her shoulders. Before it had looked like a respectable dark brown. Now, however, I could see that it was a deep shade of espresso, interlaced with strands of gold that might or might not have been natural.

Her conservative business suit had been replaced by a tight-fitting dress with a short jacket made of the same fine wool. It was black, of course, since she was on her way to a funeral. But the dress skimmed her frame in an extremely flattering manner, hugging curves that had been impossible to discern beneath a straight skirt and tailored blazer. The neckline was low, perhaps even too low for an occasion like this one, since it revealed an abundant amount of cleavage that once again was new to me.

No sensible shoes today, either. Scarlett wore black heels that were so spiky, any self-respecting dominatrix would have been proud to own them.

And while I'd never seen her wearing any makeup before, that, too, had changed. The shade of lipstick she wore was a deep brownish-red that complemented her skin tones. She'd apparently substituted contact lenses for glasses, and I noticed for the first time that her eyes were dark brown. The same tone was mirrored in her eye shadow, mascara, and eyeliner, all expertly applied.

To use an old-fashioned phrase, she looked like a scarlet woman.

"Hello, Jessie," she said casually. "I didn't realize anyone was in here."

"I was looking for a good spot to read," I said, holding up the book I'd grabbed off the shelf. "Missy asked me to stay behind while everybody else goes to the funeral. I figured I'd stay here on the main floor so I could keep an eye on the place, but it's hard to find a decent reading light anywhere in this house."

"I know what you mean," she agreed, rolling her eyes. "I constantly nagged Linus about it, telling him over and over again how bad it was for his eyes. But he always had his own way of doing things."

A heavy silence followed, no doubt the result of both of us contemplating the fact that Linus's days of doing things his own way were over.

"What are you reading?" Scarlett finally asked, craning her neck.

Good question, I thought.

I held up the book, allegedly to show her the cover but really to let *me* see it.

"Uh, *Understanding the Basic Principles of Accounting*," I said, as surprised as she probably was. Thinking fast and speaking even faster, I added, "Part of being a veterinarian means running my own business. I have a terrific assistant, but I need to learn more about the day-to-day stuff myself."

"I see," she replied, not sounding entirely convinced.

Wanting to move away from that topic in case she decided to ask me something technical, I observed, "You certainly look...as if you're ready to go." I'd caught myself at the last second, realizing that complimenting her appearance, even as a matter of politeness, wouldn't have been appropriate.

"We're all planning to go over together," she said. "The service starts at noon, and since it's still pouring, it might take us awhile to get there. I hope everyone else is running on schedule."

She flicked her sleeve and glanced at her watch. It looked as if it was made of pure gold. But something else also made it glint: Both the band and the oval-shaped face were studded with diamonds. Not those pitiful specks that I could afford, either. These were king-sized diamonds that had undoubtedly come with a king-sized price tag.

It wasn't exactly the kind of accessory I'd expect someone to be able to afford on a personal assistant's salary, even if the person she personally assisted was known for his generosity.

This bit of bling hinted at a totally different level of generosity.

And then Scarlett brushed back a strand of hair that had swooped down into her eyes. As she pushed it behind one ear, she revealed more shininess. This time, it was in the form of a diamond stud the size of a dime.

Cook's assertion that one of the other females in the household had been more than a loyal employee was starting to ring true. In fact, suddenly all the jokes about Miss Scarlet and the lead pipe in the conservatory didn't seem quite so amusing.

Just because Scarlett turns out to be stunningly sexy doesn't mean she was up to no good, I reminded myself. *You can't assume that every woman who's drop-dead gorgeous uses her looks for devious purposes.*

Still, I couldn't help thinking that Scarlett's attractiveness probably wouldn't go unnoticed by any man, even one like Linus, who had practically been elevated to sainthood by almost everyone who knew him.

As for her expensive baubles, it was possible that she came from money—or that she had an indulgent boyfriend who was closer to her own age, not to mention unmarried. Or maybe she was simply good at handling her own finances, which enabled her to splurge on a piece of jewelry every now and then. I decided to hold off on judging her.

"The funeral will probably be pretty tough," I commented, "but hopefully it will help give everyone a sense of closure."

Scarlett nodded. "Even so, I think it's going to take all of us quite some time to get over this."

"I'm sure," I agreed. "I know you're all going to miss Linus. I've really been struck by how well loved he was." Studying her carefully, I added, "It's hard to believe that anyone could have possibly intended to kill him."

Scarlett lowered herself onto the couch opposite me, sitting down gingerly as if she was taking care not to muss up her outfit.

Extending one long leg, made even longer by her S&M-style footwear, she said, "I'd be inclined to believe it was an accident if it wasn't for the fact that everyone—and I mean absolutely everyone—knew how dangerous it was for poor Mr. Merrywood to go anywhere near an egg."

I nodded. "Lieutenant Falcone talked to Cook, and the conclusion seems to be that someone stole into the kitchen and substituted a chocolate cake made with eggs for the one she'd made without any." Still watching her carefully, I added, "The question is, who?"

"I know one thing that might help the police figure that out," she said with a strange smile.

"What?" I asked, genuinely curious.

"Linus's will."

Exactly what I was itching to learn about.

"Do you know anything about who's inheriting what?" I asked, trying to sound casual. "After all, you were his personal assistant."

Scarlett eyed me warily. As our gazes locked, I got

the feeling she was debating whether or not to tell me what she knew.

Or maybe she was telling the truth when she replied, "I honestly don't know a thing about it. It's true I was involved in much of what went on in Linus's life, but that didn't include whatever plans he made for after his death."

Her response got me wondering again about Scarlett's true role in her employer's life. Had she been more than just his assistant? And if she was, did she truly care for him or was she simply seeking a way to walk away with a piece of the Merrywood pie?

But before I had a chance to ask her any more questions, Charlotte bustled into the room. As usual, she looked as if she deserved to be on the cover of a magazine, even if it happened to be the one the AARP put out. Like Scarlett, she was dressed in black. But her dress exuded dignity and good taste, with clean lines and a modest length and neckline. Her jewelry was similarly understated, even though it still managed to scream wealth: a string of pearls, a diamond-studded bangle bracelet on one wrist, a simple gold Cartier watch on the other.

"There you are, Scarlett," she said, smiling at her husband's former assistant. "You look very nice."

"Thank you," Scarlett replied, smiling back. "I decided to dress up in Mr. Merrywood's honor. I wore this dress to his birthday party. He seemed to like it."

"He was very fond of you, my dear," Charlotte said.

My eyebrows shot up. Was Charlotte, the trusting wife, really so naïve?

Or was I the one who was reading into things?

"I think everyone is ready," Charlotte said. She went over to Scarlett and put her arm around her, almost as if they were mother and daughter. "I'm glad we're all going over together. It will make this easier for everyone."

Turning to me, she added, "Thank you, Jessica, for agreeing to watch the house while we're gone. I just don't feel comfortable leaving it unattended with all those horrid reporters and photographers lurking across the bay."

"I'm glad there's something I can do to help," I replied.

But as I watched the two women amble toward the front door, where the others were gathering, it occurred to me that I'd try to do even more to help while they were gone. If things turned out the way I hoped, by the time they returned I'd be that much closer to figuring out who had killed Linus.

• • •

I stayed in my seat until the front door slammed shut. But the banging sound was still echoing through the hollow hallways of the house as I jumped out of my chair and ran up to my bedroom, taking the steps two at a time.

I found Nick stretched out on the bed. Surrounding him were Max and Lou, a laptop, a pad of yellow legal-size paper, a bunch of highlighter pens, and several textbooks so hefty they made Alvira's dumb-bells look like toys.

"Detective Popper," he greeted me, flinging his legal pad across the bed. "What insightful little tidbits have you uncovered this morning?"

I filled him in on the details he'd missed at breakfast with Missy, Townie, and Harry, marveling over how good the illicit lovers were at pretending they were nothing more than friends. Then I told him about my latest theory, that Scarlett might have been more than simply Linus's assistant—and that not all her compensation for her duties may have come from a paycheck.

"The plot is definitely thickening," he observed once I'd finished. "It'll be interesting to find out what's in the old man's will."

"My thoughts exactly," I said. "Maybe that information will help me figure out once and for all what all the intrigues in this household add up to."

Suddenly I had an idea. "Hey, you're in the process of becoming a lawyer. Do you have any secret ways of finding out what's in Linus's will?"

"Afraid not," he replied. "All you can do is wait, just like everyone else in the family. But for now, my beauty," he leered, doing a really bad Dracula imitation, "at last vee are alone." Patting the bed next to him, he added, "Come into my lair and I vill transpor-r-rt you to another world."

I grinned to show him that even though he wasn't quite ready for *Saturday Night Live*, I still appreciated his efforts. "But we both have so much to do in this world."

He sighed. "Rejected! I'm telling you, I'm beginning to wonder if I ever should have agreed to walk down that aisle."

Playfully, I punched him in the arm. "Wait a minute! You were the one who wanted to get married so badly!"

"I know," he said, turning serious. "And I must say, I haven't regretted it for a minute. Now, go chase that killer—and I'll do everything I can to learn about that pesky Fourth Amendment."

"I will," I told him. "I'm even going equipped with bait." To demonstrate, I reached into a dresser drawer and pulled out the pan of fudge Margaret had sent me upstairs with after our chat. "Actually, it's more like a bribe."

"Whatever works," he said.

Pulling *Frankenstein* off the shelf, I added, "Now, watch this."

I turned so I could see Nick's face as the entire unit moved to one side, revealing the hidden door.

His reaction didn't disappoint me. "Wow!" he cried. "A secret passageway?"

"Remember that hidden staircase I mentioned?" I threw open the door, then swept my hand through the air like a model showing off a prize on a game show.

"That is totally awesome!" Nick exclaimed. "We have to get one of those!"

"Sure," I agreed amiably. "As soon as we have a crazy aunt of our own to lock in the attic."

With that, I bounded up the stairs, carefully holding on to the fudge.

"Knock, knock," I called when I reached the top, opening the door and peering inside. "Anybody home?"

The cats certainly were. All five of them this time, sprawled across the furniture like some exotic collection of throw pillows. The Maine coon seemed to have snatched the best spot, a soft cushion on top of the already soft couch. The black cat was close by, choosing to curl up just a few inches away. The one with the luxurious coat of long white fur lay on top of the couch with his tail hanging down over the cushions, while the gray-and-black tabby, Madeira, Alvira's favorite, had staked out one of the arms. Even Muffin was among this coterie of cats, although she lay on the floor, keeping herself slightly apart from the others.

A second later, Alvira emerged from the room behind the living area. She broke into a smile as soon as she saw me. "You came back!"

"I promised I would," I said. "And I brought what you asked for."

Alvira's face lit up like the nighttime sky on the Fourth of July. "Fudge!" she cried, eagerly reaching toward the foil-covered pan in my hand.

"Not so fast," I insisted, pulling it away. "First, you have something *I* want."

She looked puzzled, but only for a few seconds. "Oh. Information, right?"

"That's right."

I sat down on the couch, placing the coveted fudge in my lap so that it was in clear view.

"I'm anxious to hear about that clue you mentioned yesterday." With a little shrug, I said, "No clue, no fudge."

"They weren't supposed to be related," Alvira said crossly. "I asked you to get me some of that fudge as a favor. I'm planning to tell you my theory no matter what."

Ah, I thought. So Alvira's closely guarded piece of information had been demoted from an actual clue to a mere theory.

I decided to remain a tough negotiator. For all I knew, her craving for fudge would quickly be replaced by a yearning for some other treat—and her determination to have me visit her regularly would cause her to delay telling what she knew even further. "In that case, let's hear it."

Alvira plopped down next to me. "If you ask me," she said with a quick nod, "the answer to the question of who killed Linus and why is in Linus's notebooks."

"What notebooks?" I asked. Yet I remained wary. While Alvira had impressed me as someone who knew plenty, I hadn't forgotten Winston's claim that her own brother had characterized her as less than reliable. I realized that I'd be wise to take whatever she said with a grain of salt.

"Linus was a fanatic about his notebooks," she said, so caught up in what she was saying that she seemed to have forgotten all about her chocolate pay-off. "Journals, I suppose you'd call 'em. Or diaries. They weren't something he told most people about, since when he first got started, he thought keeping a diary was kind of a girl thing. But even as an adult he wrote in them religiously."

I had to admit that what she was saying sounded pretty plausible. "Did he write personal information?" I asked. "Or just notes about the day-to-day workings of his business?"

"Y'got me there," Alvira admitted. "All I know is that ever since he was a kid, Linus recorded everything. I suppose his scribblings started out like any other kid's diary. He'd write about where he went that day, who he went with, what exams he had coming up, what girl he had a crush on—"

"If you don't mind me asking," I interrupted, "how do you know so much about what your brother wrote in his diary when you were both children?"

She shrugged. "How d'you think? Like any self-respecting little sister, I figured out where he hid it—under the mattress—and peeked at it every chance I got!"

I didn't doubt that part for an instant. "But keeping a diary as a child is one thing," I pointed out. "How do you know it was a practice he continued into adulthood?"

"Because I used to tease him about it," Alvira explained. "I'd say, 'Still keeping those diaries, Linus? Do you really think one day somebody's going to want to sit down and read your years' and years' worth of jottings?' And he'd always say the same thing: 'They're not for other people, Alvira. They're for me. It's what I do to keep my head straight. You could say it's my form of therapy.'"

"I see," I said. Still wary, I added, "But it sounds as if you never actually saw them. Once the two of you grew up, I mean."

"Nope. That's why I don't know if he was writing about his personal life or his business dealings. But either way," she added, her eyes narrowing, "I wouldn't be surprised if he wrote something in 'em that would help the police figure out who killed him. Maybe he was blackmailing somebody—or somebody was blackmailing him. Maybe he had a secret life none of us knew about. Maybe he was even doing something shady with the business. I'd find it hard to believe, given what I know about my brother. But when you come right down to it, who knows what other people are capable of—even people they're close to?"

Her reference to individuals who were close made me shiver. After all, those were the exact words Linus had used in his final telephone call to Winston.

That coincidence aside, I knew Alvira was right. If Linus had kept a diary, chances were good that someone who took the time to read it would find a clue to who might have wanted him dead.

I was ready to take on the task.

"Where does he keep them?" I asked. I tried to sound as if I had a casual interest—instead of letting on that it was all I could do to keep myself from racing down the stairs, grabbing the latest volume, and reading every single word.

Alvira didn't answer right away. Instead, her eyes traveled downward. "Maybe some of that fudge would help me remember."

I decided that handing over the goods at this point wouldn't hurt. She'd already told me the most important part of what she knew. I felt pretty confident that she'd spill the rest as soon as she had a little sugar in her bloodstream.

I waited in silence while she tore open the foil, acting as if she hadn't eaten for days. Just as speedily she broke off a chunk of fudge and stuffed it in her mouth. I wasn't even offended that she didn't offer me any.

I gave her about thirty seconds to chew and swallow before asking, "So is the fudge helping you remember where Linus kept his diaries?"

"Y'got me," Alvira replied with a shrug. "Like I said, he was always pretty secretive about them. That's why he stashed 'em in a place he thought nobody would look. I don't know what he did with them once he moved out of our parents' house. If you're going to look for them, you have your work cut out for you."

Glancing around the room, she added, "But I bet he brought 'em with him when he started spending more time out here. Especially the current one. And they shouldn't be that hard to find, since in a place this big, he probably figured he didn't have to hide 'em anywhere as mysterious as under his mattress. In fact, I'd bet the rest of this fudge that, as the old saying goes, they're hidden in plain sight."

• • •

As I tromped back down the stairs, I mulled over Alvira's story about Linus's diaries. While I was still ambivalent about whether or not to believe whatever she told me, the idea of her brother keeping records of what went on in his life certainly sounded plausible.

And because I was eager to get as much information as I could, I decided to accept what she'd told me as the truth. After all, the worst that was likely to happen was that I'd waste some time looking for something that didn't exist.

But until proven otherwise, I was willing to assume that they did exist—and to hope Alvira was correct about Linus not necessarily hiding whatever journals or records he kept. Once he grew up and moved away from a little sister with prying eyes, he might not have felt the need to be quite so secretive. However, there were also plenty of places to store them here in this sprawling mansion, which was so big that something as simple as a diary wouldn't stand out.

Unless, of course, someone with a great deal of determination went searching for it.

"Did you find what you needed?" Nick asked as I closed the door, picked up *Frankenstein,* and slipped it back onto the shelf.

As the gigantic bookcase slid into place, I replied, "Not yet. But I'm hoping I can still accomplish that before everybody gets back."

Especially since that person with determination happened to be me.

Chapter 10

"When spider webs unite, they can tie up a lion."
—Ethiopian Proverb

Perching on the edge of the bed, I told Nick about Alvira's claim that Linus had been as addicted to journaling as he'd been to making money. I also filled him in on Winston's take on the woman's grasp on reality.

While I half-expected him to dismiss the clue she'd given me, he seemed matter-of-fact about accepting it as the truth.

"She's his sister," he said with a shrug. "She probably knew the guy better than anybody. If she says he kept a diary, chances are it's true. Go for it, Jess."

Feeling encouraged, I left Nick in the bedroom with his law books and headed to Linus's study. I brought my two dogs with me. I figured that if anyone caught me and I needed an explanation for what I was doing in the deceased's private sanctum, my story would be that Max or Lou had run in there and I'd had no choice but to retrieve them.

And if anyone wondered why chasing my dogs involved studying the books lined up on the shelves, I'd explain that I was a passionate reader and couldn't resist looking at someone else's books to see if their taste matched mine.

Armed with an excuse that was a tad convoluted but I was pretty sure I could relate convincingly, I boldly went into the room.

"Hidden in plain sight," Alvira had theorized about where Linus kept his journals. If she was correct that I was likely to find the notebooks in the most obvious spot, then the best place to start was his study, since it was the room that served as his home office whenever he was away from corporate headquarters.

The first thing I did was switch on the overhead light. As I did, thunder that sounded like a bowling alley on a busy Saturday afternoon rolled through the house. For a fraction of a second, I thought I'd brought it on by venturing into a place where I wasn't supposed to be.

But I reminded myself that the storm had been raging for days, and I forged ahead.

I headed straight for the floor-to-ceiling bookshelves that lined the wall behind Linus's huge wooden desk. It was still covered with stacks of paper. From the looks of things, Missy and Scarlett had barely made a dent in the tremendous task they'd taken on of going through Linus's files.

As my dogs sniffed around happily, thrilled to find themselves amid a whole collection of new smells, I parked myself in front of the shelves and began studying the spines of the hundreds of books. Fortunately, Linus had been fairly organized. He'd grouped them by subject.

The fact that the books I was looking for wouldn't have titles stamped on their bindings helped. Still, I wished I'd thought to ask Alvira if he preferred spiral notebooks or bound books. At least that way I'd have had an idea of what I was looking for.

I must have spent ten minutes studying Linus's book collection, and I still didn't see anything that looked like a diary. The few volumes that struck me as possibilities turned out to be dead ends when I pulled them off the shelf to check them.

I finally gave up on the bookshelves. I glanced around the room, looking for other likely spots. Checking the doorway every five seconds, I perched on the swivel chair and opened a few drawers in Linus's desk. Next I tried the wooden file cabinets on the other side of the room. Signs of organization were here, too, mainly in the form of neatly lined-up file folders. But I didn't find a single book.

Where should I try next? I wondered, sighing loudly as I dropped back into the desk chair. By this point, I was convinced that his study was a dead end. That left the second-most obvious possibility: Linus and Charlotte's bedroom.

The idea of prowling around in there made me uncomfortable. There was something sacred about a couple's bedroom, at least as far as outsiders were concerned. Having stumbled upon Charlotte combing through old photographs and other keepsakes all by herself in that room made me even more reluctant to pry.

But the fact remained that I was lucky enough to have the entire house to myself, other than Nick, who of course would have understood, and Alvira, who didn't seem to make a habit of strolling the halls during the day. That made this the best time—and possibly the *only* time—for me to search for Linus's notebooks in his bedroom.

I still felt like an intruder as I crept up the stairs and into the master bedroom. I couldn't help wondering if the walls had eyes. At least the wallpaper in this room didn't appear to, the way it did in mine.

The first thing I did was close the door behind me to keep Max and Lou out. I wanted to get in and out as quickly as possible, and the last thing I needed was to be slowed down by the two kings of sniffing-every-single-item-within-reach.

Once that was done, I took a moment to survey the room. I noticed for the first time that this room was fairly pleasant. The wallpaper was powder blue, splashed with oversize off-white flowers complemented by tremendous green leaves. They looked like lilies of some sort. The furniture was the dark, heavy wooden stuff that filled the rest of the house, but somehow the dressers and bed in here didn't seem as clunky. The drapes were drawn tightly against the windows so they shut out the gray, stormy day.

But I wasn't here to critique the décor. I immediately set about my task. I began by checking the usual places: under the bed, inside the night table, in the top drawer of the dresser. When none of the usual hiding places turned up anything, I stood in the middle of the room with my arms folded across my chest.

Where on earth...? I thought impatiently as my eyes darted around the room.

And then I noticed the curio cabinet. In fact, I practically kicked myself for not spotting it right off the bat. The tall, slender display unit stood proudly in the back corner, its curved glass doors crystal clear and its rich wooden surfaces gleaming. It was one of the few items in this house that looked as if someone had taken care of it.

It struck me as a very good place to stash important things.

I made a beeline for it, already feeling the adrenaline rushing through my veins. Even in the dim light, I could see that it contained only a few items. But given their diversity, I concluded that they had been hand chosen for this special spot.

On the top shelf was a polar bear that looked as if it had been carved out of ice. Steuben glass, I surmised, which meant it was of the highest quality. The polar bear stood side by side with a colorful ball that reminded me of a kaleidoscope. That, I knew, was Venetian glass.

I glanced at the other items only long enough to as-

certain that the soapstone carvings of an Inuit fisherman and the graceful clear glass vase weren't what I
was looking for.

But what I found on the bottom shelf made me feel
as if I'd just been hooked up to an espresso IV.

Neatly lined up were more than a dozen of those
black-and-white marble notebooks that schoolchil-
dren have used for decades.

So they do exist! I thought, certain I'd just found
Linus's journals.

My hands were trembling as I carefully unlatched
the glass door and opened it. I reached for the first
notebook and pulled it off the shelf.

Handwritten on the front in bold black letters was
1992. I hesitated, listening to my heart thump against
my rib cage as I contemplated the momentousness of
what I was about to do.

I'd been yearning to find Linus's diaries ever since
Alvira had mentioned them. Yet now that I actually
held one in my hands, part of me felt that intruding
into someone's private thoughts was wrong.

I had to remind myself that doing so could turn out
to be the best way of finding his killer.

I opened the book, aware that blood was pounding
through my temples with alarming speed. Inside, I
found page after page of handwritten notes, along
with the date of each day's entry.

Met with Bill Everett, I read. *Looks as if merger will
go through. Lunch with Tad and Edwin. Tad's marriage is falling apart—really sad. Makes me appreciate*

my Charlotte even more. I should remember to bring her flowers more often.

I cringed. I didn't know what I'd expected, but peeking inside the head of a man in this manner— even someone I'd never met—was making me feel like a cat burglar.

Even so, I read on. I found more of the same: short, choppy sentences that summarized each day of Linus's life. While his writing style made for difficult reading, the journal was explicit about what was going on in his life. He had named names, for one thing. For another, he had recorded his feelings, however briefly, about whatever had happened in his business dealings, his marriage, and his friendships.

Which meant that Alvira's theory that his journals might contain a clue about what had been going on close to the end sounded more solid than ever.

But the day-to-day details of Linus's life in 1992 seemed too remote to be related to his alleged murder. I needed more-recent information.

So I slipped his journal from 1992 back onto the shelf and reached for the notebook that was the farthest to the right.

As soon as I pulled it out, I saw that the date written on the cover was 2007.

That can't be, I thought, staring at it. *This is much too old. What about the most recent years? Didn't Linus keep a diary throughout his life?*

I checked the shelf again, wondering if perhaps he'd run out of storage space. But the notebooks weren't tucked in that tightly. There was still a good inch left—certainly enough room to store his journals from 2008 and beyond.

Which meant he'd stored his most recent diaries somewhere else.

Either that or someone had removed them.

Yet instead of feeling defeated, I felt energized. The fact that someone had gone out of their way to conceal Linus's final diaries increased my certainty that they contained clues about his murderer's identity.

Which, in turn, increased my determination to find those missing journals.

• • •

Even though I had a feeling the notebook thief had found a really good hiding place, that didn't stop me from examining every nook, cranny, shelf, cabinet, and corner I passed. I searched the bedrooms, wondering if whoever had killed Linus had also stolen his notebooks and hidden them in their room. But I found nothing. Next I went back downstairs, figuring I'd use the rest of the time I had to prowl around, looking for any secret doors or hidden staircases I'd missed.

I was standing in the front hallway, trying to plan my strategy, when I heard the sound of voices outside.

They're back! I thought, a wave of disappointment washing over me.

I darted into the closest room, which was the sitting room directly off the hallway. Even though I wasn't doing anything sneaky at the moment, the fact that sneaky behavior lurked in my immediate past made me feel guilty.

Which, in turn, made me want to act *un*-guilty. So I sank into a big, comfy, upholstered chair in front of the fireplace, acting as if I'd spent the entire time the others were away warming the soles of my feet.

Corky sauntered into the room, wagging his tail and looking for love in all the right places. Admiral followed a few seconds later. But after a glance in my direction and a polite wag of his tail, he settled in front of the fireplace, resting his chin on his front paws.

I'd just started to fondle Corky's wonderfully soft ears when I heard the front door open, then a couple of seconds later slam shut. I stood up, planning to put on my best expression of surprise and stroll over to greet whoever had just come in. But then I heard someone say, "I'm certainly glad all *that's* over."

Instantly I froze. Something about that voice sounded off. It took me a second or two to realize that it was Gwennie's voice.

What was odd, however, was that it didn't contain even a trace of a Cockney accent. In fact, the British accent she was now using sounded decidedly upper crust.

Is it possible she's a fake? I wondered.

"It's always hard being around all of them at the same time." This time I heard a male voice I immediately recognized as Jives's. At least his accent sounded the same as usual.

Silently, I crept to the other side of the room and positioned myself in the corner, next to the door. Standing there enabled me to peer through the crack between the door and the jamb. For once, I was glad the house was so full of shadows, since it greatly reduced my chances of being spotted.

Sure enough, Gwennie and Jives stood in the front hallway, pulling off rubber boots and shaking out umbrellas.

Gwennie sighed tiredly. "I'm so glad we'll be done with all of this soon," she said as she unbuttoned a half-soaked trench coat.

"Me, too," Jives agreed. "I've had about enough of the buttling business."

What's this? I thought, frowning in confusion. *A career change on the horizon?*

"You think it's fun making beds and cleaning up after people?" Gwennie demanded shrilly, still speaking with a British accent that was light-years away on the social scale from the one I'd heard her use up until now.

An explanation came soon enough.

"And I'm *really* getting tired of speaking in that ridiculous Cockney accent," she grumbled. "I feel like a character in a Dickens novel. If I hear myself saying 'blimey' one more time, I swear I'm going to shoot myself."

"Relax," Jives insisted. A second later he moved into my line of sight, verifying my initial impression. "At least all those years of studying at that drama school in London turned out to have some use."

"He-e-ey!" she protested teasingly. "I was pretty impressive as Hedda Gabler, wasn't I? And the critics loved me as Varya in *The Cherry Orchard*." All the lightness went out of her voice as she added, "At least the ones who bothered to show up."

"I like to feel my training paid off, as well," Jives said, sounding a trifle wistful. "And I'm not talking about the rave reviews I got for my portrayal of Estragon in *Waiting for Godot.*"

My mouth dropped open.

They're actors! I thought. Which meant, fake accents aside, neither one of them was what they appeared to be.

"We'll find out how good we are at acting soon enough," Gwennie replied.

I pressed my nose even closer to the doorjamb, hoping she'd expand upon that comment a little.

Instead, she commented, "The old man got quite a send-off, didn't he?"

"I'll say," Jives agreed. "Not that I'd expect anything else, given how important the old codger was."

"You mean how *rich* the old codger was," Gwennie added jokingly.

"Y'got me there," Jives agreed with a chuckle.

"There must have been a few hundred people at his memorial service," Gwennie continued. "Even a few of those wealthy ancients we researched."

Research? My ears pricked up like I was one of the dogs.

"I think we got lucky, though," Jives said. "With the way things worked out with Linus, I mean."

"I agree completely," Gwennie said. "Still, it was interesting, meeting so many of the other people we initially identified as possibilities. Since we already knew so much about them and all."

"To tell you the truth, my favorite part of the whole event was watching Brock and Townie," Jives commented. "They're pretty good actors themselves."

"I'll say," Gwennie said. "Did you notice the big show they made of not sitting together? You'd never guess the two of them were about to get in bed together—as the saying goes."

"Missy deserves a round of applause, as well," Jives noted.

Brock? Townie? Missy? What was up with that? I wondered.

I was dying to know what they were talking about. But given the fact that I was a mere eavesdropper, I wasn't about to have any say in the matter.

The tone of Gwennie's voice changed as she suddenly said, "Goodness, the place seems so quiet." With a little laugh, she added, "I mean, even quieter than usual."

"Yes, it does feel different with the whole family gone," Jives agreed. "It's rather nice, being here all alone, isn't it?"

"I'll say."

"Too bad everyone else will be back on the next ferry," he said, his voice growing husky.

"That still gives us a bit of time to ourselves," Gwennie murmured.

She took a step closer to him, meanwhile letting her coat slip off her shoulders. As it fell to the floor, she put her arms around his neck and planted a big wet kiss on his mouth.

For the second time in less than a minute, my mouth dropped open.

Not only were Jives and Gwennie a couple of fakes, they were a *couple*!

I watched as she pressed her body against his. By the way he responded—by grabbing her bum, for lack of a better word—I concluded that they had been a couple for some time. After all, they seemed so comfortable with each other.

Unfortunately, Corky chose that moment to seek me out, demanding attention. And he chose to do so by letting out a yelp.

The jig was up. Through my peephole, I saw both Gwennie and Jives turn their heads in my direction. Both of them looked surprised—and not in a good way.

I stepped back quickly, then dashed back to my chair by the fire as quickly as I could. I dropped into it, slumped to one side, and closed my eyes.

A few seconds later, I heard the dull thud of footsteps against the thick, dust-encrusted carpet.

"Someone in 'ere?" Gwennie asked. She was back to speaking in her loud, high-pitched voice, the one that came complete with the Cockney accent that did, indeed, make it sound as if she should be dressed like a chimney sweep.

I pretended to snap awake, then glanced around the room, looking confused. "What—what time is it?" I asked in my best disoriented-from-having-just-been-unconscious voice.

"Sorry to wake you, mum," Gwennie replied shrilly. "It's about half past the hour."

I glanced at my watch, still acting surprised. Of course, the fact that she hadn't specified *which* hour gave me a good excuse.

"My goodness!" I cried. "I didn't realize it was that late!" Smiling sheepishly, I added, "Boy, I was really fast asleep."

I only hoped my acting abilities were as good as Gwennie's—even if I'd never played Hedda Gabler.

Don't you dare turn me in, I thought, glowering at Corky. Even though I've wished on more occasions than I can name that the canine segment of the population could talk, this was one time I was very glad they couldn't.

"How were the funeral and the memorial service?" I asked, still feigning grogginess.

A sudden movement in the hallway caught my eye. Peering out the doorway, I saw a long, narrow shadow that I suspected belonged to Jives. From the looks of things, he was doing some eavesdropping of his own.

"Cor, what a sad occasion," Gwennie replied, shaking her head and *tsk-tsk*ing. "There wasn't a droi oi in the place. Everybody loved Mr. M."

Not quite everybody, I thought, wondering if I happened to be talking to one of the exceptions at that very moment.

With the second exception hovering in the hallway, listening to every word we said to each other.

"I'm sure it was very emotional," I commented. "But at least everyone had a chance to say good-bye."

I heard the front door slam again, then a few seconds later saw Charlotte pass by the doorway. She seemed lost in her own world, not the least bit surprising given the fact that she'd just attended her beloved husband's funeral.

While Corky wasn't about to abandon my world-class ear-scratching, Admiral pulled himself up and trotted out into the hallway after her. Between the click of his toenails on the floor and Charlotte's loving mutterings as she greeted the dejected basset, I could tell she was heading upstairs. I figured she was probably retreating to the privacy of her bedroom.

"I think I'll go upstairs and say hi to Nick," I said, trying to sound casual as I got up out of my chair. The last thing I wanted was to let on that I couldn't wait to tell him about this new development. "The poor guy is holed up in the bedroom, studying. He could probably use some company by now."

With that, I eased out of the room, taking care not to make eye contact with Gwennie. Or Corky.

• • •

As I dashed toward the stairs, my new discovery about the Merrywoods' duplicitous servants was making my heart pound and my mind race.

I wonder if Linus caught on to Gwennie and Jives, I mused. *Maybe he figured out their true identities, which were something they were clearly determined to hide. For all I know, the two of them topped Scotland Yard's Most Wanted list!*

Still agonizing over how to find out more information about the two imposters without the benefit of the Internet, cell phones, or any other form of technology, I trudged up the staircase. I thought Nick might have some ideas about what to do with my newfound knowledge.

But instead of heading toward our bedroom, I found myself making my way toward Charlotte's room. I noticed that the door was ajar and a light glowed from inside.

While I was anxious to talk to Nick, I couldn't help feeling that I'd just been handed a valuable opportunity to talk to Charlotte without anyone else around. Part of me was anxious to offer her some company at this very difficult time. But a more calculating part was curious about whether anything had happened at the funeral that might provide me with some new information.

I tiptoed over and peered through the doorway. Charlotte was sitting in a rocking chair with a book open in her lap. From the way she was staring off and the faraway look in her eyes, I got the feeling she wasn't actually reading.

"Charlotte?" I said in a soft voice as I knocked on the door frame gently.

She glanced in my direction and blinked. "Jessica!" she cried. Her mouth softened into a smile as she added, "Goodness, you do have a way of sneaking up on people."

"Sorry," I replied, returning her smile as I stepped into the bedroom. "I saw your light on and thought I'd ask how the memorial service went."

Charlotte let out a deep sigh. "As well as could be expected, I suppose. I must say, it was wonderful to see so many of Linus's friends and business associates there. He was so successful and so well respected. I suppose I should be pleased that he had such a long, full life."

"It's nice that the children could all be there with you, too," I commented. "And Townie, of course."

"I don't know what I'd do without them." Once again, her gaze traveled off into the distance. "Especially my daughter. She's been such a tremendous source of support through all this."

"Will Missy be able to stay on a little longer?" I asked. "After Brock and Tag have gone back to their regular lives, I mean?"

"I'm sure she'll stay as long as I need her," Charlotte said.

"I guess at some point there'll be a lot of paperwork to deal with," I noted, trying to steer the conversation toward the topic I really wanted to talk to her about. "She'd probably be helpful in that area, too."

I perched on the small round stool with a needlepoint cover that was near Charlotte's feet. Doing my best to sound casual, I added, "I noticed that Scarlett has already started sorting through Linus's records and that Missy's been helping her."

Charlotte nodded. "Scarlett was always so good at keeping track of the day-to-day workings of the company." With a wan smile, she added, "I have a feeling she's the only person in the world who ever figured out Linus's system of record-keeping."

I chuckled. "I'd think someone who'd reached his level of success would have to be pretty organized, but it doesn't look that way."

"He was a very hands-on type of person," Charlotte said. "Isn't that the expression they use these days? What I mean is that he was someone who insisted upon knowing everything that was going on in his company. Not that he was controlling, at least not in a negative sense. It was more that he liked to be in control."

It was possible that he liked to be in control of his time as much as his money, I mused. Which would be consistent with keeping a journal.

I decided to leave Aunt Alvira out of this discussion. It was partly because I didn't want to implicate her in any family business without her permission. But I also didn't want Charlotte or any of the other Merrywoods to know I'd been prowling around the house, sneaking up hidden staircases to ferret out reclusive relatives.

"Charlotte," I asked, "by any chance did Linus keep any diaries or daily records or anything like that?"

Charlotte looked startled by my question. "Diaries?" she repeated. "Not that I know of."

It took all the self-control I possessed to keep from looking over at the wooden curio cabinet less than ten feet away—the one in which the diaries Linus had kept for nearly two decades were stored. We were practically staring right at them.

How could Charlotte *not* know about them? I wondered.

Unless she was hiding something.

"You're sure he never kept journals or notes about his day-to-day activities?" I asked again.

She shook her head. "As I said, I don't know a thing about any diaries." Fixing her steely blue eyes on me, she added, "Why do you ask?"

"Only because something like that might turn out to be helpful to the police," I said with a little shrug.

The muscles around her mouth tightened. "You're talking about this terrible murder investigation, aren't you?"

Before I had a chance to reply, she continued, "Frankly, I wish the police would just go away and leave us alone. Linus is dead, and nothing is going to change that. The only thing that could make it worse would be dragging my children's names into something as horrible as a murder investigation."

Her expression darkened. "I think we all know what the press would do with a story like that. They're already lined up across the bay, waiting to pounce. They'd like nothing better than to accuse one of my children of killing their father for . . . for money or revenge or who knows what."

"As difficult as all this is," I said quietly, "it's important that the police get to the bottom of any foul play that went on."

"Personally, I believe his death was accidental," Charlotte insisted. "I don't know what happened, but somehow a food containing eggs got onto this island. And for some reason, when Linus began to experience symptoms, he was unable to use one of those EpiPens that are all over the house. If you ask me, his death was the result of some terrible chain of events that was completely outside anyone's control. Having the police turn this family tragedy into a circus isn't going to help any of us!"

I was surprised by Charlotte's outburst. The strength of her reaction made me wonder if perhaps she knew more than she was willing to tell. And not only about the existence of any diaries.

"Charlotte, I can't imagine what you and the rest of your family must be going through," I said. "But you're all doing an amazing job of coping with it. And I know you'll be there to support one another no matter what happens."

With that, I rose from the stool. "Now I'll leave you in peace and go see what Nick is up to. If you'd like, first I'll see if I can find Betty. I'm sure she'd be happy to keep you company."

"Thank you, Jessica," Charlotte replied. Apologetically, she added, "I'm sorry for my little outburst. I think I'll look for Betty myself. On the ferry ride over, she and I were talking about having a cup of tea. I have a feeling she's already in the kitchen, putting together a snack with Cook."

I was still thinking about our conversation as I retreated to my bedroom. It was possible that Charlotte really did believe that her husband's death was accidental. Or maybe she suspected—or even knew—that someone in the household had plotted to kill him.

As a mother hen, maybe she was determined to protect someone she cared about—perhaps one of her very own chicks.

Chapter 11

"The lion and the calf will lay down together, but the calf won't get much sleep."

—Woody Allen

Despite honesty's reputation for being the best policy, it's not usually my first choice when I'm investigating a murder. However, this was one of those rare occasions when I decided to use the direct approach.

I did a quick survey of the rooms on the first floor and found Gwennic in the conservatory, straightening up. At least, that was the impression she was clearly trying to give. As I stood in the doorway for a minute or two, watching her, I saw that she was merely drifting around the room, humming and distractedly fluffing up the occasional pillow. Now that I knew she saw herself as an actress rather than a housecleaner, I finally understood why everything in this house was so dusty. I also decided that the only reason she hadn't been tossed out on her bum, as they say in England, was that Charlotte and Linus were so kind.

I cleared my throat. Predictably, she turned around, wearing a surprised expression.

"Cor, Miss," she cried. "Y'scared the living day-loights outta me, lurkin' about loike that!"

I stepped into the room. "Gwennie," I said, "you don't have to lie anymore—or use that ridiculous Cockney accent. I know all about you."

She must have been a really good actress, because she managed to stay in character. "Sorry, mum," she said, her voice only a little more high-pitched than usual. "Oy 'ave no idea—"

"Gwennie, or whatever your real name is," I interrupted, "I overheard you and Jives talking in the front hallway when you came home from the funeral."

Narrowing her eyes, she asked, "What did you hear exactly?"

"That you've been speaking in a phony accent—and that you're both actors who've been pretending to be the hired help when you're actually two very accomplished individuals." I hesitated before adding, "In other words, I know you're fakes."

"We 'aven't done anything wrong!" she cried shrilly, still speaking in her phony accent.

"Please stop talking like that," I said, letting my impatience show. "Frankly, I'm as tired of hearing it as you seem to be of speaking that way. I feel like I'm in

Oliver. I keep waiting for the Artful Dodger to pick my pocket while he's singing and dancing."

She didn't laugh. I didn't know if it was because I wasn't as funny as I thought I was or because she'd been caught in a lie—a lie she and Jives had apparently been living for some time.

"I also know the reason you did it wasn't something as innocent as practicing for a role," I continued.

"Why would you think that?" she asked. At least she was finally talking in her own voice.

As for her question, I suspected she was trying to find out how much I knew. I decided to go for broke.

"I heard you say something about how you and Jives would find out soon enough just how good you were at acting." With a little shrug, I said, "Sounds to me like you were both up to no good."

Gwennie stared at me. I could practically hear the wheels turning in her head.

"It seemed like such a good idea at the time," she finally said, sounding defeated. But then she brightened, as if a lightbulb had just gone on inside her head. "It was all Jonathan's idea, actually."

"Jonathan?" I asked. "Do you mean Jives?"

"That's right," she replied. "Jonathan is his real name. Anyway, he thought the whole thing up, then talked me into it. From the very start, I was against it, but he can be a very persuasive man."

As she spoke, she kept her eyes glued to my face, as if she was monitoring my reaction. I guess she wasn't seeing much sympathy there, so she decided to try another tack.

"He threatened me," she said. She now spoke in a hoarse whisper, meanwhile twisting her fingers together as if she were trying to knit with them. "When he told me his crazy idea and I said I wanted no part of it, he told me I had to go along with it. He said now that he'd told me, he was afraid I'd go to the police, and—"

"The police!" I exclaimed without thinking.

"I told him he was being silly!" she cried. "That the police wouldn't give a hoot about what we were doing! After all, it's not actually illegal."

"And what exactly were you doing?" I asked calmly.

Gwennie bit her lip. For a few seconds, she looked like a scared young woman barely out of her twenties rather than an uneducated maid who'd seen too many episodes of *EastEnders*—or a calculating actress with dollar signs where her pupils should have been. I had a feeling that, for the very first time, I was getting a glimpse of the real Gwennie.

"A couple of years ago, things started to dry up for us in London," she said wistfully. "Acting-wise, I mean. Both Jonathan and I were suddenly having a really hard time finding work. I may not be old by the real world's standards, but I'm not twenty-one anymore. I was starting to lose that blush of youth that directors love. I was drifting into that period of being too old to play the ingenue and too young to play the mother—not to mention being too youthful for any interesting character-acting roles."

"And Jonathan?" I asked, sincerely interested. "Does that happen with men, too?"

She shook her head. "That's one more area where they've got all the luck. But Jonathan had some other...problems. He can be kind of temperamental. When it comes to his acting, I mean. He sees himself as a true artist. In other words, he always thinks he's right, even when his take on the way things ought to be done is different from the director's. He had a few run-ins along the way, and he ended up with a reputation for being difficult to work with.

"That was when he came up with his big idea." With a sad little laugh, she said, "I told him from the start that it sounded like the plot from an Agatha Christie play. You've heard of her, haven't you?"

With a wan smile, I said, "I think I've heard the name once or twice."

"Anyway, his idea was that he and I should come to America, where no one knew us. Besides, most Yanks aren't very good at telling the difference between one British accent and another. He decided we should get jobs as servants for some rich family, one where the person who controlled the purse strings was really, really ancient. Then we'd do everything we could to ingratiate ourselves, with the idea that once the old man kicked the bucket, he'd include us in his will."

"So that's how Gwennie and Jives were born," I observed. I had to admit, their plan was clever. Hateful, but clever.

"That's right," she said. "Jonathan and I did some research and we came up with the name of a posh employment agency in New York City that places maids and butlers in the homes of very wealthy families. The agency was supposed to be top of the line, which it was."

Except when it comes to doing background checks, I thought wryly.

"Jonathan and I presented ourselves as two people who'd worked together before but weren't romantically involved," Gwennie went on. "They wouldn't have liked the idea of us being a couple, because they'd be worried that if we split up one of us would quit. Either that or we'd be sneaking off into the broom closet together all the time.

"Anyway, having worked together in the past seemed to make us pretty attractive candidates—that and the fact that we both spoke with British accents. Jonathan decided to mold himself after the butler Anthony Hopkins played in *The Remains of the Day.* You know, polished, dignified, and ready to do anything to please his boss."

Except carry luggage, I thought begrudgingly. Or maybe that was just the way he acted around visitors.

"As for me, I decided to play the fool with a Cockney accent," Gwennie explained. "I didn't want the lady of the house to see me as competition, so I figured acting as if I wasn't too bright—or too attractive—would be seen an asset."

I had to admit that I was impressed by the fact that she'd thought of every angle. She had even custom-designed her accent and her hairstyle for the role.

"We were presented with quite a few opportunities," Gwennie continued. "We interviewed at a number of places, but the potential employers either weren't rich enough or old enough. We had to come up with different excuses not to take those jobs. Too far from New York, not enough pay, whatever. Then this gig came up."

A dreamy smile crossed her face. "We knew right away that it was perfect. We'd actually heard of the Merrywoods, all the way over in England. Of course, we'd made a point of learning everything we could about the richest people in America. And Linus Merrywood was near the top of the list.

"We knocked ourselves out at the interview, and lo and behold we got the job. The two of us started working here a year and a half ago." Her eyes grew as big as hamburger buns as she added, "I remember the first time I set eyes on this place. I couldn't believe how huge it was. It's true that it's seen better days, but I could still see that the Merrywoods were dripping with money.

"As for Jonathan, he was positively thrilled," she went on. "In fact, I'd never seen him so happy. He was convinced we'd found the perfect way to strike it rich. All we had to do was act like two devoted servants, kissing up to the old man every chance we got, and we'd walk away with a nice chunk of money—hopefully enough to keep us both on Easy Street for a while."

Somehow, her use of the words *Easy Street* reminded me of Fleet Street—as in Sweeney Todd, the demon barber of.

"Did it work?" I asked simply.

"What?" Gwennie looked confused, as if she'd gotten lost in telling her story.

"Did Linus name you and Jonathan in his will?"

"I—I don't know," she replied, suddenly flustered. "Linus never actually said anything about it. I suppose Jonathan and I won't know whether or not our ploy worked until the reading of his will."

At this point, I was as curious as she was to know if the two of them had achieved their goal of going from bogus butler and mendacious maid to heir and heiress. After all, they hadn't been working for Linus for very long, especially compared to the family's cook.

Then again, they could have come to the conclusion that they'd already been successful in ingratiating themselves with Linus. Or maybe Gwennie had lied about knowing whether or not she and Jonathan were in the will. Perhaps Linus had even come right out and told them he'd included them.

Or maybe they'd simply gotten impatient and decided to bump off the old man and hope for the best. After all, Gwennie had told me herself that Jonathan was temperamental.

As if she had read my mind, Gwennie suddenly said, "But just because we were hoping to get a piece of the old man's fortune doesn't mean we ever wished him any harm. Or that either one of us is capable of murder."

She stood up a little straighter as she added, "Some people might see what we were doing as stealing. But stealing money is a far cry from killing someone!

"In fact," she continued, her voice wavering, "that's why I'm being honest with you. I intend to tell our whole story to the police, too. I want them to know I'm cooperating fully. If they see that I'm being honest, I'm hoping they'll believe that I had nothing to do with Linus's murder."

And Jonathan? I thought. *Is he planning to come forth with the truth, as well?*

"But there is something else," she said, twisting her fingers again. "I don't mind telling you all this because, well, I hardly know you. And since you over-heard what Jonathan and I were saying and all, I don't want you forming the wrong opinion. But would you do me one favor?"

"What is it?" I asked skeptically.

"Please don't say anything to the Merrywoods," she said, sounding almost like a scared little girl. "I actually became quite fond of them while I was working here. Not Taggart. He's slime, as far as I'm concerned. But I really have a lot of respect for Charlotte. I'd rather she didn't find out what Jonathan and I were up to."

I thought about her request for a few seconds, then said, "I don't see any reason to say anything at this point."

At least not to the Merrywoods. I was so anxious to tell Nick what I'd just found out that I was as ready to burst as an overfilled balloon.

"Thanks, Jessie," Gwennie said. "I really appreciate that." Both her smile and her gratitude struck me as sincere.

"By the way," I asked, "you told me Jonathan's real name, but you haven't told me yours."

"It's Gwendolyn." She sighed, then added, "It was hard enough living a lie day in and day out. I figured the least I could do was hang on to one piece of truth: my own name."

As if I should feel sorry for you, I thought angrily. *Playing a charade like this for months on end, all to wrangle a few bucks out of an old man.*

Pretty despicable.

Still, as Gwennie had pointed out, stealing wasn't murder. And I still wasn't convinced the two of them had carried off their plan of winning Linus over.

Yet I couldn't discount them completely. Especially if Gwennie and Jonathan had reason to believe that their plan had succeeded and that Linus had written them both into his will. If he had, one more possible scenario was that he had suddenly seen through their ruse and was planning to change the will. In that case, waiting for him to die a natural death could have cost them. Perhaps a *lot*.

So while Gwennie insisted that her confession about what she and Jonathan were up to was enough to clear her, knowing the truth had only solidified their place on my list.

• • •

Once again, I headed back to my bedroom—and Nick. I was anxious to update him, as well as to spend a little good old-fashioned quality time with him.

But as I entered the bedroom, the excited look on his face told me he had some news of his own.

"What have you been up to?" I asked, grinning.

"Plenty," he replied. "I took your request that I find out whatever I could about the dangerous liaison between Missy and Harry Foss very seriously."

"Did you have any luck?" I demanded eagerly.

Feigning indignation, he replied, "I can assure you that my impressive success in finding out everything you wanted to know had nothing to do with luck."

Grimacing, I said, "Don't tell me. It was all due to that secret weapon of yours, right? The old Burby charm?"

"Exactly." He grinned. "Hey, you're the one who told me to take advantage of the fact that I'm the next best thing since James Bond."

I chuckled. "Okay, James. What did you find out?"

"That Missy has been having an affair with Harry since the beginning of last summer," Nick said. "The two of them had run into each other a few times over the years, but they were never anything more than casual acquaintances. But back in June, it seems they were both attending some corporate function—a reception at the top of the Empire State Building—and they just clicked. Scarlett said something about their eyes meeting over the buffet table."

"It sounds terribly romantic," I said, picturing Harry and Missy gazing at each other across a dune-size mound of pasta salad. "But how can Scarlett be so sure about all this?"

"Because Missy confided in her," Nick explained.

"She told me the two of them have become pretty close. Missy was apparently dying to talk about it, and Scarlett was someone she trusted."

"Scarlett spilled the beans to you pretty easily," I observed. "So she's not as reliable a confidante as Missy thought."

"Surely you couldn't expect anyone to resist the famous Burby charm!"

"Speaking of which," I said, looking at him askance, "exactly how did you manage to get all this information out of the unassuming Miss Scarlett?"

"Nothing I can't admit to," Nick assured me teasingly. "Just a little harmless flirting. And only enough to get her talking. All those years I spent as a private eye taught me a little something about how to get information out of people without them noticing."

I sighed. "So all is not as it appears with the happy couple—Missy and her husband, I mean."

"Not if you consider the wife's extracurricular activity a good indication," Nick replied.

"The question is whether her secret love affair with Harry had anything to do with Linus," I mused.

"Maybe Missy finally decided to leave Townie," Nick conjectured, "but she needed more money to do it. After all, it looks as if Townie was the moneymaker in that family."

"True," I added. "And while Harry makes big bucks, if Linus learned his daughter was leaving a son-in-law he was fond of—and leaving him for Linus's business partner, no less—he might have disapproved to the point where he'd have fired Harry."

"Still, if that happened, Harry could have easily gotten another job," Nick noted. "So it's hard to believe that money would have been a motive."

"Unless Linus had a vengeful side and found a way to get Harry blacklisted," I said. "But here's another idea: that Harry was anxious to take over Merrywood Industries and somehow his relationship with Linus's daughter was likely to get in the way. According to Winston, now that Linus is dead, Harry is in charge of the company. Assuming that's true, that means he can run things however he pleases."

"That scenario sounds plausible," Nick agreed. "Then again, maybe Harry killed Linus for reasons that had nothing to do with Missy. Maybe he just couldn't wait any longer to take over the company."

"That could be," I said. "Harry told me himself that he and Linus disagreed on certain aspects of the business. Maybe Linus was about to take Merrywood Industries in a direction that Harry found intolerable."

Nick and I were both silent for a few seconds. I was still thinking about all the possible ramifications of Harry's affair with Linus's daughter when Nick said, "Aren't you going to ask me what else I found out?"

I blinked. "About what?"

"About the beguiling Miss Scarlett," Nick replied. "Just because I was talking to her with the goal of finding out whatever I could about Missy and Harry doesn't mean I didn't also learn plenty about her."

"Okay," I said, my eyes narrowing. "And what did you find out about her?"

"That she has a boyfriend."

I raised an eyebrow. "You mean a boyfriend as in someone other than Linus?"

Now it was Nick's turn to look surprised. "You mean Scarlett and Linus were—"

"It's just a rumor," I assured him. "Cook seems to believe either she or Gwennie was involved with Linus, but that doesn't mean it's true."

Warily, Nick said, "Frankly, I don't know if anything was going on between Linus and Scarlett. But she told me she's been dating someone seriously for almost two years. A doctor. A surgeon, in fact. An orthopedic surgeon. They met when she broke her wrist skiing."

A surgeon, huh? That meant her beau was someone who made a pretty good salary—which could explain her pricey possessions.

"He also happens to be an older man," Nick added.

"How much older?" I was back to thinking about Linus. I wondered if there was a pattern here—if Scarlett tended to go for men who were several decades her senior, including both her boss and her surgeon.

"He's thirty-five," Nick said. " 'An older guy,' she called him, even though he's around my age." Frowning, he mused, "Gee, I never thought of myself as 'an older guy' before."

"She only thinks thirty-five is older because she's something like twenty-four or twenty-five," I reassured him.

"That's a relief." Nick sighed. "Although I have noticed a few gray hairs lately."

"It's only when you notice *no* hair that you have to start worrying," I told him.

"Besides," I added, patting his hand affectionately, "I've already agreed to stay with you in sickness and in health and all kinds of other contingencies. I'm pretty sure those vows you and I took covered gray hair and baldness and everything else that comes along with you turning into an older guy."

"So I guess you're stuck with me," Nick said with a grin.

"Like glue," I said, grinning back. "Krazy Glue, the kind that never gets unstuck."

• • •

Nick and I were marveling over the fact that we were bonded for life—something I still hadn't gotten completely used to—when I heard Betty outside our closed bedroom door, calling us in a soft voice.

"Jessica? Nick? I hope I'm not disturbing you..."

"You know what she thinks we were doing, don't you?" I asked Nick teasingly.

"Another two minutes and she would have been right," he replied, moving his eyebrows up and down in a lascivious way.

I just rolled my eyes. "Come on in, Betty," I called back.

She opened the door hesitantly, then looked relieved to find Nick and me sitting side by side on the bed, fully clothed. True, my hair was mussed and our clothes were a bit disheveled. But I figured she was afraid she might find us in a considerably more compromising position.

"Sorry to bother you," Betty said, "but Linus's lawyer just arrived, and he's about to read the will. I suggested to Charlotte that she might want those of us who are outsiders to find something else to do, but she invited us to join everyone else downstairs. I thought you would be interested..."

Nick and I exchanged excited glances.

"We're interested," I assured her. "We'll be down in a second."

As she closed the door behind her, Nick whispered to me, "I think this may be the part where the plot thickens."

"Maybe we'll get some answers," I replied, less interested in the drama of the event than in the possibility that it might help me put my finger on the killer.

As soon as Nick and I put ourselves back in order, we rushed down to the first floor. Charlotte was standing at the bottom of the staircase, chatting with a man who was a newcomer to Solitude Island.

Glancing up at us, she said, "I see you two have decided to join us for the reading of Linus's will. You might as well, since I'm sure that afterward everyone in this household will be talking about nothing else."

She placed her hand gently on the newcomer's arm. "Let me introduce Oliver Withers. He's been our family attorney for years."

Charlotte made it sound as if having a family attorney was as common as having a family doctor—or a family pet. Of course, now that I was married to a lawyer, I supposed I had a family attorney of my own.

This particular one happened to look very lawyerly. While he didn't have much in the way of hair, the silver strands that remained did a really good job of staying in place. He was dressed in a conservative gray suit that had either been made for him or customized by an expert tailor. The blue in his striped black-and-blue tie was almost the exact color of his shirt. Instead of ordinary buttons at the ends of his sleeves, he wore cuff links. Gold ones, engraved with his initials.

I made a mental note to get Nick a pair of those as a graduation present.

Nick and I barely had a chance to shake the attorney's hand before Scarlett came scurrying toward us. "I see you've met Mr. Withers," she said to us. Turning to Charlotte, she added, "It's probably a good idea to hold the reading of Mr. Merrywood's will in the conservatory. That way, there'll be plenty of room for all of us."

As Nick and I followed Charlotte, Mr. Withers, and Scarlett into the conservatory, I saw that Tag, Brock, Missy, and Townie were already in attendance, along with Harry, Betty, and Winston. It looked as if Charlotte had also invited Jonathan-as-Jives, Gwennie, and Cook to sit in. That made fifteen of us in all.

The womenfolk lined the couch and filled the chairs, while once again most of the menfolk chose to stand in front of the fireplace or elsewhere in the room. Only Brock opted for the floor. He sat in the lotus position, with his legs folded pretzel-style and his feet balanced on top of his knees.

"I see that everyone is here," Mr. Withers said as his eyes traveled around the room.

"Excuse me," I piped up, having just realized that wasn't quite the case. "Shouldn't we ask Alvira to join us?"

"Aunt Alvira?" Brock scoffed. "She doesn't want anything to do with us."

"It's hard to believe she's related to us," Missy agreed petulantly. "She wouldn't even come downstairs for Daddy's birthday party. You'd think she'd want to help her own brother celebrate."

But she did help him celebrate, I thought. Quietly, with just the two of them enjoying a glass of champagne and no doubt talking and laughing about old times.

I realized I'd become quite fond of Aunt Alvira.

In fact, I was about to protest that she should at least be invited as a matter of courtesy, when Charlotte said, "After the reading of the will, one of us will go upstairs and inform Alvira of its contents."

"Then without further ado," Mr. Withers said, pulling out a pair of glasses and perching them at the edge of his nose, "I'll begin."

You could have heard the proverbial pin drop as he took a deep breath, preparing to read.

"*I, Linus Ellsworth Merrywood, being of sound mind and under no restraint, do make, declare, and publish this my last will and testament, hereby revoking all wills and codicils hereto made by me—*"

"You can skip all that," Tag interrupted. "We don't need to weed through the legalese."

"Taggart, show some respect," Charlotte reprimanded him. "Mr. Withers, please proceed in whatever way you usually do."

Eyeing his audience warily, Mr. Withers said, "I'll just skip ahead a few paragraphs. . . . Ah, here we go. *I bequeath each of the following charities the sum of fifty thousand dollars, to be used in whatever manner they choose.*" He glanced up. "There's quite a long list of organizations here. Should I read it?"

"Not now," Brock said impatiently. "You can go back to that later."

"Of course." Frowning, Mr. Withers bent his head over the will once again. "*To my dear sister, Alvira, I leave the following mutual funds, stocks, and other securities. My intention is that she maintain her present lifestyle for the rest of her days, residing in my house and using the funds from these accounts however she pleases.*"

The lawyer looked up and blinked. "There's a long list here, too. Do you want me to skip that, as well?"

"Can we please just get on with this?" Taggart asked crossly.

Mr. Withers bent his head over the document once again. "*To my children, Taggart, Melissa, and Brockton, I leave each the sum of ten thousand dollars—*"

"That's it?" Tag cried.

"You're joking!" Brock seconded.

Missy just gasped. Glancing over, I saw that all the color had drained out of her face.

"There's more," Mr. Withers said quietly. *"I encourage each of my children to donate this money to a worthy cause or to use it in some way that will benefit others who have been less fortunate—"*

"Is this a joke?" Brock exclaimed.

"Maybe there are additional provisions in subsequent paragraphs," Townie suggested.

"Why don't you continue reading?" Charlotte suggested.

With a nod, Mr. Withers went on. *"To my loyal assistant, Scarlett Sandowsky, I leave the sum of fifty thousand dollars plus the following pieces of jewelry from my mother's estate: one diamond and emerald necklace, one pair of ruby earrings..."*

Automatically, I glanced over at Charlotte. Yet nothing even close to jealousy appeared to register on her face.

I couldn't say the same for Cook. Her eyes had narrowed and her cheeks had turned the color of those rubies that were apparently going to Scarlett.

"To my right-hand man in both business and friendship, Harrison Foss," Mr. Withers went on without looking up, *"I leave my gold Montblanc pen—"*

"What?" Missy cried. "A pen?"

Harry, meanwhile, looked as if he was going to be sick.

"—as well as fifteen hundred shares of stock in Merrywood Industries," Mr. Withers continued. Glancing up, he commented, "I believe that makes him an equal shareholder with Charlotte."

Harry's look of horror immediately relaxed into an

expression of satisfaction. "Oh. Well. That's more along the lines of what Linus and I had discussed."

"*To Margaret Reilly,*" Mr. Withers read, "*who served my family and me well for so many years, I leave the sum of two hundred thousand dollars, which will hopefully enable her to retire whenever she chooses.*"

Margaret let out a cry of surprise. "Oh, my," she said breathlessly. "All that money! The man was a saint."

"And for us?" Gwennie asked, using her Cockney accent. "Did Mr. M. leave me and Jives anything?"

"I'm afraid not," Mr. Withers said. "In fact, we're almost at the end."

I stole a glance at Gwennie and the man masquerading as Jives, my stomach curdling at the horrified looks they cast at each other.

Mr. Withers cleared his throat, then read, "*I leave the remainder of my estate, including my residence on Solitude Island, my apartment at 1255 Park Avenue in Manhattan, my cars, boats, and personal effects, as well as all my financial investments, to my beloved wife, Charlotte.*"

He glanced up and said, "That's all, except for more legalese." Glancing at Charlotte, he asked, "Should I continue?"

"Thank you, Mr. Withers," she said, her eyes drifting over the forlorn expressions on her children's faces, "but I think we've all heard what we needed to hear."

Chapter 12

"Though the lion and the antelope happen to live in the same forest, the antelope still has time to grow up."
—African Proverb

The mood in the house felt oppressively heavy as the group dispersed. While those who had been the beneficiaries of Linus's generosity were obviously pleased, those who hadn't fared as well looked—well, ready to kill.

All three of Linus's children seemed dazed. It was as if they still hadn't digested the fact that their own father, who was wealthy beyond imagination, had left them an amount of money so small that it basically amounted to a slap in the face.

As for Gwennie and Jonathan, they, too, seemed to be in a state of disbelief. Yet I knew perfectly well that they had no real claim to any of Linus Merrywood's money.

Still, the fact that no one seemed in the mood for reminiscing over home movies or making idle chatter didn't deter me from seeking out a family member I had yet to have a heart-to-heart talk with. I watched Missy leave the conservatory after making an excuse to her husband about wanting to finish up the organizing she'd been doing in her father's study. I waited a minute or two, then wandered over to the study, hoping to catch her alone.

She was standing in front of the shelves behind Linus's desk, studying them. For a moment, I wondered if she, too, was searching for his missing notebooks.

"Missy?" I said quietly as I entered the room, not wanting to startle her.

She whirled around, her eyes wide with panic.

"Jessie! You scared me!" she cried, clasping her hands against her chest like the heroine in a romance novel.

"Sorry," I said sincerely. "I was actually looking for, uh, Nick. He was here a minute ago, but he seems to have suddenly disappeared."

Her fearful expression softened. "I don't blame you for wanting to keep track of that husband of yours," she remarked, sounding as if she was only half teasing. "He seems like a real catch."

"I think so," I said, unable to suppress a genuine smile. "Frankly, it took Nick and me awhile to get hitched, but now that we are, I couldn't be happier."

Missy let out a long, deep sigh. "You two are so lucky," she said, a dreamy look coming into her eyes. "There's no better time than those first few months of marriage."

Choosing my words carefully, I said, "You and Townie have been married for years, but it looks as if you two are still on your honeymoon."

Missy giggled. But I was nearly certain I detected an edge to her girlish glee, as if it was forced. "You're right about that," she said simply.

"I wonder if you could give me any advice," I continued, watching her carefully. "About how to keep a marriage happy, I mean. What's the secret of you and Townie still seeming so incredibly happy together?"

I was almost certain I saw a strained look cross her face. But a second later, the tension was gone.

"I think the secret to a happy marriage is each partner treating the other as if they were the most important person in the world," she said with a resolute nod. "And doing it every single day."

"That's pretty good advice," I replied earnestly. "I'll try to keep that in mind."

Figuring there was no time like the present, I casually asked, "What about Harry Foss? Is he married?"

I guess I wasn't casual enough. "Why do you ask?" Missy asked sharply, her eyes narrowing.

I hesitated for a moment. *Got me there,* I thought.

But I'd gotten pretty good at thinking on my feet, especially at times like this. "I have a friend who's in the market," I said. Remembering that old saying about sticking as close to the truth as possible whenever you're telling a lie, I added, "Suzanne is in a relationship with a really nice guy right now. A New York State trooper, in fact. But I'm afraid she's putting too much pressure on him and that at some point the whole thing is going to fall apart. I'm thinking that it's not a bad idea to keep an eye out for any other prospects in case that time ever rolls around."

"That's considerate of you," Missy commented.

I shrugged. "Suzanne and I have been friends for years. In fact, we met in college. So what about Harry? Is he available?"

"He's single." She sidestepped my question about whether or not he was actually available. "He got divorced about five years ago."

"And he never remarried?" I asked, sounding as surprised as I felt. "Or got into a serious relationship?"

"He's pretty involved in his work," she replied, quickly adding, "From what I can tell, that is. I don't know him all that well."

"I see." I did my best to keep all skepticism out of my voice. "What about your brothers?" I asked offhandedly. "I get the impression that neither of them is married."

Missy shook her head. "Not at the moment, anyway."

When I cast her a confused look, she added, "Brock has never been married. The man can't make a commitment to which avocado to buy, so how could anyone expect him to choose a life mate?

"As for Tag, he's the exact opposite." Missy gave a

disapproving snort before explaining, "He's already been married twice, and he's not even out of his thirties."

"What were his two wives like?" I asked.

Another snort. "Not exactly the kind of girls you'd be anxious to bring home to meet Mom and Dad. The first one, Monique, was a French model. Or so she claimed. Personally, I thought she'd found other ways of using her looks to make money—and that not all of her beauty was natural. That girl's breasts were so big, thanks to the humongous implants she got somewhere along the line, that she looked as if she were shoplifting basketballs underneath her blouse.

"That marriage lasted less than a year," Missy continued, her voice dripping with disdain. "As for the divorce, that went on for at least three. But do you think my big brother learned a thing from the experience?"

I didn't have to answer.

Missy sighed. "Their divorce lawyers were still battling it out when Tag announced all over again that he'd found the woman of his dreams."

"Another model?" I asked.

"Another *supposed* model," she corrected me. "This one was Brazilian—Mariana. She was about seven feet tall, with legs as long as palm trees." She shook her head disapprovingly. "She also had the IQ of one. But Tag didn't seem to care. I swear, he married her before the ink was dry on the divorce papers."

"But it sounds as if that one didn't work out, either," I prompted.

"No, it didn't," Missy replied. "That one lasted only a few months. And I'm pretty sure that divorce ended up costing him even more than the first one." With a sardonic smile, she explained, "That one got herself a better lawyer."

Something was troubling me. Tag clearly had a taste for expensive women and expensive toys. But when it came to the question of how he paid for both, I was mystified.

He certainly wasn't getting the money from Linus. And he didn't appear to have much of a career going.

Which made me wonder where the money for his hobbies was coming from.

"Missy," I finally asked, hesitant about pushing her even further, "is there anything else Tag is involved in besides flashy women?"

"How about *stuff*?" she shot back. "He's probably the biggest consumer of ridiculous boy toys in this entire hemisphere. My big brother is all about fun, and his version of it takes a lot of accoutrements. Fancy cars, luxurious condos in glamorous locales, yachts—"

"I'm talking about something else," I said quietly. "Something that might have gotten him into trouble."

A look of puzzlement crossed her face. "Like what?"

By this point, I had a few theories of my own. But I decided not to share them. "I don't know. It's just that yesterday I found him doing something kind of strange."

"What do you mean, strange?" she asked suspiciously.

"I happened to run into him while I was doing a little exploring," I said. "It was shortly after Nick arrived on the island. I was getting us some lunch in the kitchen, and I noticed a staircase I hadn't seen before. I couldn't resist taking a peek, since this house is so amazing. Anyway, I found Tag way up at the top of the tower. Somehow, I got the feeling he was hiding."

Missy's look of confusion melted into one of disgust. "Oh, for heaven's sake. Not *that* again. I thought that was one problem he'd finally gotten under control."

"What problem?" I asked.

I wasn't surprised when she responded, "Gambling."

Bingo, I thought. One of the possibilities I'd already come up with. "Tag gambles?"

"One more of his vices," Missy replied angrily. "My brother has brought shame on this family again and again, ever since he discovered the power of a pair of dice. It's gotten him into trouble more times than I care to think about. And there's no doubt in my mind that that's why you found him cowering in a corner somewhere.

"Oh, sure, there were times when he'd win," she noted. "That's how he financed that abomination of a car down there—among other things. And he happened to meet both Monique and Mariana when he was flush.

"But that's only one side of the coin," she continued. "I can't tell you how many times he came slinking into this house with his shoulders slumped and his head down, begging Daddy for money to pay off his gambling debts. A *lot* of money. And he'd swear up and down that he'd give it up if only our father would bail him out. 'Just this once!' he would always say. By this point it's practically become his slogan. He probably means it, too, at least when he's saying it. But before you know it, he's back at it again."

"And did your father bail him out?" I asked, genuinely curious.

"For a while. But even then, it was never without making Tag grovel. Daddy would give him a stern lecture every time. He also made it clear that the only reason he was helping him out was because the characters Tag owed money to were so—well, they were pretty unsavory. They meant business, too."

"But you make it sound as if Linus stopped paying back Tag's creditors," I observed.

"Only lately." Missy frowned. "Finally he'd had enough. So the last couple of times Tag came begging, Daddy told him he was on his own. I imagine he got the money he needed somewhere, but I don't have a clue as to how or where."

Shaking her head disapprovingly, she added, "They say gambling is an addiction, one that's as hard to break as an addiction to drugs or alcohol. Believe me, I've done tons of reading on the topic. And I have to admit that that certainly seems to be the case with Tag. But it doesn't make it any easier to deal with."

My mind was racing. Tag's fear of loan sharks could explain why he might need a lot of money fast, which he could get hold of most efficiently by killing

262 • Cynthia Baxter

Linus and benefiting from a large inheritance—at least, the one he assumed he'd be getting.

I was about to change the subject, now that I had the answer I'd been looking for, when Missy let out a wistful sigh.

"I've tried having Harry talk to him," she said. Her voice sounded far away, as if she was talking to herself rather than to me.

"Harry?" I repeated.

"That's right," she said, still distracted. "But it hasn't done a bit of good. I swear, whatever advice anyone gives Tag goes in one ear and out the other. You'd think he'd listen, especially to someone like Harry, who's such an incredible role model!"

Your loyalties are showing, I felt like telling her. *You're supposed to be saying things like that about the man you love, not the one you're secretly visiting in the middle of the night. At least in public.*

But her claim that Harry was the ideal role model for her wayward brother was one more sign that the two of them were, indeed, an item. Which led me to move her name, as well as her big brother's, a little bit higher up on my list of suspects.

• • •

Given what I'd learned about Gwennie and Jives's true identities earlier that day, I was curious to find out more about them. After all, just because Missy and Tag were looking more and more suspicious, it didn't mean I'd ruled out anyone else—especially two imposters who'd traveled all the way across the Atlantic to play their con game.

My first impulse was to run upstairs to the bedroom, pull out my laptop, and do a little Googling. But then I remembered that there was no Internet access on Solitude Island.

The more time I spent here, the more I understood how well named the place was. And there were no computers, cell phones, or even electricity, for that matter, back when Epinetus Merrywood came up with the name.

I considered asking Nick if he had any ideas, some secret technique he'd learned during the years he spent as a private investigator. But I knew, deep down, that being stranded on an island didn't leave me with a lot of options.

Which meant that if I was going to find out more about the duplicitous duo, I would have to do it the old-fashioned way: with a face-to-face confrontation with the Merrywoods' bogus butler.

So I took a few deep breaths and started checking all the rooms on the first floor. I realized that I didn't know what a butler did when he wasn't buttling—not that Jonathan had ever exhibited much skill in that department, anyway.

Given the low level of job satisfaction he was undoubtedly experiencing, especially now that he knew he hadn't even gotten a mention in Linus's will, I wasn't surprised to find him in a back room. The TV was on, his feet were propped up on an ottoman, and the liquid in his iced-tea glass looked like something other than iced tea.

I cleared my throat as a way of announcing my arrival. Jives immediately jumped out of his chair and stood at attention.

"Dr. Popper," he said, doing a really good job of not sounding the least bit surprised. "Is there anything I can get for you?"

"Jonathan," I said impatiently, "you can drop the formality. Gwennie told me all about you."

A look of astonishment crossed his face. But he insisted on staying in character as he added, "I'm afraid I haven't the foggiest idea what you're talking about—"

"Your acting skills are actually pretty good," I interrupted. "But I know that you're no more a professional butler than I am."

His shoulders slumped. "What exactly did Gwennie tell you?"

"Everything," I replied. "That the two of you are out-of-work actors who decided to put your training to good use by getting some poor unsuspecting rich guy to write you into his will."

"That's not quite accurate," he said tartly. "I merely suggested to Gwennie that since we were both between acting jobs, we might find employment as servants. That way, we'd be free to leave our jobs when another opportunity to ply our craft arose."

I sighed. Getting Jonathan to give up his Jives act was turning out to be a lot harder than I'd anticipated.

"I know even more," I said, looking him in the eye

to hide the fact that I was bluffing. "I know about your . . . past."

His shocked expression told me I'd been correct in assuming that, in addition to having a collection of eight-by-ten glossies, somewhere along the line he'd also posed for a couple of mug shots.

"I sincerely believed I had enough money to cover those checks," he insisted. "I wasn't trying to defraud anyone. As for that old woman who fell down the stairs, it was entirely coincidental that I was in her house at the time, collecting money for the Actors' Relief Fund. Scotland Yard was never able to prove any connection whatsoever, mainly because there was none."

I was pleased that he'd fallen into my trap. While he'd made plenty of excuses, I now knew that he was previously involved in schemes that involved stealing money—and possibly even crimes directed at senior citizens. And I'd learned all that without using the Internet.

"But when it came to our positions here, Gwennie and I weren't doing anything dishonest," Jonathan continued. "It's true that we told a fib about having work experience of this type, and I did give a different name on my job application, just in case Linus turned out to be one of those compulsive people who do background checks.

"But everything else was on the up-and-up," he insisted. "Gwennie and I did the jobs we were paid to do, and we extended every possible kindness to Linus

266 • Cynthia Baxter

and his family. Except for that vile assistant of his," he
added.

"What's up with you and Scarlett?" I asked.

I'd noticed that he seemed to have more disdain for
her than he did for the rest of the world in general.

"She's a snob," Jonathan sniffed, "unlike the members of the Merrywood clan. I must say, they all
treated us with respect. Especially Charlotte. Now
there's a real lady. And Brock has always gone out of
his way to make all the servants feel as if they're his
equals."

"What about the other Merrywoods?" I asked.
"And Townie?"

"Tag treats everyone the same," Jonathan observed. With a wry smile, he added, "He basically
thinks everyone on the entire planet was put here to
serve him. As for Townie, he was clearly well brought
up. He seems to have learned from childhood that a
gentleman always acts kindly toward the hired help.
That's true of Missy, as well, although she's so self-
absorbed that she probably doesn't notice there's anyone else in the room most of the time.

"But Scarlett—that's another matter entirely."
Scowling, Jonathan said, "She can be downright rude.
The night of Linus's birthday party, for example. She
was a holy terror, ordering all of us around like there
was no tomorrow. And she's not even a family member."

"Maybe she was just tense," I commented. "She
probably wanted to make sure everything went

smoothly, since it was such an important day in Linus's life."

Studying his face for his reaction, I added, "From what I've observed, she seemed to think the world of him."

"Hmph," Jonathan sniffed. "Or maybe she was tense for another reason—like she had a few tasks on her to-do list that had nothing to do with planning a dinner party."

I stared at him. I was learning that maybe the walls in this place didn't have ears but the servants certainly did. And they seemed to know plenty about what went on with the Merrywoods and their associates.

I knew I'd do well to pay attention to whatever observations Jonathan had made about the dynamics of the household.

"Are you saying you think Scarlett is responsible for Linus's death?" I finally asked. "That she's the one who switched the birthday cakes?"

"I'm just saying that I'm convinced there was more to their relationship than her making his plane reservations," Jonathan said dryly. "Much more. And when strong feelings come into play, especially in a situation that's bound to be a dead end for one of the parties...well, that person could decide it should become a dead end for the other."

Wait a minute, I thought. *Jonathan is trying to make it sound as if Scarlett killed Linus, yet he's one of my prime suspects.*

"I suppose everyone who was in the house that

night had a motive for murdering Linus," I said. "Including you and Gwennie."

"Well, we didn't kill him," he said with a little pout. "And the police have no reason to suspect us. After all, we weren't even in the will."

"Yes, but—" I quickly cleared my throat, wanting to disguise the syllables that had jumped out of my mouth. I'd started to point out that Jonathan and Gwennie hadn't learned that they weren't in Linus's will until just a few hours earlier.

Which meant there was a good chance that the phony butler's attempts at casting suspicions on Scarlett could well be a way of deflecting them from himself and perhaps from his pal, Gwennie.

After all, if there was one thing actors were good at, it was acting. And being considered a murder suspect was undoubtedly the best time for someone to muster up all of his talent.

• • •

I dashed across the main floor of the house, anxious to tell Nick about my conversation with Jonathan—especially with respect to his comments about Scarlett. I assumed he was holed up in our bedroom, studying away. But as I reached the staircase, I saw that the man who played Romeo to my Juliet was heading in the same direction. So were his two furry sidekicks, who lit up like fireworks when they spotted me.

"Nick!" I cried, stopping in my tracks. "I was looking for you!" I immediately crouched down to give Max and Lou the greeting they deserved.

"That's funny," he replied, "because I was looking for you."

Nick's serious tone caused me to glance up. His voice, combined with the expression on his face, gave me the feeling there was nothing funny about his decision to seek me out.

"Is something wrong?" I asked, still scratching two furry necks, one with each hand.

Nick's frown deepened. "Jess, I just found something I think you ought to see."

Chapter 13

W hat is it?" I asked, my mouth already dry.
"You should probably see for yourself," Nick replied mysteriously. If he hadn't looked so earnest, I'd have thought he was playing a joke.

I followed him through the house. Max padded along happily beside me, his eyes bright and his red tongue hanging out as if it were a necktie, while Lou kept darting ahead to sniff things that, to me, were invisible.

I expected Nick to lead our little parade to Linus's study or the kitchen—or at least the conservatory. Instead, he stopped when we neared the front door.

"Are we going somewhere?" I asked in confusion. Max kept glancing up at me expectantly, as if he assumed we were all going out for a walk. I scooped him up in my arms and gave him a hug, which I figured was the next best thing. As for Lou, he plopped down on the floor, no easy feat given how slippery the marble was.

Nick shook his head, then pointed to one of the two dusty, tarnished suits of armor standing against opposite walls. "This is what I was talking about."

So much for clearing up my confusion. "What about it?" I asked, examining the decrepit metal structure. It was in such bad shape that it looked as if it really could have been used in the Middle Ages.

"Look inside it."

"Why would I do that?" I asked. "Better yet, why would *you* do that?"

"I didn't intend to," he replied. "Actually, I was staring at it, wondering how the whole thing stayed together. I got up close to study it better. That was when I noticed a piece of paper sticking out of the visor. That prompted me to look a little further."

I frowned. Paper and suits of armor were definitely two things that did not go together. So I plopped Max back down on the floor and watched him embark on a sniff fest. Then, as Nick suggested, I reached for the visor designed to protect the wearer's face—one of the few pieces that appeared to open and shut—and lifted it gently.

"Oh, my!" I cried.

While I'd expected to encounter empty space, instead I found paper. Not wadded up, exactly, but not stored with any sense of order, either. In fact, what I saw appeared to have been stuffed in there, either carelessly or because someone was in a hurry.

"What is all this?" I wondered aloud.

"I didn't get that far," Nick replied. "I didn't think I was in a position to start taking stuff out."

I, however, did not possess his sense of responsibility. Certainly not his self-control. I couldn't resist reaching into the imaginary knight's head and pulling out the first thing I could grab.

I just stared at it, blinking.

"What is it?" Nick finally asked, peering over my shoulder.

"It looks like an electric bill," I said. "According to the postmark, an electric bill from two years ago."

Nick frowned. "It was mailed to this address. And the name on it is Linus Merrywood."

"Maybe Linus started paying his bills online," I suggested. "Or at least having Scarlett do it that way."

"That would explain part of it," Nick commented. "But what about the fact that Linus, or whoever did this, decided that a good place to store his unpaid bills was inside a suit of armor?"

"*Hiding* his unpaid bills is more like it," I said. "After all, whoever did this went to a lot of trouble to make sure these were out of sight."

"That's true," Nick agreed. "Which means there's bound to be other stuff in there that's much more interesting than an electric bill."

"Love letters?" I suggested, thinking of Jonathan's claim that Scarlett and Linus had been more than employee and employer.

Nick cast me a questioning look. "What do you think? Should we try to find out?"

I thought for a few seconds. "If someone comes out here and finds us, we're going to have some serious 'splaining to do," I said, quoting the late, great Ricky Ricardo.

"In that case, we'll have to act fast," Nick said, glancing around nervously. "Look, at least we can get an idea of what else is hidden in here."

I didn't wait another second. I reached into the no-longer-errant knight's face and pulled out a bunch of papers.

It immediately became clear that most of them were bills, as well. But there was also plenty of junk mail— envelopes full of coupons for car washes and pizza parlors, credit-card offers, and all the usual detritus that somehow finds its way into everyone's mailbox.

How it had subsequently found its way into some-one's personal suit of armor was another matter en-tirely.

"What does this mean?" I asked, not really expect-ing an answer.

"Maybe someone mistook Sir Galahad for Sir Garbage Pail," Nick suggested.

But my thoughts were heading in a different direc-tion. "Or maybe this is a decoy," I said. "Maybe who-ever did this stashed the real thing deeper inside."

"Good point!" Nick said brightly. "Should we keep digging?"

We took turns at reaching inside the suit of armor and pulling out papers. The next few batches proved to be more of the same—junk mail, unpaid bills, and, finally, unopened Christmas cards, all from two years before. But then, when we reached the middle of Sir Galahad's chest, we encountered a big gap.

"Is that it?" Nick asked, sounding disappointed.

"I bet it's not," I replied. Maybe my arms weren't quite as long as Nick's, but they were considerably narrower. So I stood on tiptoe and was barely able to reach way inside to the torso. I wasn't surprised when my fingers touched what I instantly identified as a stack of papers.

"Eureka!" I cried.

By rolling up the papers I now held in my fingertips, I was able to extract the whole thing at once. As soon as I held the sheaf in my hand, I studied it eagerly, certain that whatever I'd found would explain this absurdity.

"Legal documents!" I said breathlessly. "That's what the person who did this really meant to hide!"

However, as soon as I glanced over at Nick, I saw that he didn't share my enthusiasm.

"But why would someone hide legal documents?" he asked. "And look at the date. This was filed only a few months ago, back in March. It's not as if stashing away the paperwork can make a legal action go away."

He had a point. "Well...maybe Linus hid this because didn't want Charlotte to know about some lawsuit that was going on," I said, trying to come up with an explanation.

Reaching for the papers, Nick said, "Why don't we

see what this is all about? Maybe that will help us understand why someone hid it."

I held the documents so both Nick and I could read them at the same time. I was glad to have a lawyer-in-training on hand to help me decipher their meaning. But it didn't take a year and a half of law school to see that they involved one of Linus and Charlotte's neighbors in the high-rise building in New York City that housed their co-op. Just from perusing the first few lines, I surmised that the Merrywoods had put something large and bulky on their balcony that blocked their next-door neighbors' view of Central Park.

I handed the documents to Nick, then waited in silence while he read through them.

"That pretty much sums it up," he concluded as he gave them back to me. "The Merrywoods' neighbors certainly had a right to an unobstructed view. I can't imagine that Linus wasn't fully aware of that. He shouldn't have been the least bit surprised that they sued him over it, either."

"This whole thing is so strange," I commented. "Not only that someone hid these legal documents, but also that Linus and Charlotte were doing something so annoying."

Nick nodded. "And given that everyone thinks Linus was a pretty reasonable guy and the fact that I can see for myself that Charlotte's a real sweetie, it seems unlikely that they wouldn't have been more neighborly."

"That's true," I agreed. "You'd think they'd willingly take down a . . . a big plant or an umbrella or whatever else they put on their balcony as soon as their neighbors pointed out that it was a problem."

The sound of voices in a not-too-distant room made us both start. Even Lou rose to his feet, preparing to greet whoever happened our way, while Max stood at attention and wagged his stub of a tail.

Nick and I looked at each other guiltily and, without another word, began putting everything back inside the suit of armor, exactly the way we'd found it.

• • •

"That was close," Nick whispered as we tiptoed away. I'd scooped Max up into my arms again, while he had taken hold of Lou's collar to keep him from wandering off in the wrong direction and revealing our presence. The last thing we wanted was for anyone to wonder what we'd found in the front hallway that was fascinating enough to hold our interest for such a long time. "What do you say we hightail it upstairs and get away from all this?"

While I'd been planning exactly that a few minutes earlier, I'd just noticed Townie heading toward the back parlor—by himself. Since Missy's husband was barely allowed out of her sight—clearly a rule that was good for the goose but not for the gander—I decided to jump on the chance to talk to him alone.

"Why don't you take the dogs back upstairs without me?" I told Nick distractedly. "I'll catch up with you in a few minutes."

Nick's eyes traveled to the doorway through which Townie had disappeared.

"Go for it, Jess," he said. Then he took Max into his own arms, leaned over to give me a peck on the cheek, and dashed off with Lou in tow.

I found Townie standing at the dry bar in one corner of the room, pouring a pale golden liquid from a crystal decanter.

"Oh, hello, Townie," I greeted him, doing my best to sound surprised instead of letting on that I'd been stalking him. "I was looking for Nick."

"No Nick here," he replied with a smile. Holding up his glass, he asked, "Can I offer you some brandy?"

"No, thanks, I'm fine," I said. Letting my eyes drift to the window, I commented, "This storm is brutal."

"And endless," he added.

We were both silent as lightning flashed, Townie sipping his brandy and me staring out at the storm. A few seconds later a powerful roll of thunder sent the crystal glasses lined up in the cabinet clinking against one another.

"We may lose the electricity again," I commented.

Townie frowned, locking his jaw even more than usual as he commented, "As if this place wasn't already gloomy enough."

"It is pretty gloomy," I agreed. "But at least the whole family is together."

"Yes," he agreed. "That's important at a time like this." He held out his brandy snifter as if to toast the concept of families being together.

"I've been amazed at how closely knit the Merry-woods are," I went on. "Oh, sure, I can see that there are the usual family tensions."

Anxious to follow up on Gwennie and Jonathan's mysterious comment about Brock and Townie being "in bed together," a situation Missy was supposedly aware of, I added, "The tensions between Missy and Brock, for example."

Sounding offended, he insisted, "Missy may tease her brother a bit, but she certainly loves him, even though she might not always show it. In fact, it was her idea that Brock and I—"

He stopped himself midsentence, and a pained look crossed his face. I wondered if saying more than he'd intended was a side effect of drinking brandy.

"I suppose there's no reason to keep it a secret any longer," he said with an air of resignation. "It's not as if we're going to go ahead with it, anyway."

By that point, I'd definitely put on my listening ears.

"For the last few months," Townie continued, "Brock and I have been talking about going into business together."

Aha, I thought. *So Gwennie and Jonathan really are paying attention.*

"That sounds like a great idea," I commented. "I don't know Brock very well, of course, but I get the sense that he's really talented. He certainly seems dedicated to getting his jewelry-making business off the ground."

"My feelings exactly," Townie agreed. "So it

seemed to make good business sense to help him get started. It also would have been a good way of showing support for my brother-in-law. I would have been happy to subsidize the whole venture myself. It was Missy who insisted that he put up half the money."

I tried not to let my surprise show. "Why is that?"

Townie sighed. "She felt he'd be more committed if he made a financial investment in the business. That, in effect, it would help him grow up. And I suppose she was right. The problem was, I didn't know where she expected Brock to come up with that kind of money."

"What kind of money are we talking about?" I asked.

"Half a million."

I gulped. "Half a million *dollars*?"

He cast me an odd look. "It takes substantial capital to get a new business going. If you want to do it right, of course. You need to rent space, hire the right people, create a strong presence on the Internet… And besides the usual start-up costs, Brock was going to need to invest in some high-quality materials for his jewelry. He doesn't work in gold or precious stones, but the price of silver and semiprecious stones these days is nothing to sneeze at.

"For a while, things looked very promising," Townie continued. "Brock did a surprisingly thorough job of putting together a business plan. After he did, I ran some numbers and came up with the million-dollar amount. I thought it was a pretty reasonable investment, and I was prepared to jump in by myself. But then Missy insisted that her brother meet me halfway." With a shrug, he added, "I had no choice but to go along with it."

My mind was racing. So Brock needed a substantial amount of money in order to live out his dream of pursuing his current passion. And given his father's attitude toward sharing his wealth with his offspring, Linus certainly wasn't about to give it to him.

Which led to a question that was almost too painful to ask: How on earth would Brock ever come up with that kind of money?

I went ahead and asked it anyway.

Townie's response was a deep sigh. "I don't know about all the options he had. But I do know that a couple of weeks ago, Brock swallowed his pride and came here to Solitude Island to ask his father for the money. Not as a gift but as a loan."

"What was Linus's response?" I asked, even though I was pretty sure I already knew the answer.

"A resounding no," Townie replied. "Linus gave Brock his usual speech about how he was thirty-one years old and it was high time he started acting like a man instead of a child."

"Brock must have been devastated," I observed.

"He came away heartbroken," Townie agreed. "After that, he tried a few other options, like getting a bank loan. But he finally told me on Wednesday afternoon when we all arrived here at the house for Linus's birthday celebration that he wasn't going to be able to come up with the cash."

He shook his head slowly. "I felt really bad for the

guy. Brock has his faults, of course. But this seemed like a wonderful opportunity for him to finally realize his potential. I tried talking to Missy again about letting me finance the whole deal, but she refused."

Maybe because she had some plans of her own, I thought. Like divorcing Townie to run off with Harry.

And the richer the husband, the bigger her divorce settlement.

But while I felt bad that Brock's dream had fizzled out, I couldn't ignore the fact that there was one last way he could have gotten his hands on the money he needed: through a generous inheritance.

True, it was difficult to imagine the dreamy, Birkenstock-sandaled baby of the family murdering his own father. But I'd meant it when I commented to Townie that I didn't really know Brock. In fact, I didn't really know any of the Merrywoods, so I was in no position to judge who was capable of what.

Especially where money was concerned.

• • •

By the time we all gathered together for the evening meal, I wasn't sure who it was safe to sit next to. Practically everyone in the room had a motive for murder, which didn't exactly lend itself to relaxing dinner conversation. I wished I'd been able to join Max, Lou, Admiral, Corky, and Frederick instead: Cook had just summoned them into the kitchen for a private dinner of their own.

Fortunately, I ended up between Nick and Betty. But I'd barely had a chance to snap open my carefully folded linen napkin before the chandelier began to flicker.

Automatically everyone's eyes traveled upward.

"Uh-oh," Tag groaned. "There go the lights."

As if on cue, the dim lights went out, leaving all of us sitting in complete darkness.

"Do you believe the electricity has gone out *again*?" Scarlett cried.

"We should all buy stock in a candle company," Townie grumbled.

"We'll have to make the best of it," Missy said cheerfully. "Besides, it's kind of romantic, dining by candlelight. Don't you agree, Townie?"

"Frankly, it's just darned annoying," he replied. As usual, he was talking through clenched teeth, but this time at least there seemed to be a reason.

"I've got matches," Charlotte said helpfully. "Let me light the candles on this candelabra—"

In the darkness, we could all hear the sound of a match scratching against the side of the matchbox. It was actually a pleasant sound, as if the hostile darkness around us was about to be banished.

But Charlotte had barely had a chance to hold the flame up to the wick before we all heard another sound—one that, instead of warming us, chilled us to the bone.

A shrill scream, coming from some distant part of the house.

Chapter 14

"If the lion and dragon fight, they will both die."
—Tadashi Adachi

lvira? Acting up again?

A At least, that was my first thought. But the concerned expressions on everyone else's faces told me it wasn't anything that innocent.

"What *is* that?" Tag demanded.

"*Who* is that?" Townie seconded.

Glancing around the table, taking a head count, Missy added, "I don't know, since everyone is here. . . ."

"It's Gwennie!" Charlotte declared, her expression stricken. "I recognize her voice."

Within seconds all of us were on our feet, getting ready to rush out of the room. Tag grabbed the candelabra, then led the group, with Brock close on his heels. I was happy to lag behind a bit, along with the other outsiders: Betty, Winston, and Nick. The four of us followed the family as they headed in the direction from which the scream seemed to have originated.

Tag took the stairs to the second floor two at a time, with Brock still right behind him. Townie was next, with the rest of us scampering after the three of them as quickly as we could.

Even the dogs came along, dashing out of the kitchen as soon as they heard all the commotion. But, unlike the humans, none of them seemed the least bit concerned. Max and Corky darted ahead of the rest of the pack, acting like schoolkids who'd just been let out onto the playground, while Lou loped after them like the little brother who didn't know if he was welcome. Admiral lumbered along next, followed by Frederick, who had the shortest legs of any of them.

As soon as I reached the top of the staircase and rounded the corner to the left, I came to a sudden halt. The entire group was gathered just a few feet away, huddled together in the hallway. Gwennie was at the front, her head raised slightly as she stared at the wall.

"Whoa," Tag muttered, holding up the candelabra in the direction in which she was looking. "Check this out!"

I did exactly that, shuffling closer so that I now stood shoulder to shoulder with everyone else. Even though the light from the half dozen candles was dim, it was bright enough to see that, scrawled on the wall in huge letters, each one at least a foot high, were the words, *GO HOME J!* And the words were written in what looked like blood.

My stomach instantly curdled, and a wave of dizziness passed over me.

That message is for me! I thought, taking deep breaths. Automatically, I reached down and picked up Max, hoping to find comfort by holding his warm, furry body in my arms.

Then I did what any other self-respecting person would do in a situation like this: I started rationalizing.

Maybe you're not the only J *on Solitude Island,* I thought, quickly running through the names of everyone else in the household. Charlotte, Tag, Missy and Townie, Brock...There was Jives, of course, also known as Jonathan. But somehow I got the feeling he wasn't the one this note was meant for.

The fact that everyone else turned to face me reinforced my conclusion.

I was slightly relieved that Gwennie decided to turn on her mock-Cockney charm, taking me out of the spotlight for at least a little while.

"Sorry to bring all o' you running up 'ere loike this," Gwennie said, her accent thicker and her voice even more shrill than usual. "I just come up 'ere to turn down the beds for the noight, like always. Then I saw this and it scared the livin' dayloights outta me. Oi didn't mean to scream."

"I don't blame you for reacting that way, Gwennie," Brock said, turning back to the horrible writing on the wall.

"Is that . . . *blood*?" Missy asked, clasping her hands over her face.

"Blimey!" Gwennie scoffed. "If that's blood, I'm Camilla Parker Bowles! And if I was, I certainly wouldn't be married to that slimy blackguard 'oo makes even King Henry look loike a saint!"

"So it's *not* blood?" Missy's voice was a near whisper, but at least she was able to bring herself to peek out from between her fingers.

"Not from the looks of it," Gwennie exclaimed. "Not from the smell, either."

With that, she horrified absolutely everyone by running her index finger through the scarlet smear and sticking it in her mouth.

"Ew!" Missy once again covered her face with her hands.

"Good heavens!" Charlotte cried.

Even the men looked revolted. As for me, I instinctively buried my face in Max's fur.

"Ketchup!" Gwennie announced triumphantly. "Heinz, if you ask me. Full o' those nasty chemicals that are probably wot really did poor ol' Mr. Merrywood in, Gawd rest 'is soul!"

The fact that we were all once again in an escapade involving food wasn't lost on me. Scanning the faces, I realized that Cook hadn't bothered to race upstairs with the rest of us to see what the commotion was all about.

"Okay, everybody," Townie said, breaking into my thoughts. "Whoever did this made his point. Or her point. If it was one of you, I think I speak for the rest of us when I say that if this was meant to be a practical joke, no one is amused."

"And if it was meant to be a threat," Tag inter-jected dryly, "next time use something a little scarier than Heinz ketchup."

"This isn't funny, Tag," Charlotte insisted. "And I don't think this was meant to be a practical joke, al-though to be perfectly honest, I don't know what it was meant to be."

Turning to me, she added, "If it was meant for you, Jessica, I hope you won't think that I'm the one who doesn't want you here. The same goes for the rest of you—Betty, Winston, Nick, and even those lovely dogs of yours. You're all welcome here. I hope you can put this ridiculous business behind you. In fact, I hope we all can."

"Hear, hear," Brock mumbled.

"Why don't we all go back to the dining room?" Scarlett suggested. "I'm sure Cook has prepared a lovely meal, as usual, and it's a shame to let it all go to waste."

Personally, I wasn't in a hurry to eat anything Cook had prepared.

"Oi guess Oi'm the one 'oo'll be cleaning up this mess," Gwennie said with a sigh. "I 'ope this comes out of the wallpaper. It's silk, inn't it, Missus Merry-wood?"

"Don't worry about it," Charlotte said vaguely. "Just do your best. And even though most of the walls in this house are indeed covered in silk, this isn't one of them."

"Good thing," Gwennie grumbled. "Otherwise Oi

could scrub me fingers to the bone and it still wouldn't keep from stainin'.'"

The group and our canine entourage made its way back to the dining room, all of us moving considerably more slowly than we had while storming up the stairs. There were so many of us that we broke into smaller groups, with the members chatting among themselves. I still had Max in my arms, and my lovely loyal Lou was at my side. Nick, who's at least as loyal, immediately made his way over to me and put his arm around me.

"Are you okay, Jess?" he asked, his eyes clouded with concern.

"I'm fine," I said, even though I wasn't completely sure about that.

Betty and Winston came up on my other side.

"Jessica, Winston and I both feel absolutely terrible," Betty said, softly enough that the others couldn't hear. "We're the ones who got you into this in the first place. If you and Nick want to pack your things and leave right now, we won't blame you one bit."

Glancing over at Nick to make sure he agreed, I replied, "No, I'll stay."

"Really?" Winston said, sounding as surprised as he looked.

"You don't know Jessie as well as I do," Nick told him with pride. "Somebody telling her in no uncertain terms that they'd prefer it if she left is exactly the type of thing that makes her even more determined to stay—and to accomplish what she came here to accomplish."

He squeezed my hand. "And the fact that she won't let anyone bully her is only one of the ten million reasons I love this woman."

I smiled wanly. Not that I didn't appreciate Nick's loyalty. It was just that at the moment, I wasn't completely sure that opting to stay on Solitude Island was the right decision.

To be honest, if Lieutenant Falcone hadn't charged me with doing my own murder investigation, I might have taken this warning written in blood-red ketchup as my cue to leave.

But for the first time ever, he'd invited me to prove to him just how good I was at solving crimes, and that changed everything. In fact, his belief in me—or perhaps his determination to show me once and for all that I wasn't the sleuth I thought I was—made me unwilling to back down.

Even in the face of tomato-based threats.

I had trouble focusing on the conversation going on around me once we all sat back down to dinner. But it wasn't the message someone had written for me in pretend blood that kept me so preoccupied.

It was the realization that so far I'd been working pretty hard to find out all I could about other people in Linus Merrywood's inner circle, but I *hadn't* thought to find out what the man himself was really like.

True, I'd made plenty of assumptions about him, based primarily on what other people had told me. One interesting thing was that, even though he had a lot of money, he apparently hadn't been anxious to share it with his kids.

Then there was his love life. He might have been having a fling with his attractive young assistant. Or—just as likely—he was a loyal, loving husband to his wife, who had clearly adored him.

As I shoveled in spoonful after spoonful of vichyssoise—another dish Margaret had mastered—I obsessed about the kind of man Linus Merrywood really was. Aside from the way he'd conducted himself—or perhaps as a result of it—had he been the universally loved patriarch that people kept saying he was? Or had there been another side to him?

Maybe this house was filled with secrets, deceptions, and downright lies. But there was one person I was pretty sure would tell me the truth.

• • •

After dinner, Nick and I walked away from the dining room in silence. I was lost in thought, plotting my strategy for confronting Alvira—and hoping she'd be able to give me some insights into Linus Merrywood.

I was so absorbed in my own thoughts that I did a double take when I found myself face-to-face with another senior citizen. Instead of Alvira, I was looking at Betty. Winston was right behind her. It would have been difficult to decide which one of them looked more distraught.

"I hope you're not too upset, Jessica," Betty said, reaching over and patting my arm comfortingly.

"That silly message on the wall was probably noth-

ing more than somebody's idea of a practical joke,"
Winston added, "even though it was a very *bad* idea."

"I'm fine," I assured them. "Believe me, it takes
more than a few smears of ketchup to scare me off."

"I'm sure that's true," Betty agreed. "But Winston
and I still feel terrible that we dragged you into this."

"When we asked you to come to Solitude Island
with us, we never dreamed that someone would
threaten you," Winston said.

"Don't *worry,* you two," I insisted, draping my arm
around Betty's thin shoulders and giving her a
squeeze. "Actually, the whole thing is pretty funny,
when you think about it."

Neither of them looked convinced. "We appreciate
your bravery—and your determination," Betty said,
hugging me back. "But, honestly, if you and Nick decide to pack up and just get the heck out of here, Winston and I would both understand—"

The ringing of the doorbell made the four of us
freeze.

"Who could that be?" I asked, even though I already had a pretty good idea.

The others must have, too, since we all hurried
toward the front hallway. We stopped right before we
reached it, preferring to do a little reconnaissance before revealing our presence.

"Oh, dear," Betty whispered, peering through the
doorway that separated us from the front hallway.
"It's that horrid homicide detective again."

"Falcone," I said, the two syllables coming out like
a groan.

Sure enough, when I did some peering of my own, I saw that Lieutenant Falcone was standing right inside the door. Even though he'd barely come into the house, he was already exhibiting his usual charm by scowling at Jives.

"I suppose it's a good thing that he's working on the case so hard," Betty commented softly.

"I'm sure he's doing everything he can to solve this," I whispered back. I couldn't resist adding, "Including calling in his experts."

I watched as Falcone stomped his feet loudly, all the better to splatter drops of rain over the marble floor, the walls, and even the ceramic urn. I hoped the sudden influx of moisture wouldn't cause whatever ancient material it was made of to dissolve.

"Sorry to bother everybody on a Saturday evening," he told Jives, not sounding the least bit sorry. He thrust his arm out, handing over the wet raincoat he'd just peeled off.

"We're all glad that you and your staff are working 'round the clock," Jives drawled. Gingerly accepting the sopping garment and holding it as far away from his body as he could, he added, "I'll just hang this up. In a bawth-tub."

Glancing at the others, I said, "Let me talk to him alone."

"Gladly," Betty said. She turned and skittered away, dragging Winston along with her.

"Are you sure you don't want some moral support?" Nick asked. "I know this guy isn't exactly your favorite person."

That was certainly true enough. But tonight I had some solid information to share with him.

"Thanks," I told him, "but this is one time that Falcone is treating me with what could be loosely defined as respect."

Nick gave my shoulder a quick squeeze of encouragement, then dashed off.

"Docta Poppa," Falcone greeted me loudly as I stepped into the hallway. For a change, he looked genuinely pleased to see me.

"Hello, Lieutenant," I replied. I realized that my heartbeat had suddenly sped up. While I had some information to share with him, I hoped the reason he was making a house call was to report that he'd found some important evidence of his own. Maybe even evidence that was important enough to identify Linus's killer.

"So what's wit' all this rain?" Falcone muttered, barely glancing at me as he angrily brushed a few remaining drops off the sleeves of his jacket. Not only was it a bad fit, it screamed polyester. "And what about that friggin' ferry? You'd think people who have this much money would build themselves a bridge!"

"Rough seas?" I asked politely, trying to hide my glee over the fact that the man had truly met his match in Mother Nature.

His response was a glare. "If the press wasn't still all over this, watchin' every move we make, I woulda sent somebody else in my place." Glancing around as if wanting to check that no one was listening, he added, "But I also wanted a chance to, y'know, check in wit' you. Whaddya got for me, Poppa?"

Plenty, I thought. I had a ne'er-do-well son with a couple of expensive ex-wives, a passion for overpriced toys, and a serious gambling problem, and his baby brother, who was looking for a windfall to support his current fascination with beads. I had a seemingly loyal daughter who was secretly playing footsy with Daddy's right-hand man, trying to cover up her dalliance by lavishing undue amounts of affection on her husband.

I also had a cook who claimed devotion to her boss but as queen of the kitchen was the person who served the birthday cake that killed him. Two other servants, as well, who were in reality actors looking to make a financial killing. I had a personal assistant who went back and forth between playing the lady and the tramp with alarming facility, and a CFO who had started to doubt the number one man's ability to run the show.

The only problem was, I didn't have anything conclusive. And apparently Falcone didn't, either.

"I consider everyone who was in the house the night Linus died a suspect," I told him, after giving him a quick summary of everything I'd learned since his visit the day before. "The problem is, I haven't been able to figure out which one of them is the murderer."

Disappointment flashed across his face. "I was hopin' for more, Poppa. What about evidence? Any chance you uncovered somethin' the rest of us missed?"

I debated whether or not to tell him about Linus's diaries. But it took me only a second or two to decide to come clean. After all, whatever I might think of Falcone personally, he and I had the same goal: seeing Linus Merrywood's killer brought to justice.

"Has anyone mentioned Aunt Alvira?" I asked.

His puzzled look gave me my answer.

"She's Linus's sister," I explained. "She lives in the attic."

He stared at me. "You're kiddin' me, right?"

"Nope."

By this point, his expression had morphed into one of annoyance. "So what you're tellin' me is that we got another suspect, right in this house."

Actually, I hadn't even entertained the possibility that Alvira could be the killer. But while my gut told me she was innocent, I realized I couldn't completely discount her as a suspect. After all, she was one more person who had been in the house the night of the birthday dinner.

It dawned on me that I might have been terribly naïve in not considering the idea up until now.

"Then I guess I got one more person to talk to," Falcone said.

The very idea filled me with alarm—until I realized that if there was one person who could hold her own against Anthony Falcone, it was Aunt Alvira.

"Alvira gave me the only real clue I've come up with," I noted.

"Which is?" he prompted impatiently.

"Apparently Linus Merrywood kept a diary

throughout his life," I explained. "Alvira thought he might have written about something that was going on that could provide some insight into who might have wanted him dead—and why."

"And does it?" he asked.

"I . . . I don't know," I had to admit. "I haven't been able to find it."

His beady eyes narrowed slightly. "This Alvira sounds like she might know somethin'. Maybe even more than she's lettin' on."

"Would you like me to show you to her room?" I offered.

"I think I can probably find it," he said scornfully. "Trackin' down people who are hard to find is one of the things I'm good at."

I hesitated, debating whether or not to help him out. But, once again, I decided that there was no point in holding out on him.

"I have a feeling this is something you haven't encountered before," I told him. "I'd better take you there myself."

• • •

"Yer kiddin' me, right?" Falcone muttered as he stood in the bedroom, his eyes the size of headlights as he watched the bookshelf move aside to reveal the secret door.

Nick and I exchanged an amused look. Max and Lou, meanwhile, were completely blasé about their surroundings. The moving bookshelf might have once held their interest, but by this point it was old news.

"Who designed this place, anyway?" Falcone demanded. "I feel like I'm in one of those old-time black-and-white horror movies."

"My theory is that Epinetus Merrywood, who originally built this house, was really worried about security," I replied. "I have a feeling the reason this house is so full of spooky features is simply that he wanted to be sure he had plenty of places to hide."

"Sounds a little neurotic, if you ask me," Falcone commented. "Hey, maybe there's a system of tunnels underneath the house! You know, so he could escape if the redcoats were coming. Or even invaders from another planet."

He chuckled, as if he was proud of his uncharacteristic display of imagination. I ignored him, flinging open the door and gesturing toward the secret staircase.

"Alvira's up there," I told him, making a sweeping gesture with one arm. "I hope you're not allergic to cats."

"*Madon'*," he muttered. But he started up the stairs.

While I was acting as blasé as Max and Lou, I was actually pretty jumpy as I waited for Falcone to come back down. I sat on the edge of the bed with Nick, engaging him in mindless small talk and distractedly petting the dogs. I'd come to feel protective toward Alvira, and I didn't want Falcone bullying her. I also hoped he'd come to the same conclusion I'd come to: that she couldn't possibly have had anything to do with her brother's death.

I jumped up as soon as I heard his heavy tread on the wooden steps. "So?" I asked a few seconds later, when he emerged from the doorway. "What's your take on her?"

"Hard to say," he mumbled. "In fact, even harder than the rest of them. She was his sister, and from what I can tell she had nothin' to gain from killin' the guy. Besides, although she was in the house the night of his death, it sounds like she pretty much stays up there in her cozy little attic all the time. If she did go downstairs, chances are somebody else in the family woulda seen her and commented on the unusual occurrence."

Unless she's as good at sneaking around as she claims, I thought. She'd told me herself that she was a good spy—and, frankly, I believed her.

But that wasn't information I was prepared to share with Falcone, since I was concerned about him harassing a sweet old woman I was still pretty certain was innocent. So I held my tongue.

I could hardly wait for Falcone to leave. I was anxious to get up to the attic and see for myself how Alvira had withstood his interrogation. Fortunately, he didn't hang around for very long before offering to find his own way out. In fact, from the way he high-tailed it out of there, I got the feeling that even seasickness-inducing boats had started looking better to him than haunted houses.

As soon as I heard his footsteps on the stairs that led down to the main floor, I turned to Nick.

"I'm going up to talk to Alvira," I explained. "She's

a tough lady, but I want to check on her. I also have a few questions of my own."

"No fudge this time?" Nick joked.

"I think Alvira is as committed to finding out who killed Linus as I am and that she's anxious to do whatever she can to help."

For the third time since I'd arrived on Solitude Island, I climbed the hidden staircase.

"You're back!" Alvira greeted me with a huge grin. "I was hoping you'd stop by again."

"I told you I enjoyed spending time with you," I said, "and I meant it."

"You're my second visitor in a row," she commented.

"You're a popular person." I couldn't resist asking, "So what did you think of Lieutenant Falcone?"

She cast me a scathing look. "It's people like him who make me glad I decided to lock myself away in an attic. Now, how about a nice cup of tea?"

"Tea sounds perfect," I said sincerely.

I wouldn't have minded if Aunt Alvira was in the habit of adding the same secret ingredient as Betty was: a shot of Jack Daniel's.

"I've even got cookies!" Alvira exclaimed.

"No, thanks," I told her. "I'm not really hungry."

"They're chocolate chip!" she said.

If there's anybody better than Jack Daniel at soothing the soul, it's Mrs. Fields. In fact, I decided to wait until both Alvira and I had been fortified by the butter, sugar, and caffeine food groups before popping the big question.

300 • Cynthia Baxter

Once she'd made a pot of Earl Grey—another expert at elevating people's moods—we got settled on the couch. In front of us on the coffee table was a tray laden with delicate porcelain teacups decorated with pink-and-purple flowers, a teapot in the same pattern, and a plate of those chocolate chip cookies she'd promised. Alvira's cats joined us, too, with the exception of the eternally shy Muffin. The Maine coon honored me by jumping up onto the couch to sit next to me, while the black cat curled up at my feet. The other two—the white longhair and the gray-and-black tabby—kept their distance, preferring to watch the action from afar.

I jumped right in as soon as Alvira had poured the tea.

"Alvira," I said thoughtfully, "even though you rarely venture downstairs, you seem to know more about the people in this house than just about anybody."

"I think what you mean is that I'm willing to say things nobody else is willing to say," she said, cackling. "Probably 'cause at this point I've got nothing to lose."

Narrowing her eyes at me, she asked, "So what's on your mind? I can tell there's something—or somebody—in particular you're interested in."

"That's right." I took a deep breath. "Linus."

"What about him?"

"Ever since I learned about what happened Wednesday night, I don't think I've heard anyone say a single bad thing about him. Oh, his kids have their complaints, of course. Mostly about—"

"Money, right?"

I didn't try to hide my surprise. "Yes. How did you know?"

"Because those three have been griping about the same thing since they were old enough to understand you can't buy a candy bar without a handful of change," she grumbled. "But you know what I think?"

I had a feeling that, whether I wanted to know or not, I was about to find out. Fortunately, I couldn't have been more eager.

"What?" I asked.

"That my brother did the absolute right thing," she replied with a firm nod of her head. "Linus was trying to teach them the value of money—and especially the value of earning it for yourself rather than being handed a blank check. True, his lessons never really took hold with those kids of his. But that wasn't his fault.

"In fact, he was a terrific father," Alvira continued. "Given the fact that the man ran a huge company, he could have chosen to put all his energy into work. In-stead, he always made time for them. He never missed a school play or a graduation or even a meet-the-teachers night. He made sure he spent time with them every evening, except when he was traveling. Telling them bedtime stories was part of his nightly routine. Making sure they brushed their teeth, too."

"What about his marriage?" I asked. I didn't want

to overstep any lines. But Alvira appeared to be someone who had no qualms about speaking the truth—
about anything. "Were things between Charlotte and
Linus as wonderful as they seem?"

"Better," Alvira said without missing a beat.
"Those two were made for each other. You never saw
two people who were more caring or more loving or
more involved with each other. They both would have
done anything for the other, no questions asked."

"What about Linus as a businessman?" I asked. "I
heard he gave lots of his money to charity. His time,
too. But what about the people he worked with day in
and day out?"

Alvira sighed. "I'm afraid I'm starting to sound like
a broken record—if somebody like you who grew up
with CDs even knows what that means. His employees loved him. He ran Merrywood Industries like one
of those old-fashioned paternalistic companies. You
know, the kind that gives every employee a turkey at
Thanksgiving? Only he gave his employees something
even better: stock. Even the people at the very bottom
owned a piece of the company, however small.

"He didn't have to do it that way, of course," she
added. "But my brother was always idealistic. In some
ways, he was the least likely of all the family members
who were in the running to take over the business. But
he rose to the top, like the cream. He managed to run
a successful company and do it without compromising his convictions."

"I believe everything you're telling me," I told her,
"but somewhere along the line, Linus made an enemy.

Do you have any idea at all who that might have been?"

"Nope." With a little shrug, Alvira said, "That's why I was hoping you'd be able to get hold of his diaries. I thought if something was going on that Linus never told any of us about, at least he would have written about it. Still no luck, huh?"

"No, I'm afraid not."

"Keep searching," Alvira said. "I'm convinced that if you're going to find the answer, it'll be in those notebooks."

As with everything else, I couldn't help but believe that Linus's sister knew what she was talking about. But that only made my inability to find the most recent journals—the ones that were likely to provide me with some insights into who might have wanted to kill Linus—all the more frustrating.

Which made me all the more determined to keep on looking.

Chapter 15

Even though Saturday night is supposed to be party time, all the members of the household were unusually somber for the rest of the evening. Funny how finding a note written in fake blood can take the fun out of family time.

Charlotte, Betty, and Winston gathered in the sitting room near the front door for coffee and brandy, while Townie and the three Merrywood siblings retreated to the small parlor in back to play Scrabble. Nick and I, meanwhile, decided to make ourselves at home in the front parlor.

I relished the feeling of the two of us having this corner of the house to ourselves as we curled up on the couch in front of the fireplace, with Max and Corky lying next to me and Lou and Admiral on the floor in front of us. I wished Frederick were there, too, but he'd chosen to stay with Betty and Winston.

"This is cozy, isn't it?" Nick commented. "Or at least it would be if there wasn't a murderer in the house."

"I'm still convinced that everybody who's here is a suspect," I said. "Aside from us, of course, plus Betty and Winston."

Nick nodded. "I hate to say it, but from what you've told me, it sounds as if any one of Linus's kids could be guilty."

Thoughtfully, I said, "Of the three of them, Tag strikes me as the most desperate. After all, he's the one who's got the loan sharks after him. There's no doubt in my mind that those guys can be pretty scary. Tag thought so, too, so much that he hid in a dusty old tower. That gives him a strong motivation for doing whatever he thought was necessary to get his hands on some cash—fast."

"True," Nick agreed. "But his baby brother was desperate for money, too, because he wanted the chance to live out his dream—not to mention to finally show everyone in his family that he wasn't the screwup they all thought he was."

Nick frowned. "One person I keep coming back to is Harry Foss," he said. "He certainly had a strong motive, since now that Linus is gone, he's going to step up to the number one spot at Merrywood Industries."

306 • Cynthia Baxter

"And he can bring his lady love, Missy, along with him," I added. "A woman who just happens to be Linus's daughter."

"Which makes her a suspect, too," Nick said. "After all, she could have taken on the task of getting rid of Daddy to pave the way for her lover boy."

"Which brings us to Townie," I said. "Maybe he thought he could make big bucks off Brock's new venture. But unless Brock could find a way to come up with the cash they both needed to get it off the ground, it wasn't going to happen."

"What about Miss Scarlett?" Nick asked. "The other woman?"

"We don't know that for sure," I reminded him. Still, I was as suspicious as he was that their relationship went beyond simply employer and employee.

"Then there's Charlotte," I said. "After all, she's the one who inherited the bulk of Linus's estate."

"True, but I don't think her lifestyle is going to change much, now that her husband is gone," Nick said. "It certainly won't be any better. I get the feeling she really loved the old man. Out of all of them, I think she's the one who's taking this the hardest."

"Except possibly Cook," I added ruefully. "Margaret seems to have had strong feelings for Linus."

"She also inherited a lot of money from the guy," Nick observed. "I know Falcone didn't consider her a suspect, at least not at first. But then we all found out what was in Linus's will. It seems to me that inheriting two hundred thousand dollars and being able to retire after decades of cooking and cleaning up would give anybody a pretty strong motive."

"Jives—or Jonathan, his real name—and his side-kick, Gwennie, were also looking for a payday," I commented. "And for all we know, the reason they left England was that Scotland Yard was after them."

"Good point," Nick agreed. "They could have a long history of doing this. Pretending to be a butler and a maid in order to get jobs with a wealthy family, ingratiating themselves with the person who controls the money, and then once they're sure they've been written into the will, moving things along a little faster than nature intended."

I sighed. "Goodness, that's a long list. Have we left anybody out?"

"Alvira," Nick replied. "We can't discount her as a suspect."

I was silent as I thought about how convinced I was that she hadn't had anything to do with Linus's death. Despite her quirkiness, or maybe because of it, she struck me as a good example of what you see is what you get. I couldn't imagine her wishing ill of her brother.

Besides, she didn't appear to have anything to gain from his death. Though most people wouldn't be satisfied with her lifestyle, she seemed perfectly content.

She had also gone out of her way to help me with my investigation by volunteering information about Linus's diaries. While his most recent journals had yet to appear, I couldn't imagine why she'd bring them up if there was even a chance they contained something that incriminated her.

Then again, I'd been wrong about such things before. Maybe she was simply trying to deflect suspicion. In fact, she could have been the one who hid the volumes Linus wrote over the last few years.

With a deep, pensive sigh, I said, "We should probably go to bed. But first I'm going to see if I can rustle up something warm. Herb tea or hot chocolate, maybe. Can I get you anything?"

"No, thanks," Nick said amiably. He stood up and stretched. "I'm wiped out. I can't even promise that I'll manage to wait up for you."

"After only five months of marriage?" I teased. "I guess the honeymoon is over."

• • •

Since arriving on Solitude Island two days before, I'd learned that Cook was in the habit of leaving food out for the family pretty much around the clock. As soon as she and Gwennie cleared away the breakfast things, she'd fill the urn that was kept on the sideboard with fresh coffee in case anyone needed another caffeine hit. She did the same after lunch and dinner, as well, adding a few snacks such as fruit or freshly baked scones.

So as soon as Nick went upstairs, I made a beeline for the dining room in search of something warm and soothing that would help me fall asleep. I needed something to counteract the list of suspects Nick and

I had been agonizing over, which I kept running through over and over again in my mind.

I was still ruminating about each person who'd earned a spot on that list as I stood at the urn. While I filled a delicate china cup with hot water and then dunked a peppermint tea bag into it, I stared off into space. Or, to be more accurate, I stared at the gigantic oil painting on the wall behind the sideboard.

Not that it was anything even close to pleasing to the eye. Like most of the other pictures that hung throughout the house, this one featured an unpleasant-looking individual who was probably a member of the Merrywood clan.

This particular portrait was of a sour-faced woman in a dark dress with a high collar. The only relief from complete dreariness was a narrow band of lace that looked as if its main purpose was to cause a skin rash under her chin. Her black hair, as smooth and shiny as Falcone's on a good hair day, was pulled back into a severe bun. Her lips curled downward in a frown, and her dark eyes looked cold and disapproving. The perfect complement to her dour expression were her eyebrows, so thick and dark that it looked as if a couple of caterpillars had gotten lost and ended up on her forehead.

But it wasn't the woman in the picture that had caught my attention. It was the narrow black line barely peeking out from the bottom left corner.

That thin line was something I'd never noticed before. As I sipped the hot tea, I realized that the reason was that the painting was slightly askew. It could have been the result of the house shaking from all that thunder—or perhaps a miracle had occurred and Gwennie had decided to do some dusting.

I leaned closer to get a better look and saw that there were actually two lines that formed an *L*. In fact, from where I stood, it almost looked as if someone had cut into the wall—and that those cuts had been carefully laid out so that they'd be hidden by the painting.

With my free hand, I reached up to touch one of the lines. And discovered that that was exactly what had happened.

This wall opens! I thought in amazement, pulling back my hand as if I'd just made contact with something hot. *Behind this painting there's a door!*

I guessed that it most likely opened onto a safe. That certainly made sense, given the fact that on the other side of this wall lay the bowels of the house, rather than the exterior or another room. I could picture the huge chunk of metal nestled among the pipes and electrical wires, practically bursting with the family's treasures. Maybe jewels, maybe stocks and bonds, maybe stacks of cold, hard cash.

Or maybe something else that Linus or someone else in the household had felt was important.

By this point, my heart was beating as fast as if I'd been hitting the coffee urn rather than sticking with herb tea. I glanced around furtively, wondering if I dared dig a little deeper.

It appeared that no one else was around. At least at the moment. Yet the other members of the household were just a few rooms away. I knew that if someone popped out of nowhere, I'd have a hard time coming up with a convincing reason for why I'd taken down a huge painting and was desperately trying to pry open the wall behind it.

So I filed my discovery away in the back of my mind—but not so far back that I couldn't retrieve it the next time an opportunity arose to do a little more poking around. In the meantime, I decided to head upstairs to see if that husband of mine was still awake. But as I left the dining room, I determined to find the earliest opportunity to test my abilities as a safe-cracker.

Chapter 16

"Some people lose all respect for the lion
unless he devours them instantly.
There is no pleasing some people."

—Will Cuppy

B y the time I crawled into bed, Nick was fast
asleep, just as he'd predicted.

So much for a romantic getaway, I thought
with disappointment. I pulled the blankets up to my
chin, which involved slightly displacing one half-
asleep Dalmatian and one Westie who had been
awake only thirty seconds yet already looked ready
for an impromptu game of Slobber All Over the Tennis Ball.

Despite the alleged soothing effects of herb tea, I
expected that once again I'd have trouble falling
asleep. But it turned out that investigating a murder

was even more exhausting than putting in a long day treating animals. I'd barely found a comfortable spot on the pillow before I felt the pleasant sensation of being sucked into unconsciousness.

In fact, I fell into such a deep sleep that when I finally snapped awake, I was completely disoriented. After only a second or two, I remembered where I was. But I had no idea what time it was—or what had woken me up.

A nightmare? I wondered, puzzled by the tightness in the pit of my stomach and the disturbing feeling that something was wrong.

I was still trying to remember what I'd been dreaming about when I heard the sound of barking dogs.

I knew immediately that they weren't my dogs. Max and Lou were both still lying down, but their heads were up and their ears twitched as if they, too, wondered what was going on.

It must be Corky and Admiral, I thought.

It sounded as if they were somewhere downstairs. And from the crazed way in which they were both barking, it seemed as if something was very wrong.

"Nick?" I whispered without turning my head. "Do you hear that?"

The silence that followed told me he was fast asleep. Either that or he was too frightened to speak, by something he knew and I didn't.

"Nick?" I cried. I looked over, anxious to see which of the two scenarios was correct.

Neither, it turned out. He was gone.

"Nick!" I leaped out of bed, not sure what alarmed

me more: the dogs going nuts downstairs or the fact that my husband had vanished.

As if on cue, the frantic barking started up again. Instinctively I rushed to the window, vaguely aware that the wooden floor beneath my bare feet was so cold that it felt as if I'd gone ice-skating without any skates. But I ignored the discomfort as I pulled back the drapes and peered through the fog hovering outside the windows. Dawn had started to break, providing me with enough pale gray light to see the property surrounding the house.

My eyes quickly lit on two figures hurrying across the lawn.

"It's Jonathan and Gwennie!" I cried. "They're fleeing the island!"

I squeezed my bare feet into the sneakers I'd left by the side of the bed. Then I grabbed my Polarfleece jacket off the back of the chair and pulled it on over my flannel pj's.

My heart was pounding as I raced along the hallway and down the stairs. I was huffing and puffing by the time I reached the front door. While Gwennie and Jonathan had left it unlocked in their haste, my hands were shaking, which made forcing my fingers to function in even the simplest way nearly impossible.

I finally managed to turn the knob. I threw open the door and encountered a wall of thick fog. I also realized for the first time that a light drizzle was dripping through the dismal gray clouds.

But I wasn't about to let a little rain get in my way. I zipped up my jacket and charged out the door.

I immediately started jogging toward the dock—the same direction in which Gwennie and Jonathan had appeared to be headed. As I ran, I focused on the rhythmic *thump, thump, thump* of the rubber soles of my sneakers hitting the irregularly shaped slabs of slate, which told me I was going the right way. The cold, damp air made the insides of my nostrils tingle. I had to strain to see through the fog, so thick in some areas that I felt as if I was running through a steam room. Up above, seagulls circled, their raw screams cutting the silence.

As I neared the edge of the island, the fog cleared enough that I could see the waves of Peconic Bay. They lurked just a few feet away, so dark and turbulent and ferocious they seemed to be daring anyone to try to get across them.

But I wasn't the one who was planning to leave. I scanned the shore, searching for the dock. I finally spotted it, a low rectangle jutting out into the swirling waters with the dilapidated boathouse at the end. Gwennie and Jonathan were already trudging across the ragged planks of wood, from the looks of things making their way toward the dinghy docked next to the ferry.

Now that I was closer, I saw that Gwennie was dragging a large suitcase behind her, its wheels bumping across the uneven wood of the dock. In the other hand she was hauling what looked like a canvas gym bag. From the way she struggled with it, it must have weighed forty or fifty pounds. In fact, both bags were so stuffed they looked ready to burst.

As for Jonathan, he was carrying a suitcase that was even bigger than Gwennie's. Just as full, too. But it appeared that he was also bringing along a few souvenirs of his stay on Solitude Island. A small Oriental rug was rolled up and tucked under one arm, and sticking out of the oversize tote bag slung over his shoulder was a Chinese porcelain vase that I could only assume was a valuable antique.

The idea that they were not only running away but also stealing from Charlotte made me run even faster.

"Hey!" I cried as I grew near enough for them to hear me. "Stop, you two!"

Automatically they froze, looking back over their shoulders with panicked expressions. But as soon as they saw it was me—as in *only* me—they turned away and kept heading toward their getaway boat.

Still, they were weighed down by their suitcases and the rest of their booty, which gave me enough time to catch up with them before they reached the dinghy.

"Stop!" I demanded one more time. I grabbed Gwennie's shoulder and pulled, so that she had no choice but to face me. Out of breath, I asked, "Where do you think you're going?"

"We're just going to Long Island for the day!" Gwennie whined. "We've got a bit of shopping to do."

I didn't bother to point out that the only retail establishment likely to be open at this hour was 7-Eleven. Instead, I lunged toward the gym bag she was carrying.

"Hey, what do you think you're doing?" she cried. "That's not your—"

But before she had a chance to stop me, I'd pulled open the zipper far enough to see that stashed inside were clothes folded so loosely and unevenly that they'd obviously been tossed in. But I was much more interested in what was sitting on top of them: a small burgundy-colored rectangle that I immediately recognized.

"Since when do you need a passport to go shopping?" I demanded, grabbing it and holding it up in front of her face.

"When you use traveler's checks?" she replied meekly.

"You give that back to Gwennie!" Jonathan ordered, without a trace of his usual British gentility. Instead, he sounded like a Dickens character. One of the really nasty ones, like Bill Sykes or Uriah Heep.

"I don't think you two should be going anywhere," I insisted. "Not when the police explicitly said that no one should leave Solitude Island."

"We don't care what you think," Jonathan sneered, yanking Gwennie's passport out of my hand. "Why don't you mind your own business and go back to bed?"

"I'm not letting you leave this island!" I exclaimed. My eyes darted around as I searched for the means to prevent them from escaping. I'm not sure what I had in mind—a rope, a drill I could use to put a hole in the dinghy—but I certainly didn't spot anything that might be helpful.

I didn't even have a cell phone on me. Then I remembered that it wouldn't have done me any good, anyway.

"Come on, Gwennie," Jonathan barked. "If we're going to make that flight, we'd better get a move on."

I had just opened my mouth once again, hoping some argument I hadn't yet thought of would come flying out, when I heard what sounded like voices in the distance.

At first I thought they were only those annoying seagulls again. But a second later I realized they were human voices. Male ones.

I heard dogs barking, too. And then: "Jessie! There you are!"

That was a voice I recognized.

I turned, still trying to process the fact that I wasn't alone out here with Gwennie and Jonathan after all. A few more seconds passed before Nick emerged from the thick swirls of fog, his cheeks flushed and his eyes wild. Brock, Tag, and Townie followed right behind him. Nick had brought Max and Lou with him, while Corky and Admiral trotted along behind the group.

"What's going on?" Nick demanded. "The front door is wide open. What are you doing out here?"

He'd barely gotten the words out before his eyes—and everyone else's—traveled over to the dinghy and the two people who were dumping so much luggage into it that it would be a miracle if the thing didn't sink as soon as they climbed in.

Which I had no intention of letting them do.

Gesturing at Jonathan and Gwennie with my

thumb, I cried, "They're the ones you should be ask ing! But before we give them a chance to answer, I suggest that you gentlemen escort these two back inside."

• • •

"I can't believe Jonathan and Gwennie were trying to escape," Nick said as we sat side by side in front of the fire he'd built in our bedroom fireplace.

The tattered Oriental carpet was just big enough and just soft enough to provide a comfy cushion. And leaning against the bed kept our backs from suffering. Our canines sat beside us, Lou dozing with his chin resting on his paws and Max gazing at the fire like some prehistoric cave dog who couldn't get over such a wonderful invention.

"They're not going anywhere now," Nick commented. "Not with Brock and Tag keeping them practically under lock and key until Falcone gets here. Imagine poor Townie having to take the boat over to Long Island just to use his cell phone."

"Trying to sneak back to England while everyone was asleep doesn't do much to make them look innocent," I noted.

"Neither does Gwennie's claim that the only reason they were trying to leave is that they didn't do anything wrong," Nick added. "All they'll say is that they had nothing to do with Linus's murder and they didn't want to be accused."

"Thanks for helping me reel them in," I said. "You

...nd the other guys showed up in the nick of time—no pun intended."

Nick grinned. "Glad I could help. When I came back here and saw that you were gone, I got nervous. That message that was left for you in pretend blood sure didn't help."

"Hey, where were you, anyway?" I asked. "When Corky and Admiral's barking woke me up, I looked over on your side of the bed and you were gone."

"I went down to the kitchen to get something to drink," he replied. "You were fast asleep when I left, and I did my best to be quiet."

"And here I was afraid you'd been spirited away by poltergeists," I said.

"Nothing that dramatic," Nick assured me. "Now, why don't we try to get a little more sleep? I'd say we earned a couple more hours."

A minute or two after we climbed back into bed, Nick's breathing became low and even, a sign that he was already asleep. A few seconds later, Max began making wheezing sounds, and soon afterward Lou started to snore.

But I wasn't even close to falling asleep.

I couldn't stop thinking about how Gwennie and Jonathan's attempt to sneak away from Solitude Island—to head back to England, no less—made them look as if they were the ones who had killed Linus.

Yet as guilty as they appeared, I couldn't conclude that they were the killers. Not when there were so many other people in this house who could have been at least as motivated as those two.

The fact that I still couldn't put my finger on Linus Merrywood's murderer made me more determined than ever to put all my energies into finding those missing diaries.

After all, I was running out of options.

And given the fact that it was now Sunday and I had a life to get back to, I was also running out of time.

• • •

I spent the next two hours searching for the missing diaries. I brought Max and Lou with me as I sneaked around from room to room, once again planning to use them as my excuse if anyone happened upon me in a place where I didn't belong. How else could I keep them from getting into mischief—such as treating some innocent needlepoint pillow or other family heirloom as a chew toy?

As for why their owner was prowling around all the common areas and bedrooms, opening closed doors and rummaging through the occasional drawer, that was something I hadn't yet found a way to explain.

Still, I hoped that if I did my snooping quickly and quietly, I wouldn't find myself in that difficult position. And as my search progressed, that part was going fine. The part that *wasn't* going even close to fine was tracking down those darned notebooks.

Where are they? I wondered for the thousandth time.

I wasn't ready to accept the possibility that they

could have been destroyed, since that would mean giving up on the one good lead I had so far. Instead, I stubbornly clung to the belief that they still existed—and that I could find them, if only I looked hard enough.

Yet I finally decided I had no choice but to admit defeat.

I've looked through this entire house, I thought. *Every shelf, every cabinet, every closet. Short of prying up the floorboards or rummaging around in the basement, if there even is one, I don't know where else to look.*

I was about to head back upstairs to snuggle in bed beside Nick. But then I realized that I wasn't quite out of options.

I had yet to look in the safe—or whatever it was—hidden behind the oil painting hanging in the dining room.

Frankly, I'd had high hopes that those missing notebooks would turn up somewhere else. My résumé might include a few unusual skills, but safecracking wasn't one of them.

Still, now that the idea had popped into my head, I wasn't giving it up. I'm kind of like a terrier in that way: unable to let go of something once I've got it in my jaws, even if I'm starting to feel as if it will pull out all my teeth.

"Come on, Max," I said quietly, knowing that Lou would follow. I was about to try something that would be *really* hard to explain away, and I was going to need all the help I could get.

The dining room wasn't the easiest spot to conduct a treasure hunt, since anyone could venture in at any time, through either the doorway that opened onto the hallway or the one that led to the kitchen. Taking down a huge oil painting and tapping on the wall behind it wasn't exactly standard operating procedure for houseguests.

I hoped the members of the Merrywood clan who hadn't been involved in preventing Gwennie and Jonathan from fleeing would sleep in. As for Cook, as dedicated to the Merrywoods as she was, even she needed a break. And Sunday morning seemed like the perfect time for her to take it.

Despite all these rationalizations, once my entourage and I had stolen into the dining room, I closed the door to the hallway and checked to make sure the kitchen door was closed. My hands were clammy as I planted myself in front of the same painting I'd stood at the night before, my eyes focused on the telltale break in the wall peeking out from behind the ornate gilt frame.

I hoped Max and Lou would act as lookouts, barking or at least wagging their tails if anyone approached. But Lou seemed absorbed in the croissant crumbs he'd found pushed into a corner, no doubt the result of Gwennie being better at sweeping onstage than at actual sweeping. As for Max, he was busy looking for some goodies of his own, sniffing the Oriental carpet with the intensity of a pig rooting for truffles.

So I was pretty much on my own as I reached up

and grabbed hold of the picture frame. As I lifted it off the wall, I let out a grunt. The thing was a lot heavier than I'd expected. Awkward, too, since the portrait of the scowling woman—whose fashion sense had just earned her the nickname Morticia—was more than four feet high and close to three feet wide. Maneuvering it through the air and over the coffee urn made me look like a comic actor in a silent movie.

The fact that I was experiencing difficulty prompted Max to come running over, wanting to see if he could help or, even better, engage me in a game. His interest in what I was doing piqued Lou's, and before I knew it, my struggle with the painting was made even more complicated by the two four-legged creatures dashing around me in circles and wagging their tails excitedly.

Even with all that canine distraction, I somehow managed to set the painting safely on the carpet without breaking any antiques or making enough noise to bring the entire household running. In fact, so far the only person who was aware of what I was up to was the woman in the painting. While she didn't look the least bit happy about it, at least she wasn't about to stop me.

But once I'd managed to wrestle Morticia to the ground, I had a much bigger problem: finding a way to open what I could now clearly see was a door that had been cut out from the wall. I stared at it for a few seconds, wishing an idea would simply come to me out of the blue.

Surely Nancy Drew encountered something like

this along the way, I thought, growing more and more frustrated. If only I could remember how she figured out this kind of thing.

But at the moment I couldn't remember the details of any of Nancy's successes, much less one that had specifically involved burrowing through plaster or picking locks. And I seemed incapable of coming up with any ideas of my own. The fact that my dogs had also decided to do their best to engage me in playtime, rather than going back to their crumb hunt, made it even harder to focus.

Finally, I reached up and pounded the wall lightly, hoping I'd hit a button or a switch or some other device that would open the door and reveal the safe on the other side. Nothing happened.

Then I remembered that I'd already encountered another throwback to the Nancy Drew years here in the Merrywoods' spooky mansion: the hidden staircase. And I'd gained access by taking a copy of *Frankenstein* off the bookshelf. In other words, the mechanism that did the trick was located someplace other than on the door itself.

I glanced around, desperately hoping that something would catch my eye. But there were no bookshelves in the dining room. No books, either. And as hard as I tried, I didn't spot anything else that looked as if it might be capable of opening the hidden door.

Once again, I was wondering if I should just pack it in and go upstairs to spend what was left of the weekend with Nick. But my ruminations were interrupted by the sound of Max letting out a yip.

"Quiet, Max!" I whispered.

When I looked down, I saw that he and Lou were struggling to beat each other under the table, no doubt because they'd just smelled another tasty treat lying somewhere in the vicinity. The force of two dogs charging through the linen tablecloth that reached nearly to the floor threatened to topple the coffee and tea urns, which I knew were filled with hot liquid.

"Okay, you guys," I told them impatiently, "if you're going to act like boors, I might as well help you. At least that way you won't cause any more damage than you absolutely have to."

I got down on my hands and knees to pull back the tablecloth and help them find whatever it was they were both so determined to scarf up. As I did, I noticed a chunk of a muffin. Even though I don't generally let my dogs eat people food, it was small enough that I knew it wouldn't do them any harm.

Max darted under the table and grabbed it—not surprising since he's smaller, faster, and more determined than Lou. He was still chewing happily as I started to drag them both out of there.

But I froze when I noticed a small white button on the wall, about a foot above the floor.

The button was directly underneath the door.

"Eureka!" I muttered, feeling a surge of excitement as I crawled a little farther under the table. When I got closer to the button, I pressed it.

Up above, I heard something move.

"Double eureka!" I cried, hoping that what I hoped had happened had indeed happened.

Sure enough, when I crawled back out, I saw th
the secret door had swung open. Even so, I warned
myself against getting too excited, since there was still
that safecracking thing to deal with.

I stood up, my heart pounding so hard that I knew
it wasn't even trying to listen to what my brain was
telling it. I leaned forward to get a better look at what
was behind the door, my eyes prepared for a hard
metal safe that would probably turn out to be impenetrable.

I blinked in confusion.

There was nothing there.

And by nothing, I don't mean nothing as in a wall
with no safe. I mean *nothing*.

On the other side of the secret door was a gaping
square hole.

A wave of disappointment came over me. But only
a second or two passed before my entire mood shifted.

Oh. My. God. I found a secret passageway.

Maybe Epinetus Merrywood really *had* built a system of underground tunnels, as Falcone had joked.

By this point, my heartbeat had escalated to the
jackhammer mode. In fact, I was convinced it had to
be even louder than that little bark Max had let out.

What should I do? I thought, my mind racing.

But I already knew the answer to that question.

Chapter 17

"At 20 a man is a peacock, at 30 a lion,
at 40 a camel, at 50 a serpent,
at 60 a dog, at 70 an ape, and at 80 nothing."
—Baltasar Gracian

I t took me about one and a half seconds to convince myself that Max and Lou would be fine closed up in the dining room without me. Knowing those two, they'd probably find a nice comfy spot on the Oriental carpet and snooze once they realized their favorite playmate wasn't around anymore.

The next step was a little harder. Whoever had designed this secret passageway clearly had access to a stepladder, since the bottom of the opening was a good four and a half feet off the floor. I, however, wasn't that lucky.

So I grabbed one end of the table and lifted it

enough that I could pivot it on one leg, moving it away from the wall at a wide angle. Then I grabbed one of the dining-room chairs, dragged it over to the space I'd created, and climbed up onto it.

If anyone comes in, it's all over, I thought. There was no way of hiding the fact that I'd just rearranged the furniture in the room.

The first thing someone would see was the open door, meaning they'd immediately know what was going on—especially since I had no intention of closing the door to the secret passageway and sealing myself in.

But I wasn't about to worry about that now. After all, how many times in my life would I be handed the chance to explore a secret passageway?

Yet while the concept sounded thrilling at first, it didn't take me long to change my attitude. As soon as I climbed through the opening in the wall and lowered myself onto the ground on the other side, I realized that this wasn't exactly going to be a pleasant stroll.

For one thing, it was dark. Completely dark. I took only a few steps before I discovered that whatever light there was in the dining room wasn't going to do much to help me find my way.

I had no flashlight. Not even a candle.

I wasn't willing to turn around, however. Not when I wanted to do this as fast as possible. Besides, for all I knew, it would be a dead end. And even if that turned out to be the case, I wanted to find out as quickly as I could, go back to the dining room, close

330 • Cynthia Baxter

the secret door, put the furniture and painting back where they belonged, and get the heck out of there before anyone found out what I'd been up to.

So I kept going, feeling my way by running one hand along the wall and telling myself that, sooner or later, I'd come across a light or a window or something else that would enable me to find out exactly where this mysterious secret passageway led.

It was hard to tell how far I'd crept along, taking care not to fall. It could have been five minutes or it could have been fifty—I simply had no way to gauge the time.

In addition to not having any light, there was no noise, either. I was surrounded by complete silence.

These walls must be thick, I thought.

As I patted them, I realized they were no longer covered in plaster or drywall or whatever else had made them perfectly smooth during the early part of my trek. I was now touching the rough surface of what felt like stone. Cold, hard, unyielding stone.

And I still didn't know where I was or where I was going.

Suddenly a horrible thought occurred to me. What if this secret passageway led to a dead end—and I returned to the dining room to find that a sudden draft had blown the door leading back into the house shut?

In other words, what if Linus's killer had noticed that sending me a message in fake blood hadn't succeeded in getting me off the case—and decided to try something more effective, such as sealing me inside the bowels of the house?

I can't worry about that now, I insisted to myself. *I've come this far, and I've got to see this through.*

I'd barely had a chance to form that thought before I felt the top of my head brush against something hard.

Something *really* hard.

"Ow!" I cried, without thinking.

It wasn't until after I'd let out that yelp that I realized I should probably be as quiet as I could. For all I knew, I wasn't alone in here.

But at the moment I was more concerned about the fact that, when I'd reached up, I discovered that the ceiling in this section of the passageway was much lower. And with every step I took, it got even lower.

The walls were getting closer together, too.

Okay, I thought, crouching down to keep from doing any more damage to my head, *so you're moving through a tunnel that's getting smaller and smaller, and there's no light and the walls are so thick no one could hear you even if you screamed—*

It was at that point that I realized I was right about not being alone in there. I heard a skittering sound that could only be the pitter-patter of little feet.

Rodent feet.

"Eeek!" I cried, as something soft and furry brushed against my ankle.

You're a veterinarian, a voice inside my head scolded me. *You're supposed to love animals.*

Not rats, another voice shot back. *Especially when they're running around at the bottom of a dark, damp secret passageway.*

I paused, wondering if maybe it was time to head back and see if the door to the dining room was still open. But, rats or no rats, I wanted to find out where this darned thing ended up.

I kept going, walking with one hand to the side and one above me. Even though I'd been walking with my knees bent about as far as they'd go, I finally had no choice but to crawl.

The ground was made of mud. With puddles. And plenty of stones.

Between my wet, sore knees, the rats I kept picturing, and the fact that the space I was moving through kept getting smaller and smaller, I was starting to give serious thought to the increasingly appealing concept of giving up.

It was only about five seconds later that I spotted the light.

It was a tiny speck, off in the distance—so tiny that at first I thought I was hallucinating. Or maybe seeing a glimmer reflecting off some nasty rodent's eye.

Whatever it was, the sight of it motivated me to go on. I could hear my own breathing as I became more and more excited over the prospect of actually finding— well, the light at the end of the tunnel.

As I crawled along, aware that I'd be picking dirt and pebbles and who knew what else out of my knees for days, the small spot of light kept growing bigger. The walls around me got lighter, too.

Finally I was close enough to see that I was looking outside, into the fog. Just beyond the opening was the dock.

So this secret passageway was built to be another way out of the house. It led directly to the dock—and the boats that could get people off the island.

Epinetus Merrywood's taste in architecture might have been good for making a quick escape, but when it came to my search for answers, this hadn't exactly turned out to be the pot of gold at the end of the rainbow.

Yet even though my first reaction was disappointment, I decided that I couldn't completely rule out the possibility of finding something of value at the end of this rainbow. Especially since I quickly realized that while the tunnel led to the dock, it also led to the boathouse at the end of the dock.

The tiny wooden structure had no function other than storing tanks of gas, rope, oars, and other boating supplies. Which made it a place where, I suspected, hardly anyone ever went.

Especially in winter.

Since I'd discovered that the latest editions of Linus's diaries were missing, I'd been looking for interesting and unusual hiding places. And I couldn't ignore the fact that I'd just found myself right outside something that fit that description perfectly.

• • •

Does it have to rain every minute of every day I'm here on this island? I wondered crossly as I ventured outside the tunnel.

Even though I made a mad dash for the boathouse,

I couldn't stop the cold rivulets that trickled down the back of my neck, unpleasant as icy fingers. My feet were already wet from sloshing through puddles, but that didn't mean it felt any better to go squeaking across the damp boards of the dock in sopping sneakers.

I made a mental note to dress more appropriately the next time I decided to climb through a wall into a dark, damp, rat-infested tunnel that spat anyone who walked through it out into the rain.

All the same, I was glad that fog still enshrouded the island, since it would help keep me from being noticed by anyone who happened to look out the window and wonder why one of their houseguests was running around in the downpour like a maniac.

The boathouse was in a state of deterioration, probably because Linus and Charlotte didn't use it much now that the kids were grown. It looked as if a single substantial gust of wind could reduce it to a bunch of wooden planks littering the dock and floating out to sea. The fact that it hadn't happened over the past few days of nearly constant storms struck me as miraculous.

The door had been painted blue—about a hundred years ago. Peeling paint chips clung to the rough-hewn wood for dear life.

I placed my hand on the door, hoping I wouldn't get any splinters. Then I pushed, holding my breath and expecting it to be locked.

Instead, it gave way as soon as I applied a little pressure.

I stepped inside, immediately searching for a light switch. I didn't see one. In fact, it appeared that this little wooden shack wasn't wired for electricity. Even so, with the door open, there was enough light to find any old notebooks that happened to be lying around.

Doing that wasn't going to be all that difficult, either. The boathouse was tiny, with barely enough room to turn around—literally.

The place was packed to the rafters, positively stuffed with everything any boater could ever need. Coiled ropes hung from big rusty nails that protruded from the walls at odd angles, along with a few plastic buckets that smelled as if their last few occupants had been unlucky fish. Lying on the floor or on the built-in wooden benches that encircled the interior were folded-up tarps, a couple of oars, and a rusted metal box that looked as if it had been designed to hold fish-hooks and other fishing supplies. There was a lot of other paraphernalia, as well, but, not being a boater, I couldn't readily identify the purpose of any of it.

Aside from all that junk, the crowded little building wasn't exactly the most pleasant place in the world to conduct a search. The interior was draped in cob-webs, and as I looked around, a spider the size of a gerbil lowered itself from the ceiling about three inches away from my nose. Fortunately, I'm not an arachnophobe.

But while I wasn't afraid of spiders, I *was* afraid of getting caught. I did my best to conduct a hasty search, picking things up and looking under them.

336 • Cynthia Baxter

Nothing. I crouched down and looked under the built-in benches, but that didn't yield any hidden treasure, either.

And then I noticed a shelf in the back left-hand corner. It was small, just big enough to store a stack of well-worn books. When I pulled them down and leafed through them, I saw that they contained nautical charts.

I was about to put them back when I realized there was something else on that shelf. Four slender volumes had been lying on their side, directly underneath the map books. But since they were smaller, they had pretty much been concealed.

Even before I picked them up, I knew exactly what they were.

Black-and-white notebooks. Linus's missing diaries.

Just then a powerful gust of wind blew the door shut. At least, I thought it was a gust of wind. Alarmed, I turned and tried the doorknob, afraid that someone had spotted me, followed me—and decided to lock me in.

But the door opened easily, which meant it really had been just the wind.

While it was damp and cold and just generally creepy inside, I couldn't wait to read these notebooks. Especially since I now had a sense of how much trouble someone had gone to to hide them.

My heart was pounding ferociously as I opened the most recent notebook and began to read.

• • •

My first reaction was surprise over how difficult it was to make out a lot of the words that were scrawled across the page.

It took me only a second to realize why I was having such a hard time. The handwriting in Linus's earlier journals had been easy to read, characterized by clear, precisely formed letters. The page in front of me, however, was much sloppier. The *T*s weren't always crossed, the *I*s weren't necessarily dotted, and the sentences he'd written didn't always begin with capital letters.

Maybe he was in a hurry when he wrote this, I thought.

As difficult as his prose was to read, I forged ahead.

I planned to spend the morning working in the garden, he wrote. *But I couldn't remember where Charlotte had stored the tools. So instead I came back inside and read the paper.*

Then Charlotte invited Harry and Scarlett for lunch, his writings continued. *I could hardly follow what they were saying. Something about a merger. I was too embarrassed to ask what they were talking about.*

There was more, but I couldn't make it out, given how badly his handwriting deteriorated.

I supposed poor Linus had started to experience the symptoms of old age. Maybe he'd developed arthritis in his hands and found it hard to hold a pen. He was certainly becoming forgetful.

I read on. At least, I tried to. By this point there were more words I couldn't make out than words I could actually read.

I frowned. Maybe he was taking medication—or dealing with some ailment other than arthritis that affected his dexterity. I made a mental note to ask Charlotte, figuring that she had decided not to mention either of those possibilities for some reason.

I flipped further ahead in the notebook. I was now looking at the last few pages Linus had written before he'd died—or before he'd decided to stop keeping a journal. I looked for the date of the last entry but couldn't find one.

That was odd, I thought. He'd been so conscientious about dating every entry before this.

Confused, I started checking backward. There were pages and pages of undated entries. Instead of organized reports of what he'd done that day, the pages were filled with scribblings, all in the same wild handwriting. It looked as if he had just rambled on about anything that had come into his head.

After backtracking nearly a quarter of the way through the book, I finally found an entry that was dated.

October 12 of the previous year. More than thirteen months before his death.

There weren't thirteen months' worth of entries written in the pages that followed, though. Which told me that Linus had, indeed, stopped keeping up with his daily journal at some point.

Yet someone had clearly gone to a lot of trouble to

hide them. Given the sorry state of the boathouse, it didn't strike me as possible that there could be any other reason for them to be here. Even if the outbuilding had been in better shape, it was much too small and packed with junk for anyone to consider it a hideaway. At least not anyone over the age of eight.

Which made the effort that had gone into stashing them in this unlikely place all the more mysterious. Unless, of course, whatever that person wanted to keep a secret had occurred much earlier, back when Linus was still recording all the details of his life.

All these unanswered questions fueled my determination to find out what, if anything, Linus had written in his notebooks that might be tied to his murder. I started to read again, this time starting with the page dated October 12.

Charlotte says the children were flowers in the garden are not coming spring the dogs keep barking someone else on the island…

A wave of heat washed over me.

Gibberish, I thought. Linus was writing nonsense. Why would he choose to write something like this, something that was completely meaningless?

And then I realized what I was looking at. He hadn't *chosen* to write this way at all. Over the past year, it wasn't only Linus's handwriting that had deteriorated.

So had his mental faculties.

In fact, while I was certainly no expert, I was pretty sure that what I was looking at was a sign that in the final months of his life, Linus had suffered from Alzheimer's or some other form of dementia.

I felt as if I'd been punched in the stomach.

Oh, my, I thought. *That poor man. Poor Charlotte, too.*

I even felt sorry for his three children. At least, until I reminded myself that my discovery didn't do a thing to remove suspicion from any one of them.

Still, the ramifications of what I'd just found out were mind-boggling. Not only for Linus's wife and children, either.

If the man's writings were any indication, in his final months Linus Merrywood had been in no condition to run a huge corporation.

My mind was reeling as I tried to sort through all the possible scenarios that simple fact unleashed. My thoughts immediately went to Harry Foss.

What if Linus had become unable to run the business in a responsible way yet had refused to step down as president and CEO? Was it possible that Harry had seen the impending eruption of chaos throughout Merrywood Industries as a reason to kill a man—even one for whom he had so much respect?

Or perhaps Scarlett had taken it upon herself to remove him from power. After all, she was as close to Linus as Harry had been. If Linus was losing his ability to run the company, she could have had the same motivation as Harry.

I was about to consider all the other suspects on my list—including the members of the family as well as the three staff members at the house—and how this new information might have affected them when I heard a noise. It sounded like a soft footstep, as if someone was walking on the dock.

Horrified over being found here in the boathouse with Linus's diary in my hand, I turned. Standing in the doorway amid the thick fog was Charlotte.

The expression on her face was stern. As for me, I was pretty sure I looked really guilty, since that was exactly how I was feeling.

"Hello, Charlotte," I said. "I—I was just—"

"I know what you're doing, Jessica," she replied matter-of-factly. "Exactly what you've been doing ever since you got here."

Gesturing toward the notebook in my hand, she added, "Only this time, you hit pay dirt."

"I can explain everything!" I insisted. "It all started because Betty and Winston were concerned about what happened to Linus. From the very start they were certain there was foul play, mainly because Linus called Winston right before he died and told him he thought someone was trying to kill him."

"I know all about that phone call," Charlotte said with an eerie calmness. "That one and many other calls he made."

What other calls? I wondered.

Yet even though I didn't understand that last part, I wasn't about to start asking her questions. Not when, at the moment, she was the one who had the right to be doing the asking.

"I have a feeling you know quite a bit, Jessica," she continued, "thanks to all the prying you've done while you were in my house. As my guest, I might add."

"It wasn't my idea," I insisted. "Like I said, Betty and Winston were concerned about Linus's death. They asked me, as a favor to them, to—"

It was only then that Charlotte pulled her hand out from behind her long skirt, the same one she'd been wearing the first time I met her. As she did, I saw that she had something in her hand.

A sick feeling came over me as I realized what she was holding: the silver dagger that up until recently had been hanging in the front hallway.

Chapter 18

"A lion sleeps in the heart of every brave man."
—Turkish Proverb

I decided to pretend I hadn't noticed that Charlotte was holding a weapon. True, it was a weapon that probably hadn't been used to hurt anyone for a good century, if not longer. Still, the point looked sharp enough to kill.

Instead of acknowledging that the person who'd come after me was armed, I did my best to converse with her as casually as possible. My goal was to act as if being caught in a dilapidated old boathouse shrouded in fog, reading personal journals that someone had clearly gone to a lot of trouble to hide, was an everyday occurrence.

"Anyway," I went on, completing my sentence as soon as I got my bearings, "I was only trying to help."

"Is that one of Linus's journals?" Charlotte asked, gesturing toward the black-and-white notebook in my hand. I noticed that her tone of voice had changed. Instead of sounding accusing, it now sounded vague and faraway. Dreamy, almost. "It looks just like all those others he kept throughout his life."

So she *had* known about the journals.

But even though she hadn't been truthful with me, I didn't see a reason to be anything but honest. Especially since I'd been caught red-handed.

"Yes, that's exactly what this is," I replied calmly. "These others, as well. They're the diaries from the final months of his life."

"Have you read them?" she asked.

I nodded, since, once again, I had no choice but to admit what I'd been up to.

I decided to take a direct approach. "Your husband had Alzheimer's, didn't he?" I asked, holding up the notebook that had clued me in.

"That's right," Charlotte replied. "Alzheimer's or some other type of dementia. I didn't want anyone to know."

"Why not?" I asked, sincerely curious. "It's a serious illness; people who have it have no control over it. Surely you don't think anyone would have thought less of him."

"It wasn't my decision to keep it quiet; it was his," she replied sharply.

Her voice softened as she added, "I'm sorry, Jessica. I don't mean to sound so cross. It's just that this is something Linus and I discussed at length. How all this would be handled, I mean. He'd been experiencing symptoms of dementia for at least two years. He went in and out of a state of confusion. When he was his usual, sensible self, he was actually quite willing to talk about what it all meant."

Charlotte's grip on the dagger loosened. In fact, her entire body slackened, as if she was suddenly drained of all energy.

"My poor Linus," she said in a breathless voice, sinking onto the wooden bench. "These last two years have been so difficult. Every day became a trial. At first, it was just little things, the kind everyone experiences as they get older. He'd forget where he'd put his keys or whether he'd hired a new gardener or whether he'd already read that day's newspaper. He'd forget what he had for dinner the night before—or even the name of the restaurant where he'd eaten it.

"Oh, we laughed about it at first," she went on, her eyes clouded. "He joked about how he was getting old and that it was a good thing he had a wife who was fifteen years younger to help take care of him. But after a while it stopped being funny."

Charlotte was silent for a few seconds, as if she needed to get her bearings. "Over time, those amusing things Linus kept doing like losing his keys became more serious. He started forgetting important things, mostly the details of his business—meetings he had scheduled, the names of his company's different divisions, even the names of people he'd worked with for years. Decades, in some cases.

"Fortunately, the people closest to him did a

wonderful job of covering for him," she continued. "Harry, mostly. But Scarlett, too. They both took care of the things Linus simply wasn't capable of dealing with any longer. Harry went to meetings in his place, and he read every document that came across Linus's desk. He even spoke to people on the phone on his behalf, telling them Linus was out of town or tied up in a meeting.

"As for Scarlett, she began to accompany him everywhere. She did a valiant job of concealing what was going on. She got in the habit of sitting next to him at business luncheons so she could feed him clues like the name and title of the person they were talking to. Both Harry and Scarlett could see the writing on the wall, but they were able to ward off the inevitable. At least for a while.

"But then Linus started to forget things that were even more basic," Charlotte went on. "Like how old the children were. I remember the first time I noticed that. It was a Sunday afternoon last winter. Linus had fallen asleep in front of the fire with *The New York Times Magazine* in his lap. I was in the room with him, reading the rest of the newspaper. When he woke up, he turned to me and said, 'Is Tag home from school yet?'

"I told him that he was confused because he'd nodded off and he'd been dreaming." Charlotte's voice had become strained, as if simply remembering such a heartbreaking event still caused her great pain. "But I knew that wasn't the case. By that point it had become impossible not to understand what was happening to him. How could I not, when it was right in front of my eyes every day?"

"Did Linus ever see a doctor?" I asked.

Charlotte shook her head. "He seemed convinced that there was nothing anyone could do. I kept showing him articles about promising new drugs, but he refused to believe any of it. I think he'd begun to think of himself as an old man. He had pretty much become resigned to what he saw as his fate."

"What about the children? Were they aware of what was going on?"

"I didn't say anything to the boys," Charlotte replied. "But Missy was another story. She and her father had always been close, and she came to visit much more often than either Tag or Brock. She could see for herself what was happening to him. And it hurt her as much as it hurt me. Still, I don't think even she understood how far it had progressed. How badly it affected him, either."

"Is that why you hid the notebooks?" I asked. "To keep Missy from finding out?"

Charlotte looked startled. "I didn't hide Linus's notebooks. I knew he'd kept a journal for years. He kept them right in our bedroom. But it wasn't anything we ever talked about. And I just assumed that at some point he'd stopped—probably because it simply became too difficult for him."

"He did stop," I said, glancing down at the notebook I was still holding in my hand. "But not until fairly recently. Still, I can see by what he was writing the difficult time he was having."

"To stand by and watch a man deteriorate like that, someone who was so capable and so strong, was painful beyond belief," Charlotte said, shaking her head sadly. "But it turned out that the way he was for all those months paled beside what happened to him over the past few months."

I waited in silence, able to see for myself how hard she was wrestling with the demons in her head.

"Starting last spring, poor Linus became afraid of everything." She swallowed hard. "Even things that didn't really exist. At least not outside his own mind."

"Are you talking about paranoia?" I asked.

Charlotte nodded. "I can't think of anything else to call it."

"What was he afraid of?" I asked gently. The image of all those bills and legal documents stuffed into the suit of armor in the hall flashed through my mind.

"Linus became convinced that all kinds of people were out to get him," Charlotte explained. "At first it was people he knew. He thought Harry was trying to destroy him. Then he became convinced that Scarlett was stealing corporate secrets and selling them to his competitors. It reached the point where he didn't trust anyone at work.

"But it got even worse," she continued, her eyes distant as she gazed off at something I couldn't see. "He began to distrust the children. He would rant and rave about how they were trying to steal from him. He believed they were determined to take away this house and all his money. Then it spread. He decided all the usual suspects were after him: the FBI, the CIA, even

the Boy Scouts. He must have been in one of his para-
noid states when he hid those notebooks. In here, of
all places."

"But why here?" I asked.

"I can't be positive," she replied, "but he probably
wanted to put them in a place where no one would
find them—including the servants. He didn't want
anyone to find out, even though you only had to
spend five minutes with him to see it for yourself. I'm
sure he chose the boathouse because in his muddled
mind he decided it was a place he could reach in an
emergency by using the secret passageway that his an-
cestors had built into this house.

"You see, it all ties in to the later stages of his illness," Charlotte went on. "It got to the point where
he was terrified all the time. He would drink cup after
cup of coffee at dinner every night because he was
afraid to go to sleep. He talked about having locks in-
stalled everywhere, but I kept telling him that no one
could get onto this island without our permission.

"Given the state he was in, it's not surprising that
he also began to mistrust the servants. Even Cook,
who had been loyal to him and this entire family forever. I know she thought the world of him. I'm embarrassed to admit that I've even thought at times that
she had a crush on him."

"Charlotte, did Linus also begin doing things that
were...strange?" I asked cautiously.

"What do you mean?" she asked, sounding suspicious.

I hesitated, wondering how much to reveal about

all the papers Nick and I had found stuffed inside the suit of armor—including legal documents.

But it didn't take me long to decide that I had nothing to lose. "I understand your neighbors initiated a lawsuit over something he put on the balcony of your apartment in the city."

"Oh, dear," Charlotte said, her face crumpling. "That . . . that contraption he built last winter. It was a monstrosity he constructed out of cardboard and coat hangers and aluminum foil. He was convinced it would help keep away the evil forces that were after him.

"I tried every way I could think of to make him understand that what he was doing made no sense. But logic didn't mean much to him over this last year or so." Raising her eyes to meet mine, she said, "The man suffered, Jessica. He was so terrified. It was horrible to witness."

The more I listened to Charlotte describe what Linus's final days had been like, the more compassion I felt. Not only for Linus but also for her. Charlotte had watched the man who was the center of her world, someone she had loved and shared nearly her entire adult life with, fade away before her eyes.

"Then there were the physical changes," she went on. "He lost the ability to take care of himself in even the simplest of ways. I was afraid that if I brought him to a hospital, he'd be forced to live in a horrible state for a long time. He couldn't stand to be reduced to such humiliation."

"It must have been awful for you," I said, sincerely sympathetic.

"It was," she said sadly. "But it was even worse for poor Linus. He became someone else—or, even worse, nothing more than a shell. He was frightened and unhappy all the time. No one should have to experience what that man experienced. *No* one. Which is why someone had to do something to help him."

I froze. Those words—and the way she said them—shot through me like an electric shock.

Suddenly everything was clear.

"You killed him, didn't you?" I asked calmly.

For a few seconds, she simply stared at me.

"You have to understand," Charlotte finally replied, "that he wasn't Linus Merrywood anymore. He was already gone."

"She loved him," another voice interjected.

Startled, I looked up and saw that Missy had appeared in the doorway of the boathouse.

"Mother thought the world of him," she continued. "She couldn't bear to watch him suffer."

"You knew about this?" I asked, surprised.

Missy nodded. "Mother and Daddy had a relationship that was truly special. They were practically the same person. The two of them adored each other. In fact, I don't know how she's going to manage without him."

She kept me fixed in an intense gaze for what seemed like a very long time before she said, "Whatever she did, it was only because she loved him so much. She couldn't bear to see him in such agony."

Turning to her mother, Missy said, "Why don't you give me that silly dagger, Mummy? Surely you didn't expect to use such an ancient thing, did you?"

"I don't know what I was thinking," Charlotte said, looking distraught. "I just need everyone to understand."

"Jessie understands," Missy assured her in a soothing voice. "And we can trust her, Mummy. She's not any danger to us. She's not going to say a word."

Meekly, Charlotte handed the dagger to her daughter.

I held my breath, afraid that Missy might change her mind. For all I knew, she could impulsively decide she needed to do what she believed her mother was incapable of doing.

But I started to breathe again when she leaned over and put the dagger in the corner, out of her reach as well as her mother's.

When she stood up straight again, she turned to face me.

"I finally figured out what you were up to, Jessie," Missy said in a low, even voice. "All those questions you were asking, those private conversations you held with every member of the household . . . I tried to discourage you. That's why I wrote that ridiculous note on the wall, hoping you'd get the hint.

"I know that didn't dissuade you, but I think you understand now," she went on, studying me anxiously. "And I'm right, aren't I, Jessie? About Mummy and me being able to trust that you're not going to tell anyone?"

• • •

"A nice hot cup of tea—that's what you need," Margaret insisted.

I had to agree. Since I hadn't been wearing a jacket or gloves when I'd followed the yellow brick passageway out to the boathouse, I was chilled to the bone.

It was a relief to come back into the house with Charlotte and Missy, the three of us talking loudly about the quick tour of the grounds we were all pretending we'd just taken. Missy had made a beeline for the dining room to let Max and Lou out and put everything back in order, and Charlotte had retreated to her bedroom.

I, meanwhile, headed into the kitchen to find a way to warm up my insides, now that my outsides were coming out of the deep freeze. I also needed time to think about the morning's events.

The cup of Earl Grey went a long way in warming me up. After Margaret had set me up with an entire pot of tea and toddled off to let me recover on my own, I eagerly slurped it down, marveling over its effectiveness. In fact, I'd pretty much shaken off the chill and was deep in thought about what I'd learned in the boathouse when I felt a warm, comforting hand on my shoulder. I also heard the *tip-tip-tip* of paws against the kitchen floor.

"There you are," Nick said, leaning over to plant a kiss on my cheek. "When I woke up and found that you were gone again, I didn't know what to think."

Both Max and Lou seemed ecstatic to see me,

almost as happy as I was to be reunited with them. Max jumped up and gently placed his paws on my thigh, craning his furry white neck in an attempt to cover my face with sloppy, wet dog kisses. Lou staked his claim on my other thigh, resting his chin on it and gazing up at me adoringly. His tail was in high gear, making me glad there were no antiques in the vicinity.

As the dogs settled beside me, one on each side, Nick plopped down in the seat next to mine. Reaching for my hand, he asked earnestly, "So tell me: What have you been up to?"

"What makes you think I've been up to anything?" I asked, trying to keep my tone light.

"The look on your face," he replied without missing a beat. "I can read you like a book, Jess, and from what I can see you've been up to plenty."

I was still trying to come up with a creative explanation when I was saved by the bell—the doorbell, in fact, its chime echoing through the otherwise silent house.

"Falcone," Nick said, stating the obvious.

My feeling of dread about his arrival on the scene was even greater than it usually was.

Less than two minutes passed before Margaret reappeared. "Sorry to interrupt the two of you," she said, "but that detective is back again—and he wants to talk to you, Jessie."

I rose from the table with Max and Lou flanking me like the Secret Service, and Nick close behind. As soon as my entourage and I stepped into the hallway, I spotted Lieutenant Falcone standing by the door.

He was bent over, pulling a pair of rubber boots off his shoes. For balance, he was holding onto the suit of armor, clinging to the knight's shoulder as if he was a close friend. He was also muttering to himself, no doubt taking it personally that the rain still hadn't let up.

"Lieutenant Falcone!" I greeted him heartily, trying to hide my nervousness.

He nodded at me, then Nick, peering at us both with his dark, piercing eyes. "Sounds like you had some excitement around here this morning. I understand a coupla the people I tol' not to leave the island didn't take me seriously."

"Gwennie and Jonathan," I agreed, nodding. "I found them heading to the dock early this morning with their clothes and their passports."

"Seems to me that doesn't do much for their claim that they had nothing to do with Linus's murder," Nick commented.

"I'll question them again, but I still got nothin' on 'em," Falcone said with an air of resignation. "No hard evidence, not on those two or any of the other suspects."

Turning to me, he said, "What about you, Docta Poppa?" he asked. "Did *you* get anywhere with figurin' out who killed Linus Merrywood?"

I remained silent. I could feel Nick's eyes on me, as if he, too, was eagerly awaiting my answer. But I wasn't just stalling. I was giving the question serious thought.

Ever since my encounter with Charlotte and Missy

in the boathouse, I'd been dreading this moment. There was a part of me that was anxious to show Falcone the stuff I was made of. That part wanted to reply with a resounding *yes*, then launch into all the details.

Yet there was also another part of me that wasn't prepared to turn Charlotte in. I had lots of reasons, not the least of which was the fact that even imagining her spending the rest of her life in prison was horrifying.

But that wasn't the real issue. I believed in my heart that she had not committed cold-blooded murder. She had loved Linus with all her heart, which was the only reason she had done it.

As I replayed in my mind the conversation she and I had in the boathouse, I realized that, when you came right down to it, I didn't know for sure that Charlotte had killed her husband. Not really. After all, she hadn't actually admitted to anything. She certainly hadn't come out and said that she was the one who'd brought a birthday cake into the house that was made with the one ingredient that was guaranteed to put an end to her husband's life.

And I couldn't rule out Missy as the murderer. After all, she, like Charlotte, had been torn apart by what was happening to Linus. And while she was a far cry from Betty Crocker, I remembered her mentioning that when she was a Brownie, Cook had taught her and the rest of her scout troop how to bake. It was possible that she had whipped up two egg-laden chocolate cake layers in her kitchen at home, then brought them with her to Solitude Island. Or perhaps she'd simply brought two ready-made layers of chocolate cake to Solitude Island after picking them up at a bakery or supermarket on Long Island.

If either of those scenarios had occurred, Missy's reasons could have been merciful. Like her mother, she could have wanted to put an end to Linus's suffering. Then again, she could have done it for some entirely different reason. Maybe Charlotte was protecting her daughter.

The bottom line was that neither woman had confessed. And I had no other proof.

My silence lasted long enough that Falcone opened his mouth one more time, as if to remind me that he didn't have all day, or something along those lines.

But before he had a chance to speak, I looked him in the eye and said, "I'm sorry, Lieutenant Falcone, but, no, I didn't."

Beside me, Nick exhaled, making me realize he'd been holding his breath.

As for Falcone, his response was a smirk. "So, Docta Poppa, this turned out to be one case even you couldn't figure out."

"I'm afraid you're right."

He sighed. "Too bad. You were kinda my last hope, believe it or not. I've been in this business long enough to know that this is one of those difficult cases that has too many suspects and not enough hard evidence. It's possible that even if I put my best people on it, we'll never get to the bottom of this."

358 • Cynthia Baxter

"I guess sometimes that's just the way the cookie crumbles," I said with a shrug.

He looked at me with his beady little eyes. Somehow, I got the feeling he could see right through me.

But I did a pretty good job of staring right back.

The sound of footsteps finally caused me to turn. Betty and Winston came into the hall, their faces tight.

"Jessica, is everything all right?" Betty asked.

"Everything's fine," I assured her. "Lieutenant Falcone just stopped by to make a routine call."

"Yeah, I was hopin' our little amateur sleuth here would have cracked the case," he told them. "But I'm afraid she let us down."

There was that smirk again, the one that usually made my blood boil. For some reason, it didn't bother me in the least this time.

"Now, if you'll all excuse me," he said disdainfully, "I'm gonna take a look around."

I waited until he'd walked off before turning to Betty and Winston.

"I'm sorry I disappointed you," I told them.

Betty grabbed my hand and gave it a squeeze. "Jessica, you could never disappoint me."

"Hear, hear," Winston seconded. "You know we both think the world of you, Jessica."

I squeezed Betty's hand in return. "I think it's time we packed up our things and went back to our own lives," I said. "The best thing we can do at this point is to leave this family alone to mourn."

The other three nodded, all of them muttering their agreement.

Even though I was suddenly overcome with a desire to go home, I lingered in the hallway for a few more seconds. I studied Betty and Winston's faces, then fixed my eyes on two of the members of my beloved menagerie, Max and Lou. Finally I focused on Nick, trying to freeze this moment in my mind and hold on to it as something to cherish forever.

It really was time for all of us to get back to our own lives. And I was looking forward to sitting down to Thanksgiving dinner in a few days with this family of mine, one that consisted of dear friends and beloved animals and most of all a man I truly loved. After all, I knew that I had plenty to be grateful for.